D1241953

A Little Bit Dangerous

Rogues of Fortune's Den
Book 1

ADELE CLEE

A Little Bit Dangerous
Copyright © 2023 Adele Clee
All rights reserved.
ISBN-13: 978-1-915354-31-0

Cover by Dar Albert at Wicked Smart Designs

Chapter One

Fortune's Den
Aldgate Street, London

The first rays of dawn crept through Christian Chance's window, a golden trespass into the dark shadows of his bedchamber. The promise of a new day did nothing to restore his vigour. How could he move with a spring in his step when he carried the heavy burden of guilt?

He studied his form in the looking glass, brushing imagined dust from the sleeves of his black frock coat before straightening his cravat. His gaze fell to the diamond stick pin sparkling in the muted light. It wasn't so much a symbol of wealth but of how far he'd come from the urchin surviving on scraps in the rookeries.

Careful not to wake the household, he stole through the lavish hall of the gaming hell he owned with his three brothers. All was quiet. Eerily so. Was his eldest brother Aaron waiting to pounce? Did he know Christian meant to break his sacred rule?

Many men want us dead.

You'll tell me where you are at all times.

There must be no secrets between us, no lies.

Knots formed in Christian's stomach as he slipped out onto Aldgate Street and closed the door gently behind him. While he would not be without his kin, a man had to forge his own identity. What was there to fear? Visiting a museum at dawn was hardly a dangerous pursuit.

He spotted Lucius Daventry's unmarked carriage waiting near St Anne's churchyard. The burly coachman atop the box scoured every dark doorway. When working for the most skilled enquiry agent in London, one might die if they didn't keep their wits.

"I admire a man who's prompt," Daventry said as Christian dropped into the seat opposite. "Did anyone see you leave?"

"No. Aaron crawled into bed at three this morning." He gripped the overhead strap as the carriage lurched into motion. "My brother has a sixth sense and will undoubtedly know I'm missing."

As children forced to make their home in a dank alley, Christian had often woke in the dead of night to find Aaron watching him.

"I wouldn't want to cause a rift between family," said the man who possessed the Lord's benevolence and Lucifer's lust for vengeance.

"I shall explain the situation to Aaron upon my return." It would be a heated conversation. A clashing of swords. A battle of wills. "Rest assured, nothing would ever come between us."

Guilt flooded his body as a disturbing memory flooded

his mind. Four boys thrown out of their dead father's house and left to fend for themselves. Their stepmother hiring thugs to cart them away before the body was cold. At the tender age of sixteen, Aaron became a father to his kin overnight.

No matter what happens, I'll keep us safe.

We'll always have each other.

"I'll need you for a few days." Daventry's commanding voice snapped Christian from his reverie. "Will that pose a problem?"

Damn right it would.

Aaron would raise every objection.

Christian shrugged. "No, providing I find the work rewarding. Other than mentioning an issue with a rare artefact, you've not told me how I might assist you."

"My business at the museum is confidential. I must know you're committed before I can explain the matter in detail."

The comment roused Christian's suspicions. Daventry employed a host of agents who all worked on private cases. Was it not better to trust one of his own men than a mere acquaintance?

"The truth is, I've no one with your knowledge of Egyptian artefacts. No one with your attention to detail." Daventry spoke as if he'd heard Christian's silent question. "The curator approached me with serious concerns, concerns I feel compelled to investigate."

Damnation! Daventry knew how to pique a scholar's interest.

"My knowledge comes from books and scientific lectures. I missed out on a formal education when that evil bastard died." Despite being the grandson of an earl, Christian had dined in doorways, not the halls at Oxford or Cambridge.

A sly smile touched Daventry's lips. "If you take this job,

3

the education you gained in the rookeries will serve you better."

"Job?" The desire to feel useful in his own right swayed him towards accepting the position. "I thought you needed advice."

Daventry narrowed his gaze. "What I ask of you will test your mental and physical limits. If you're not up to the task, tell me now."

He knew damn well Christian would accept.

A skilled enquiry agent could sense a man's restlessness.

No one wanted to admit to being weak.

"I cannot abandon my responsibilities at Fortune's Den." Christian kept the accounts, dealt with paperwork, and fought alongside his brothers when reprobates caused trouble. Family always came first.

Daventry smiled. "I'm sure you can keep everyone happy. Besides, I have someone waiting at the museum to assist you. Considering the delicate nature of the problem, I need the matter dealt with quickly."

Christian fell silent while considering his dilemma.

What did Daventry want him to do?

Document the artefacts?

Read detailed letters proving provenance?

Study endless reams of text?

As the carriage trundled along London's streets, Christian noticed the haggard costermongers setting up their handcarts. He knew homeless children would be out stealing the odd apple or two while the sellers' backs were turned.

The need to live in a just and fair world ran like blood in his veins. It was why he admired Lucius Daventry, undoubtedly why he nodded and said, "I can spare three days."

"I may need five," Daventry countered. "Though if you're as efficient as your brothers claim, you will achieve the task in three. And you must swear to keep the details confidential."

Christian imagined the tense meeting with Aaron.

You'll not keep me in the dark.

What the devil does Daventry want with you?

"You have my word. I shall not discuss the matter in any depth." It was time Aaron learned to trust Christian's judgement. So why did his heart ache? Why did he feel like a soldier deserting his comrades? "Most people think I'm a rogue, but I'll not break a vow."

To the *ton*, anyone forced to spend more than a night in the rookeries was a scoundrel. Anyone disowned by their titled family was a villain.

"If I'm to trust you with the truth, do I have your word you will see this job through to the end?" Something in Daventry's tone implied the *job* was more complicated than Christian had been led to believe.

Christian pushed aside any reservations and nodded. "Don't expect me to stab my thumb and make a blood oath. Now tell me what the hell this is about."

Daventry smiled at Christian's impatience. "The museum's curator has asked me to investigate an incident of fraud. He believes some artefacts purchased during his brief absence last month are forgeries. Though the provenance comes with a seal from the Grand Vizier in Cairo."

"The Grand Vizier?" That in itself was odd and raised many questions. "He would have required a substantial amount of money in return. How much did the museum pay for the artefacts?"

Daventry glanced out of the window. "We'll be there shortly. It's better if I explain everything then. But the Vizier is gathering funds to wage war in Syria, which may explain why he sanctioned the trade."

"Or a corrupt official used the seal without permission."

Daventry arched a brow. "Continue thinking like an enquiry agent, and you will have no issue gaining the answers we seek."

They arrived at Montagu House in Great Russell Street, home of the British Museum, a grand palace befitting a nobleman of the first rank. Christian followed Daventry through the entrance that looked like a gateway to a Gothic monastery and across the deserted courtyard to a door tucked away in a shadowed corner.

"The curator is expecting us," Daventry said as they descended the stone staircase to the basement. "You're to examine the documents away from prying eyes. Should anyone ask why you're here, you're to say you're writing a thesis on Ancient Egypt."

They were met by a middle-aged man with brown wavy hair and impressive side whiskers. Through beady black eyes, he scanned Christian's physique and muttered his frustration.

"I need a scholar, Daventry, not one of your lackeys."

Christian firmed his jaw. It wasn't the first time a man had presumed he was more brawn than brains. "Insult me again and you'll feel more than the whip of my tongue. As you're keen to judge on appearances, perhaps it would help if I wore spectacles."

The fellow paled. "Forgive me. This whole business has left me desperate for answers. Based on Daventry's choice of assistants, one cannot help but feel flustered." He jerked his head to the closed door behind him, dragged a handkerchief from his pocket and mopped his brow.

Daventry smiled. "Any man would find himself anxious when left alone with such a compelling woman." He turned to Christian. "Cornelius Brown is the curator here and our client."

Under normal circumstances, Christian would have bid the man good morning—but manners be damned. Daventry hadn't mentioned hiring a woman.

Intrigue and annoyance fought for supremacy. Not wanting to mimic Brown's small-minded bigotry, Christian asked a sensible question. "Does your assistant know something of Egyptology?"

"Yes. Relatively more than you do," Daventry replied. "Now, are we to stand in the corridor all morning, or shall we get to the matter at hand?"

Christian silently cursed. No wonder Daventry had demanded a sworn oath before revealing the nature of the work. Doubtless the bluestocking wished to make her mark on the world, and he'd be forced to work with a termagant for five blasted days.

"I've left her reading the consignment list," Brown whispered.

"You didn't think to invite someone from the Society of Antiquaries to examine the documents and artefacts?" Surely their members were qualified to give an appraisal.

Brown's gaze shifted left and right as if the walls had ears. "Two members were involved in the purchase and movement of the artefacts. I don't know who to trust. To save time, I shall explain more once you've met Miss Lawton."

Lawton?

The name chilled Christian's blood.

Sir Geoffrey Lawton was the devil incarnate. A wicked man who had refused their plea for help sixteen years ago. Yes, he had a daughter, but the girl Christian remembered was sent away to school. He had not laid eyes on her since.

Indeed, he ignored the churning of unease in his stomach.

Stop fretting. Lawton is a fairly common name, he told himself as they entered the windowless room. And yet, there was nothing *common* about the exotic woman seated behind the oak desk.

Brown and Daventry greeted her while all Christian could do was stare at the vision of loveliness in the candlelight.

Miss Lawton's lustrous dark hair was swept back in a simple chignon. Beneath delicately arched brows, her sensual brown eyes had the power to bring a man to his knees. And then there were those soft lips, lips so full they made his cock weep.

Miss Lawton stood, and he'd be damned if his mouth didn't fall open when gazing upon her curvaceous silhouette. "Mr Chance, good morning. I believe we used to be neighbours." She scanned his face, his hair and physique as if recalling their last interaction fondly. "Your cook made the best shortbread biscuits. You used to leave a parcel for me by the garden gate."

Hell and damnation! She *was* Lawton's offspring.

Anger flared in Christian's chest. Biscuits? All she remembered was bloody biscuits, not her father's sordid affair with his stepmother? Did she think a sweet memory might eradicate sixteen years of pain?

By God, Aaron would tear her to shreds, whip her with the sharp edge of his tongue to remind her of her family's failings. She had tainted blood. Lucifer's blood.

"They were Shrewsbury biscuits, and I tied the parcel from the branches of the apple tree overhanging your garden," he said coldly. By God, he would throttle Daventry for putting him in this damned predicament. "Yet for me, the bitter memories are the most prevalent."

He'd not thought of those biscuits since he'd sat huddled with his brothers in a dank alley, his limbs shaking, hunger gnawing at his belly like a rabid dog.

The lady appeared confused. "While the details may have

8

become muddled over time, your kindness has always remained with me."

"Kindness?" He was surprised she knew the definition.

"Your gifts were a distraction during a difficult time, sir."

What a pity she had not returned the favour when he found himself destitute. Perhaps if she acknowledged her father's beastly misdeeds, he might feel something other than contempt.

Daventry cleared his throat. "Studying Egyptian artefacts is somewhat of a hobby. Is it not, Miss Lawton?"

A flicker of an unnamed emotion passed over her striking features, but she kept her composure. "There were many books on the subject at my mother's villa. I used to lock myself in the library and read for hours. Particularly when she had guests."

"I'm told Positano is breathtaking during the summer months," Daventry said.

She closed her eyes briefly, as if desperate to feel the warmth of the Italian sun. "The natural world never disappoints. Sadly, I cannot say the same for people."

Christian had never ventured farther than London. A fact that added to his growing annoyance. "Time is of the essence. I'm not here to indulge in sentimental waffle. Might we examine the documents?"

He needed to return to Aldgate before midday. And a man might choke on his own bile if forced to spend a few hours with Sir Geoffrey Lawton's offspring.

Daventry drew Brown aside and spoke quietly before saying, "We'll fetch the two artefacts in question. Examine them and make notes on what you would expect to find if they were original treasures. Compare them to the detailed descriptions documented in the files. That should suffice this morning."

The men exited the room, leaving Christian alone with Miss Lawton.

The atmosphere changed.

Tension wrapped around his chest like a poacher's noose, the tightness making him aware of every drawn breath. An urgency to know why a woman would come to the museum at dawn prompted him to ask the most pressing question.

"What are you doing here, Miss Lawton?"

She blinked, her long lashes fanning her flawless olive skin. "I believe we're about to examine ancient artefacts to determine if they're fakes, sir."

"I know that. Why are you not at home in bed?" Much to his chagrin, he imagined her hair loose, the soft, dark waves cascading over a crisp white pillow.

Miss Lawton's heavy frown did not deter from her physical appeal. "Because I'm being paid to examine the artefacts. Are you unwell, Mr Chance? You seem preoccupied." She raised her chin in defiance. "If you have an issue working alongside a woman, I suggest you discuss the matter with Mr Daventry. I assure you, I have the skills needed to solve this case."

"Your skills are not my primary concern." No, his main issue was the fact he found Lawton's daughter appealing. Aaron would string him up by the ballocks for consorting with the enemy.

"Does your obvious reluctance to work with me stem from a fear of ruining my reputation? Again, you have no need to worry in that regard." Her light laugh sounded empty. "I shall not force you to the altar."

His laugh dripped with disdain. "I wouldn't marry you if you were the last woman on earth." Hell, his family would disown him. He'd be an outcast, left to wander the wilderness alone. A modern-day Judas.

Her sharp intake of breath caught him by surprise. "And I could never marry a man so callous he would hurt an innocent lady's feelings."

His conscience crawled from its cavern, squinting against the cold light of day. "You cannot be surprised by my vehemence."

Water welled in her warm brown eyes. "Can I not? In all honesty, Mr Chance, I find it hard to believe you're the sweet boy I remember."

Was this woman trying to provoke him?

"That sweet boy died years ago. Hardships may scar a man's soul. Injustice kills his spirit."

Miss Lawton's lilac skirts swished as she rounded the desk. "You're rambling, sir, and clearly angry, though I'm unsure what it has to do with me. Might you speak plainly?"

Christian stepped back, keen to keep some distance between them. "I did, yet you found it offensive."

"I found your delivery offensive. Explain your motivation for making such a comment." Her vivacious voice held a trace of her mother's Italian heritage, a soft lyrical cadence he found soothing. "I cannot see how we can work together if we do not discuss the root cause of your animosity." She shrugged. "Perhaps you dislike those with Italian blood or those born on the wrong side of the blanket."

"I'm not that shallow," he snapped.

Then he remembered she had been sent to a ladies' seminary and doubts crept into his mind. Was she aware of her father's antics? Did she know the man had conspired with his lover to make children homeless?

"I hate your father with a vengeance," Christian admitted. "I've considered pouncing on him in a dark alley and giving him the beating he deserves." But revenge was a dish best served cold. And Aaron intimated he had set events in motion to ensure Lawton's downfall.

Miss Lawton's gaze slid over his broad chest. "Might I ask why?"

"Why?" Did she really not know, or was she as cunning as her kin? "Surely you know what happened the day my father died?" He could recall every harrowing detail.

"When was that, exactly?"

Christian frowned. "The May of 1815."

The significant day was carved into his memory.

Not because he gave a damn about his reprobate father but because it marked the day his life changed course. The day an eleven-year-old was forced to stop snivelling and become a man.

"I was sent to Bramling Seminary in the April."

"But you returned home for the holidays."

The lady touched her abdomen as if she had an ache she couldn't ease. "You're mistaken, Mr Chance. I've not seen my father for sixteen years. This is my first trip to London since then."

Christian stood statue still. The information did not fit the narrative he'd told himself all these years. The story he had repeated many times put Isabella Lawton at her bedchamber window, watching as her father and his lackeys bundled four helpless boys into a cart.

He scrubbed his hand down his face. It was too early in the morning to deal with a range of conflicting emotions. It was too painful to revisit the past.

"Then I shall spare you the details," he said bluntly. "With your father's help, my stepmother threw us out. We spent a month on the streets before Aaron found us lodgings."

Miss Lawton's large brown eyes widened. "You were

homeless? But what about your inheritance?" She swallowed hard. "How did you survive? How—"

Christian raised a hand to silence her. "Enough. The rest is history." Though he still wanted to scrub his skin red raw every time he bathed. "Now you understand the reason for my vehemence."

"Indeed." She tucked a stray curl behind her ear, and for a moment he glimpsed the girl he once knew. "My father is the spawn of Satan. Please do not think my ambitions are in any way aligned with his."

"Doubtless when he discovers you're examining Egyptian artefacts with me, he'll prevent you from returning here tomorrow." To Lawton, women were good for one thing. So why had he given his daughter permission to visit the museum? Or was that why they were working in a dim basement at dawn?

Her prolonged silence sent a shudder of unease through him. If Lawton could throw an earl's grandsons onto the streets, what would he do to the daughter encroaching on a man's world?

"Does your father know you're here?" he reiterated. Worse still, did he know she would be working alongside a man he considered his enemy?

Miss Lawton swallowed excessively. "No, Mr Chance. My father has no idea where I am." Her snort of amusement carried more than a tinge of fear. "I have no idea where *he* is and daren't ask the neighbours."

Lawton was missing?

Christian's pulse rose a notch. Had Aaron buried the beast in a shallow grave? Had he kept the secret to himself to avoid incriminating his kin? Was that why Christian could not shake the feeling of impending doom?

Chapter Two

"To be more precise, sir, my father thinks I'm at my mother's villa in Positano." Isabella closed her eyes against a wave of nausea. Despite spending a lifetime fleeing one nightmare after another, the last two months had been a living hell. "I journeyed to London five weeks ago, shortly after my mother's funeral."

The Conte di Barasian had given her an ultimatum.

Leave his house or become his mistress.

Aware she was without funds, the conte had presumed she would accept his scandalous offer. But having watched the drunken fights and seen her mother's desperation to keep a man who mistreated her, Isabella would rather die in the workhouse than succumb to the same fate.

"My condolences for your loss." Mr Chance's voice quivered as he expressed his sympathy. Perhaps his thoughts had turned to his own tragic past. When he was five, his mother died from a mere tumble down the stairs.

"It was more an inconvenience," she admitted, not to make him feel better. Sofia Bianchi was as cruel and as self-absorbed as Geoffrey Lawton. "I rarely saw her during the

14

years I lived there. She encouraged me to keep to my room until she grew so sick she needed a nursemaid."

Give me the wine, Isabella.

But your hand is shaking, mamma.

Stupid girl. Look! You have spilt some on my bedsheets.

"You're staying in Hill Street?" Mr Chance said as if it were the last inn on the road to Hades. While his tone lacked vehemence, the air between them crackled with hostility.

Before she could answer, Mr Daventry returned with the curator. The latter pushed a wooden trolley while Mr Daventry held the door open then removed the white sheets to reveal two rare artefacts.

On the top tier was a stone tablet.

On the bottom stood a small figurine.

The items captured Mr Chance's attention, his curious gaze fixating on the sandstone slab. "Good God! Is that a fragment from the Dendera Zodiac? It resembles Denon's sketch of the ceiling he drew in a temple in Thebes."

Isabella knew it couldn't be the zodiac.

That treasure was kept at the Royal Library in France.

"Sadly, no." Mr Brown peered into the corridor before closing the door and turning the key in the lock. "Though it's certainly an astrological chart. They said it came from an ancient temple in Amarna."

Mr Chance put on a pair of metal-rimmed spectacles he had removed from his coat pocket and inspected the stone.

Isabella's attention strayed to the impressive figure of a man, not the artefact. Christian Chance was nothing like the boy she remembered. Gold-blonde hair skimmed his shoulders as if he meant to defy convention. Like the fake artefacts found in the back alleys of Cairo, his rugged physique had been carved on the streets of London. She had never seen a man fill his coat in quite the same way—like a skilled tailor had spent days shaping the material around every hard muscle.

Mr Brown removed two pairs of gloves and a folio of paper from the trolley and placed them on the desk. "There are more candles in the drawer. You have until ten o'clock to make notes, not a minute more. Then I must return the artefacts to the display cases."

Mr Daventry offered Isabella a warm smile and gestured to the table in the far corner. On a tray was a flagon and a platter laden with fruit, bread and cheese. "There's food and refreshment. I know you often forget to eat, Miss Lawton."

She did not forget.

Food was a luxury she could ill afford.

"Don't eat while examining the documents," Mr Brown stressed, flapping like a mother hen. "You'll find paper, ink and the necessary implements inside the desk. You'll lock the door. Open it for no one. Heaven forbid someone should learn these items are forgeries."

"We'll return before ten," Mr Daventry said calmly.

Mr Chance drew his pocket watch and studied the face in the candlelight. "One cannot rush such things. What if we need more time?"

"Then you must return tomorrow at dawn."

Mr Chance glanced at her as if he would rather walk the plank than suffer a second meeting. "Then let's pray we accomplish the task today."

Being in her company must be a dreadful reminder of what his family had lost. She was the link to a past he did not wish to revisit. How could one not hate the offspring of one's enemy?

Questions flooded her mind.

None of them related to the artefacts sitting on the trolley.

Concentrating on the task ahead would be difficult when

she longed to hear Mr Chance's sad story. Not just because she hoped he was happy now. His clothes were new and expensive. From the size of his broad chest, it was years since he'd missed a meal.

But victims found solace with other victims. One did not feel so alone knowing fate had dealt someone else a dreadful blow. Perhaps his determination to improve his circumstances would give her the courage to forge ahead.

Mr Chance crossed the room, muttered sharp words to Mr Daventry and locked the door behind the retreating men. He lingered there momentarily, huffing and sighing as if deciding how best to breathe to conserve his energy.

It was her first time alone in a locked room with a man—except for Mr Griffin. But he'd been more interested in inspecting her skirts than discussing her plans for the future. Had she not escaped the seminary, she might have suffered Abigail's fate. As with other pupils, the girl had found herself married to a lecherous oaf.

Mr Chance turned to face her, and the room felt suddenly small. "Shall we begin by examining the ushabti?"

Impressed that he had identified the figurine correctly—and had not issued orders as men were wont to do—Isabella agreed. "I know enough to make a thorough assessment."

Mr Chance drew another chair closer to the desk and pushed his large hands into the gloves supplied by Mr Brown. "We should begin by listing the features we'd expect to find in a funeral figurine."

Such objects were hardly rare. Relatives placed them in tombs, believing they acted as servants to the deceased in the afterlife. No one knew how many one might need when reaching a higher plane.

"Yes," she said, her gaze flitting between the striking man and the juicy red apple on the far table. At the prospect of sating her hunger, her stomach growled like an angry bear. "Would you mind if I ate first?"

His deep frown said he did mind. "You eat. I'll study the artefact."

Pride battled the stomach pangs. It took every effort not to race across the room and gorge herself silly. Still, she would struggle to concentrate until she had food in her belly, and so surrendered to her body's needs.

Her hands trembled as she sliced the bread. The first mouthful did more than chase away the cramps. It soothed her restless spirit.

"When did you last eat?" Mr Chance stared at her, not the delicate figurine in his hands. "Don't lie to me. I know the look of the famished."

"Two days ago." She offered an explanation before he demanded one. "I need what little money I have for lodgings. A woman alone won't last the night on the streets." And she had no friends in London.

"You don't need to educate me on the dangers. But you have a home in Hill Street. Why the devil would you need lodgings?"

Isabella swallowed a piece of bread. "When my father sent me to the seminary, he told Miss Blunkett not to send me back. When I reached eighteen, she was to find me a husband. In short, my father doesn't want me. Should he return, he'll throw me out. Now do you understand why food is an afterthought?"

Mr Chance cursed under his breath. "Surely his servants are not so callous as to refuse you a meal." He placed the figurine on the trolley, removed the gloves and crossed the room. "Have they mentioned when he might return?"

She watched the man pour a small glass of wine from the

flagon. He handed it to her and waited until she had downed the contents before prompting her to continue.

"There are no servants." She had spent weeks alone in a cold, empty house, everything shrouded in white sheets. It was like living amongst ghosts. "I had to break a windowpane in the basement door to gain entrance."

Mr Chance rubbed his sculpted jaw. "I know Lawton left London for a time but was seen again last month. To my knowledge, he owns no other properties in town."

"He must be abroad. His armoire is empty." She bit into the apple, the loud crunch accompanying her satisfied hum.

"You can't go on like this," Mr Chance snapped.

"That's why I'm being paid to examine the artefacts." A chance meeting with Mr Daventry at the servants' registry changed everything. "Mr Daventry is aware of my unfortunate situation and wishes to help."

"Does he?"

She knew that tone: cynical, suspicious. "Oh, it is not what you think. Mr Daventry is devoted to his wife. His offer of help is merely a benevolent gesture."

"Everyone knows how Daventry feels about his wife. That's not the issue. Knowing of my history with your father, I can't help but wonder why he asked for my assistance."

"Perhaps because you have a knowledge of Egyptian artefacts."

He turned to look at the stone tablet, and she stole a glance at his impressive physique. Her mother's Italian lover smelled of wine and sweat. Mr Chance smelled of amber and leather. A masculine scent. Memorable. Much like the man.

Seeking a distraction, Isabella wiped her hands on a napkin. "We should begin examining the pieces. I've wasted too much time already."

Mr Chance agreed.

They wore the gloves Mr Brown supplied and sat on opposite sides of the desk to study the ushabti. Mr Chance placed the figure carefully on the smooth surface, positioning the candle lamps to gain an optimum view.

Isabella took paper and a pencil from the drawer, ready to make notes. "I'll not risk an ink spillage," she said, jotting down the key points. "The material is undoubtedly porous. First, we should determine if the piece is hollow."

"It's solid. The only way to know for sure is to hit it with a hammer, though I don't think Mr Brown would approve."

She laughed, their gazes locking across the desk. Heavens! She had never seen eyes so blue. "I'll tick solid. Do you agree it's Egyptian faience?"

"It appears so, but without breaking it in two, we cannot confirm that with any accuracy." He pointed to the symbols carved on the figurine's body. "Based on what we've learnt since Champollion deciphered the Rosetta Stone, the hieroglyphic markings here look genuine. I'll bring my notes tomorrow."

"Tomorrow?" Curiosity burning, Isabella dared to look him in the eye. Would he not find every reason to stay away? "Why return to the museum when I sense you're here under duress?"

"Daventry made me swear an oath to complete the task." He scoffed, the sound carrying the contempt of a man tricked by a knave.

"He wasn't completely honest with you. Is that not grounds to renege?"

Though his blue eyes hardened, they still shone like Murano glass. "When a man's had his dignity stolen, he has to work hard to gain respect. I'd no more break my word than I would sever my right arm."

Isabella fought to stop her chin hitting the floor. In her

experience, men fell into two categories—sly scoundrels and brutal beasts. Mr Daventry excepted, she had never met one with morals.

He's not the boy you remember, she reminded herself. She knew not to make presumptions based on words and a handsome countenance.

"My reasons for returning tomorrow are less virtuous," she said, turning her attention back to the ushabti to prevent Mr Chance seeing the utter desperation in her gaze. "I need money, and a lady has limited ways of gaining funds."

As Mr Chance was not an errant knight come to solve her problems, he returned to the matter at hand. "Based on other sketches I've seen, this funeral figurine is of similar proportions."

Isabella picked up the pencil and began making a rough sketch of the piece, noting the elements they believed made it genuine. "The wig is the correct shape and length. Some fakes fail to mimic the tomb owner's mummified remains."

"You're skilled with a pencil." Mr Chance's claret smooth voice stole her attention, his compliment catching her off guard. "Did you take lessons at the seminary?"

Isabella snorted. "The only thing I learnt at the seminary was how to outwit a crook. I doubt the tutors at Cambridge took a fee for forcing their students to marry."

"Having forgone a formal education, I wouldn't know."

Darn it! She had forgotten about that. "Well, if it's any consolation, I've never met a decent man who studied at Cambridge. And I'm told the food is foul."

The corners of Mr Chance's mouth twitched. It was as close to a smile as she was likely to muster. "Worse than spoiled fish?" he teased.

She nodded. "Spoiled fish nibbled by rats. That's not all.

At night, they drag you out of bed and shove your face in a bucket of excrement."

The glint of amusement in his eyes held her captivated. "It makes the pokey room above Mrs Maloney's bookshop seem idyllic." And yet, the thread of pain in his voice was unmistakable.

"Hardships make us stronger. You're a survivor, Mr Chance. I'd rather wear that medal than one gained in a spelling contest."

He stared at her for a heartbeat too long. "By the sounds of it, Miss Lawton, you should wear the Gold Cross."

This sudden camaraderie was surprising. Like opposing sides meeting on the battlefield during a brief cease-fire, both realised they had more in common than they'd initially thought.

"Perhaps one day we might compare scars, sir. In the hope they might eventually heal." She spoke metaphorically, yet his gaze roamed over her figure.

Men often looked at her as if she were a sumptuous piece of pie. It always turned her stomach. With Mr Chance, she felt a strange pang of excitement.

"Well, we would not get a medal for concentration," she joked. "We seem to stray from the task far too easily. And I do need to get paid."

Mr Chance frowned. "How can you be so jovial when you're starving? Lawton might return at any moment and toss you out onto the street."

Because if she didn't laugh, she would cry, and tears were as helpful as a sponge poker. "Sadness consumes energy I can ill afford. Spending the day sobbing in bed won't help put food in my belly." Her mother had been fit for nothing after a heated argument with the conte. "Surely you adopted the same attitude when sleeping on the streets."

His eyes glazed like he'd become lost in a daydream. Yet she knew whatever he envisioned had the makings of a nightmare.

"We should resume our studies before Daventry returns," he said, avoiding further discussion on the subject. "It's fair to say we can find no physical evidence to suggest the ancient ushabti is fake."

"The figure is holding farming tools, which fits with what we know." One needed a means of feeding oneself in the afterlife. Some forgers made the mistake of thinking a person needed jewels when dead.

They continued to examine the item before moving to the documents proving provenance. There were pages of diary entries detailing the dig, evidence found when surveying sites and intricate maps of the area.

Mr Chance inspected the Grand Vizier's seal, and Isabella offered him a magnifying glass from the drawer so he might consider it closely.

"Without visiting Cairo, there's no way to prove that's the Vizier's signature and seal," she said. Mr Brown would not fund a lengthy trip abroad.

Mr Chance met her gaze, and the dratted fluttering in her chest began again. "If someone is bold enough to forge the Vizier's signature and ensure the artefact looks genuine, then he has more to lose than money. How much did the museum pay for the ushabti?"

Isabella found the consignment sheet and the invoice. She stared at the figures on the pages, wondering if there might be a clerical error. "The museum paid thirty pounds for the ushabti. I would have expected ten times that amount for one with the Vizier's seal."

Mr Chance gave a curious hum. "Over the years, I've learnt to trust my instincts. This might be a genuine artefact or an excellent forgery. But a feeling in my gut says there's much more to this than meets the eye."

Keen to play devil's advocate, she said, "The Society of Antiquaries might have hired archaeologists to bring pieces home for study. It would explain why they sold them to the museum for a bargain price." Acquiring knowledge was more important than monetary gain.

"Men interested in culture and science do not forge a vizier's signature."

"It could be genuine."

"If the Grand Vizier was amassing funds to wage war, he would have demanded a much higher price." He placed the figurine on the desk. "Are we expected to believe he had nothing in his private collection to sell?"

Mr Chance had a point.

Relatives might bury the deceased with up to a hundred figures in a tomb. There was nothing rare or original about this one.

"Did Mr Daventry say why the curator suspects these are forgeries?" Her employer had been quite vague when discussing the task. A desperate woman knew not to ask questions.

Mr Chance sighed. "No. Daventry seems reluctant to reveal his source. Until an hour ago, I knew next to nothing about the case."

Interesting. The man wore a diamond stick pin and did not need money. What prompted him to accept? "And yet you agreed to help him. May I be so bold as to ask why?"

"One tires of routine."

Boredom had not brought Mr Chance to the museum at dawn. She suspected his motives were far more complex.

But how did one understand a conundrum?

Like a geyser, anger bubbled beneath the surface. One

could feel the pressure building, his temper waiting to explode and make every bystander stagger back. Then the atmosphere settled, and one glimpsed the considerate gentleman who stopped to pour a thirsty lady wine.

"You may disagree," he said, "but I don't think we'll find the answers we need by studying artefacts or reams of documents."

"How else might we determine if this is fake?"

He fell silent for a moment and sat rubbing his firm jaw. "We'll list those involved in the sale and begin there. I can source information easily. You'll be surprised what you can learn from men who owe you money."

Mr Chance seemed keen to forge ahead on his own.

Doubtless he wished to place some distance between them, but she could not afford to lose her salary.

"Mr Daventry said one can find clues in the strangest places. In all fairness, we have only scanned the paperwork. I shall continue to examine the documents while you take the bold approach."

His shoulders relaxed in relief, though he was polite enough not to sigh. "It makes sense to work separately."

There was no reason to take offence. Despite a past acquaintance, Mr Chance was a stranger, and she had spent a lifetime being shooed from the room.

So why did her throat tighten?

Why did she feel the twisting ache of disappointment?

"It does." She took up her pencil to make a list of those involved in the excavation and shipment. "It might take a while. Eat while I scan the documents."

"I'm not hungry." That was a lie. His stomach had grumbled twice in the last ten minutes. "You may take my share home. I'll examine the stone slab while I wait."

It took effort not to gasp or look him keenly in the eyes

and express her gratitude. *How kind*, she thought of saying. But he would make light of it, suggesting the food would only spoil.

"Mr Brown will probably take it for his supper," she said, trying to focus on the page of script in front of her. "Mr Clarke and Mr Woodrow from the Society of Antiquaries led the excavation in Amarna and obtained the Vizier's seal. Sir Henry Warnock studied the area's geology and supervised the local labourers."

"Who chartered the ship?"

She glanced up, expecting to find Mr Chance studying the treasure on the trolley, but he was slicing cheese and wrapping it in a napkin.

"Mr Quigley chartered the ship, *The Marigold*."

"Did he work on the excavation?"

She shrugged. "I'll need more time to read the documents. Mr Moses Snell captained the ship. It appears he owns the vessel."

Mr Chance crossed the room and placed the wrapped food on the desk beside her. "Do you have a list of names I can take with me?"

She glanced at the food parcel, then at the charismatic man who would likely scoff if she drew attention to the gesture. "Yes. Just let me find the name of the cartographer and I'll—"

Isabella stopped abruptly as her gaze fell to the name of the man who had mapped the area. She blinked, wondering if hunger could affect one's eyesight.

Hearing the hitch in her breath, Mr Chance braced his hands on the desk and leaned forward. "What is it? What have you found?"

Isabella swallowed hard. This complicated matters. This new development left her shaking to the marrow of her bones.

"You might find this a shocking coincidence, sir. I assure you, I was as ignorant as you when I arrived here this morning."

"Miss Lawton," he snapped, cringing at the sound of her name. "Tell me who mapped the area."

She put a hand on her abdomen to settle her roiling stomach. "Sir Geoffrey Lawton was the cartographer. My father mapped the dig site."

Chapter Three

"Tell me this is Daventry's idea of a sick joke." Just when Christian had a plan to distance himself from the beauty seated at the desk, a plan to appease his brother, they'd added Lawton's name to the suspect list.

Miss Lawton's hand came to rest gently on her throat. "I don't understand why Mr Daventry didn't mention it before."

"He couldn't have known Lawton mapped the area." Christian didn't want to think ill of a man most people admired. "Or maybe Daventry didn't consider it important."

"No. It certainly puts me in a difficult position." She worried her lower lip, the look in her dark eyes shifting from fear to utter bewilderment. "My father will think I'm conspiring against him."

Christian considered the problem.

Perhaps it would work to his advantage.

"All the more reason you should study the paperwork while I make enquiries elsewhere." If her father discovered she had broken into his home and was prying into his affairs, she might find herself in a French convent, not a seminary.

"Based on past circumstances, it's impossible for us to work together."

Yet she put him at ease.

She was interesting, intelligent and had courage abound.

"Impossible for you," she corrected.

"Yes, impossible for me." Nothing mattered more than family loyalty. "It's not personal, *madam*." He couldn't bear to call her Miss Lawton.

"Of course it's personal." Her laugh echoed the emptiness that consumed him of late. "I'm being punished for my father's misdeeds. Though I understand why, it hardly seems fair."

Fair! Rather than hurl accusations meant for her father, he fell silent. The lady did not press him further but returned to her studies.

For two hours, they spoke of nothing but the notes relating to the excavation. Twice, she moved to the table in the corner, poured another glass of wine and munched on bread.

Christian took the opportunity to flick through the documents, hunting for other clues. But his thoughts strayed to his rumbling stomach, and how he'd forgotten what it was like when one's body cramped with hunger.

He made a mental note to order groceries on the way home and have them delivered to Miss Lawton's abode in Hill Street. Based on her faded gown, he would lay odds she'd come to London with nothing more than a valise. He could send a modiste to the house and pay the bill, but that was a step too far.

Daventry returned with the flustered curator. "Well, did you note anything of interest?"

Christian considered grabbing Daventry by the throat and

pinning him to the wall. "We believe the artefacts are genuine but were shocked to find they were purchased so cheaply."

Brown chuckled. "Mr Purton is an experienced haggler."

"Purton?"

"My assistant. He took care of the museum during my brief absence."

Christian turned to Miss Lawton but she was already adding the assistant's name to the suspect list. No wonder Daventry had hired her. She had a keen eye, a curious mind and a body made for sin.

An odd sensation came over him. A desire to see her again. A deep sense of regret for being quick to insist they could not work together.

What did she do when home alone at night? Sit in the darkness? Sleep to keep the hunger pangs at bay? Who stoked the fire and heated the water?

Through every tragic experience, Christian's brothers had offered continued support. Miss Lawton had no one. That thought hit like a sharp stab to the gut.

"Mr Brown, may I ask why you were absent?" she said.

The curator frowned. "I went to Bath to examine a recent haul of Roman coins. Surely you don't think Mr Purton is involved in a conspiracy to defraud the museum?"

"How can he defraud the museum when the artefacts appear genuine, sir?"

The lady met Christian's gaze. Something in her expression made him take note. One did not spend time on the streets without learning to read people. The lady believed Purton had another motive for purchasing the artefacts while his employer was miles away in Bath.

Christian explained why they thought the ushabti was genuine. "We need more time to examine the tablet, but we've decided it's better if Miss Lawton continues to work here. I shall investigate the men involved in the excavation and sale."

Daventry frowned. "For what purpose?"

"A man's business dealings say a lot about him. We should establish if anyone has a reason to import forged treasures." The motive wasn't money. Not when they were sold for a paltry price.

"And you failed to mention my father mapped the area," Miss Lawton said, her tone accusatory. "You cannot expect Mr Chance to work with the daughter of his nemesis."

Daventry scanned the breadth of Christian's shoulders. "Mr Chance has a backbone of steel. It would take more than your family connection to deter him from a task."

While Christian felt the inner flush of shame, Miss Lawton jumped to his defence. "I think you underestimate the power of past trauma."

Daventry shrugged. "Based on your history, you have suffered dreadfully at your father's hands. You're willing to cast personal feelings aside in the name of justice."

Miss Lawton snorted. "Because I'm starving."

When Christian woke this morning, he did not imagine he would come to pity his enemy's daughter. Nor did he expect to feel responsible for a relative stranger. Worse still, he felt an inner tug of loyalty to someone other than his kin.

"You cannot expect us to uncover evidence when you're withholding information," Christian said, his temper rising. He faced the curator and pointed at the items on the trolley. "What made you suspicious enough to hire enquiry agents? If you want my help, you'd better have a damn good reason for dragging me here."

Brown took to wringing his hands and muttering like a Bedlamite.

"Tell them," Daventry said, not the least bit fazed.

Brown avoided eye contact. "They'll think I've lost my mind."

Daventry snorted. "Trust me, I've heard stranger things."

It took the curator a moment to gather his wits, then he blurted, "A ghost! A ghost accosted me in the courtyard." He screwed his eyes tightly. "She came at me, all pale face and haunted expression. She warned of sinister goings on at the museum. Mentioned the artefacts by name."

The mind played tricks. Tiredness, thirst and an excessive amount of wine might make a man hallucinate. "If she spoke to you, why the devil would you assume she was a ghost?"

"She was barefooted and wore a white flowing gown." Brown cupped his hand to his mouth and turned away from Miss Lawton to whisper, "There were spots of blood on her dress."

"I *can* hear you, sir. I'm a woman, not an imbecile." The lady shook her head and tutted. "In all likelihood, she was suffering from a sickness of the mind and lives in a house near here. Did the white dress resemble a nightgown, perhaps?"

Brown shrugged. "She was there one minute and gone the next."

"So she ran away?" Christian tried to establish.

"More floated than ran."

Fear had probably left the man delirious.

Miss Lawton closed the folio of papers, sighing like she'd had a wasted morning. "Did the ghost say the pieces were forgeries?"

"I can't recall what she said, not verbatim. It was late, and she caught me off guard." He pursed his lips in thoughtful contemplation. "She mentioned not trusting the men who sold the treasures of Amarna."

Amarna? That was too specific to be a coincidence.

Christian could see why the curator had jumped to conclusions.

"Now you've confirmed the artefacts are genuine," Daventry began, but Christian stopped him.

"They appear genuine. We agree we cannot be certain."

"But you're right to consider trying other lines of enquiry." Daventry sounded like a proud father. "You cannot storm Somerset House and demand to speak to the Society of Antiquaries. Not without evidence of misconduct. And it's pointless questioning Purton until we know what we're dealing with."

Miss Lawton stood. "In my experience, bribing those on the lower rungs of the social ladder is easier. We should find the ship's captain and crew. They're often party to gossip."

Daventry grinned and clapped his hands. "Excellent. You will accompany Mr Chance to the shipping office at the docks tomorrow. I'm told *The Marigold* recently returned from a trip to France. Let the captain believe you're considering hiring him to move cargo."

Hellfire!

Daventry treated them like chess pieces on a board, his every move strategic.

"Mr Chance would prefer to work alone, sir."

Christian sighed. Currently, Mr Chance didn't know his arse from his elbow. To make matters worse, he'd started thinking in the third person.

"Mr Chance gave his word he would see this matter through till the end, madam. As a man of honour, he will do whatever is necessary to get the job done."

Curse the devil to Hades!

Daventry was a master manipulator.

Christian might have argued, but one look at Miss Lawton's large brown eyes and his reserve crumbled. "I'll visit the shipping office with Miss Lawton, but on one condition." He couldn't have her wandering around the docks alone. Until they'd got to the bare bones of this problem, he needed to know she was safe. "I must be honest with Aaron."

Daventry contemplated the trade, his narrowed gaze shifting between Christian and Miss Lawton. "Very well. You can mention Sir Geoffrey but cannot reveal the other men's names. Not until we have proof of treachery."

Somewhat relieved, Christian agreed.

"You'll visit me in Hart Street tomorrow and inform me of your findings." Daventry turned to the beguiling lady in lilac. "My carriage is outside, Miss Lawton. Allow me to escort you home."

"Thank you, sir. That's most kind."

Christian inwardly groaned. "I'll take a hackney." Daventry would have him squashed next to Miss Lawton, their thighs touching every time the vehicle bounced through a rut in the road.

Daventry nodded. "You know my man Gibbs. He'll be at your disposal while you're conducting the investigation. I'll arrange for him to collect Miss Lawton at nine o'clock tomorrow before calling at Fortune's Den."

"Have him park outside the churchyard."

Gibbs was handy with his fists and would be a useful companion when navigating the docks. Unlike other servants, the coachman spoke his mind, which made him an asset, not a liability.

"We'll return the artefacts and leave you to gather your things." With that, Daventry and Brown wheeled the trolley out of the room and left Christian alone with Miss Lawton.

The lady rounded the desk as the men's footsteps receded, worry lines appearing on her brow. "Don't listen to Mr Daventry," she said, touching him gently on the upper arm, her dainty fingers resting against his bicep. "There's honour in sticking to your principles. There's honour in refusing to do anything that makes you uncomfortable."

Christian froze.

Battling a rush of conflicting emotions left him dumbfounded.

He wasn't unused to a woman's touch. He had sex—had kept a mistress until a few months ago—though it was always a physical act, a release, not something that caused a flurry of strange sensations.

"I'll tell Mr Daventry I shall visit the shipping office with Mr Gibbs." Her fingers moved slowly, not quite a caress, more a gesture of reassurance. "If he'd rather you take the job, I shall find other work. You shouldn't have to suffer for my father's misdeeds."

Mother of all heaven!

There was a God!

Good people did exist.

"That's settled then," she said, swallowing hard and snatching her hand away. "I wish you every luck for the future, Mr Chance. I pray you find comfort in—"

"No!" He reached for her, gripping her wrist before his brain engaged. "We'll visit the shipping office together as planned. I don't give a damn about breaking my oath." Daventry had hardly been honest himself. "But I'll not see you starve because of my selfish pride."

That would make him a hypocrite. And he'd not sleep a wink tonight thinking about her alone in that blasted house.

Miss Lawton glanced at where his fingers touched her bare skin, her breath quickening. "My problems are not your concern. I'll find a way out of this mess. I always do."

He imagined her sitting alone in a dark room, muttering to

herself, not seated around the huge dining table at Fortune's Den discussing the problem with siblings.

"My sister Delphine would never forgive me if I did not see you financially secure." And he suspected she was too proud to accept charity.

Miss Lawton frowned. "Your sister? I'm sure I would have recalled a girl living next door."

"Delphine is our adopted sister. She's close to your age, six and twenty." Delphine had wandered up to them in the alley one night, crying so hard it had taken an hour to settle her. "We've taken care of her for the last sixteen years."

Tears welled in Miss Lawton's eyes. "Then she is perhaps the luckiest lady alive." She tugged her hand free. It felt so natural to touch her, Christian had forgotten he held her wrist. "Take some time to think about this dilemma. I'll wait in Mr Daventry's carriage until a quarter past the hour. Don't feel obliged to come."

Daventry returned. The flustered curator bustled them out of the basement and shooed them through the courtyard to Great Russell Street. Christian watched Miss Lawton climb into Daventry's conveyance, relief racing through him when he noticed she gripped the food parcel.

She smiled at him as the carriage passed, and he'd be damned if he didn't wave. She was, without doubt, the most beautiful woman ever to make his acquaintance, yet it was not just her exotic looks that held him spellbound.

He could still feel the imprint of her tender touch. His heart still thumped hard in his chest at the depth of her benevolence. He'd never known such kindness. Kindness from a woman who had every right to hate the world.

Needing air, he walked as far as Newgate Street before hailing a hackney. The closer he came to Aldgate, the more his stomach churned. Aaron professed to have a heart of steel.

Yes, he would unleash his tightly reined temper, but he always erred on the side of common sense.

Aaron was standing outside Fortune's Den when Christian returned, his muscular arms folded across his chest as he stared at the premises opposite.

Christian straightened his spine and came to stand beside his brother. Solving the curator's ghostly mystery would be easier than dealing with his current problem.

"The Burnished Jade didn't open last night," Aaron said, his tone curious, though the bulging vein in his temple spoke of an inner rage. "Have you been to see Lovelace to find out why? Tell me someone shot the bastard and dumped his body in the Thames."

"I've not been to see Lovelace."

Aaron continued to look straight ahead, though tension stretched between them. "Then you've been to throttle Bentham and demand he keeps to his repayment plan."

"I visited Bentham two days ago, as you well know. The dandy has a bruised eye as proof. You saw it last night." Though Christian hated arguing with the brother who'd saved them, it was time Aaron accepted his siblings were no longer children. "Why don't you say what's on your mind?"

Aaron turned his head slowly. His intense stare had the power to shred a man's soul. "What did Daventry want with you? It must be important. Why else would you break the sacred rule?"

"We should discuss this inside, not on the street."

Aaron snorted. "We slept on the street for a month. It's where we forged our bond. It's where we made our pact. It's where you dabbed blood from the cut above my left eye and swore nothing would ever come between us."

Christian's stomach twisted into knots.

He had never forgotten the sacrifices Aaron had made.

He'd watched his brother take a beating just to earn a few shillings. Watched Aaron draw on his inner strength to beat an opponent twice his age and win a prize large enough to cover six months' rent.

"Like you, I'm not perfect. You broke the rule once."

Aaron cursed. "Fear does that to a boy."

It was a memory Christian wished he could forget. Him waking in the darkness to find Aaron missing from Mrs Maloney's pokey room. In a panic, he'd rushed to wipe mist from the window. That's when he saw Aaron hurrying along Lime Street, his meagre belongings in a sack thrown over his back. For a reason unbeknown, his brother had stopped abruptly and glanced back at the second-hand bookshop.

Don't leave us!

We need you!

It was as if he heard Christian's silent plea.

Dashing tears from his eyes, Aaron returned to Mrs Maloney's room. He reassured Christian all was well and urged him to go to sleep.

"Life can be unbearable even for the most hardened," Aaron confessed. "I'm a sinner and have never proclaimed to be a saint. This isn't the same, and you damn well know it."

Finding it impossible to vent his frustration, Christian said, "I'll wait for you in the drawing room where we can talk like civilised men."

For good measure, he stroked the lucky horseshoe hanging above the gaming hell's door, entered the drawing room and made for the table lined with crystal decanters. A cask of brandy would not ease his agitation.

Being as stubborn as a mule, Aaron came marching through the door ten minutes later. He did not sit down but stood before the fireplace, his stance defensive, his hands clasped behind his back as if he fought the urge to throttle someone.

"Everything I do is for the good of this family," Aaron said. "Need I remind you I foiled a plot to kidnap Delphine? Shall I name the men who would love nothing more than to see us dead?"

Christian relaxed back on the sofa and sipped his brandy. He would not be drawn into an argument. "I don't know where we would be without you, but I'm twenty-seven and quite capable of making a decision that affects my future."

"Your future? Your future is here with your family, not playing an enquiry agent for Lucius bloody Daventry."

If there was one thing Christian despised, it was hypocrisy. "Only last month we assisted Daventry with the problem at Chadwick's Auction House. You brooked no argument then."

"Because Daventry had information I wanted. It was a trade of services, nothing more." Aaron firmed his jaw. "And that lunatic Smith could have shot you. Is that not enough to deter you from this madness?"

They were straying from the topic. "I gave Daventry my word I would examine Egyptian treasures at the museum. As you know, I have some knowledge of the subject. I left early this morning, not because I had something to hide, but because the curator insisted I conduct my studies before opening hours."

The frown lines in Aaron's brow softened, albeit prematurely. "I'm not averse to helping Daventry on occasion. The man is a useful ally. But you should have left a note."

"Next time, I shall." Christian tossed back the remains of his brandy and inhaled sharply. It was better to make a full confession now. "The matter is more complicated than inspecting the artefacts."

Aaron's brow quirked. "Oh?"

Christian explained the curator's late-night interlude with a ghost. "Doubtless she'd taken too much laudanum."

Aaron laughed. "Or the curator had."

"The fellow believes the artefacts purchased last month might be fake. Bought from a market in Cairo, not pulled from an excavation site."

"Are they fake?" Aaron's shoulders relaxed and he came to sit in the chair. "Does the museum not have men trained to check provenance? You're more an enthusiast than an expert."

"That's why Daventry had me work with his assistant." A vision of the exotic beauty slipped into Christian's mind. The strange tug in his loins and his chest proved worrying. "She is extremely knowledgeable." Attractive, funny and kind.

Aaron laughed again. "Thank God all Daventry's female agents are married. They say the man is an expert matchmaker."

Christian swallowed past his growing reluctance to reveal his partner's identity. "She's not one of Daventry's agents but someone he met at the servants' registry. She arrived from Italy mere weeks ago with barely a penny to her name. When we met this morning, it was clear she hadn't eaten for days."

A muscle in Aaron's cheek twitched, his expression growing wary. "I suppose you gave her money."

"No, but I placed an order with the grocer."

Aaron offered no complaint.

"And arranged to have it delivered to Hill Street," Christian added.

Aaron jerked like someone had prodded him with a hot poker. "Hill Street?" He paused, his suspicion growing. "I know every resident. None lease properties to tenants."

"Her father sent her to a seminary sixteen years ago and

told her never to return. He's away from home, so she broke into the empty house to take refuge." In all honesty, Christian had never met a woman so courageous. However, being destitute left one with few options.

Amid the taut silence, Aaron merely glared. Like Satan rising from the underworld, he stood slowly, the dangerous glint in his eyes warning Christian to remain seated.

"I can tolerate some things," Aaron said, his tone as lethal as a blade. "You want time away from Fortune's Den? Take a trip to Brighton. You want to test your mental prowess? Tutor children who cannot afford an education. But don't expect me to condone your newfound friendship with Lawton's offspring."

Aaron made for the door.

Christian jumped to his feet. "Where are you going?"

"To throttle Daventry and evict Miss Lawton from my house."

Confusion curbed Christian's temper. "Your house? Miss Lawton lives at number six." Aaron had purchased number seven, their father's old abode, and now leased the property for a pittance.

Aaron whirled around, his eyes as dark as the devil's soul. "Lawton isn't away from home. He's short of funds and living in Gerrard Street at the secret house he bought for his mistress."

"Since when?"

"Since the beginning of April."

"April? But that's a month ago! Why the hell didn't you tell me?"

"Because it's complicated. I told you I would deal with Lawton in my own good time. And when that bastard jumps off a bridge into the Thames to escape his creditors, no one will accuse us of a crime."

Christian knew Aaron was working to ruin Lawton behind the scenes. "But Miss Lawton has nowhere else to go."

A growl rumbled in Aaron's throat. "That's Daventry's problem, not mine. Either way, I'd rather burn in hell than let that woman remain in my house."

Chapter Four

The water was lukewarm at best. By the time Isabella had heated enough to fill a bucket, the measly amount swimming in the bottom of the bathtub had cooled. She gritted her teeth and climbed into the copper vessel.

Mother Mary!

Bathing in a shift would not banish the goose pimples. She took the plunge and quickly immersed herself, though it was more like sitting in a puddle than lavishing oneself in the conte's marble pool.

It's only temporary, she told herself.

Fortune favours the bold.

Mr Daventry had promised her more work, enough so she might secure lodgings within a week or two. She had to pray her father was in Egypt, playing cartographer to a wealthy lord, and wouldn't be home for six months. With luck, he might fall down a shaft, never to be seen again.

Wickedness, it is in the blood.

One day, it will find you and drag you into the pits of hell.

Her mother's stark warning echoed in her head. It was a

mantra the woman repeated when she'd drunk too much wine and began bemoaning her fate.

And yet, despite every attempt to remain virtuous, to learn from her mother's mistakes and avoid the pitfalls of a romantic affair, yesterday Isabella had felt the first stirrings of desire.

Mr Chance was a conundrum. A piece of hieroglyphic script she felt compelled to translate. Nothing about him made sense. He was a walking monument to contradiction. Kind yet hard-hearted. Amiable yet stern.

Hearing his sad story had roused her pity.

Knowing her own kin had a hand in making children homeless left her sick to the pit of her stomach. Wickedness was not in her blood. Though she would have been powerless to act against a tyrant.

Memories of a cruel man flooded her mind. Geoffrey Lawton had never raised a hand to her, but indifference hit harder than any blow. He knew how to make a person feel worthless. Those last few days at home had been the worst.

She closed her eyes and conjured an image of a biscuit parcel hanging from the apple tree. He had remembered. At first, she had been deliberately vague, too embarrassed to admit the truth, too scared to confess such gifts were amongst her most treasured memories.

Her thoughts drifted to the food hamper the grocer's boy had delivered yesterday afternoon. A gentleman had ordered the goods, given her name and address, but the boy knew nothing more.

Perhaps Mr Daventry meant to ensure she didn't starve to death.

Yet she wondered if Mr Chance was her secret benefactor.

She scoffed aloud. Fanciful notions were for the weak-minded. A woman without means had to keep her wits. So why couldn't she stop thinking about the handsome gentleman? Like everyone else in her life, he seemed keen to avoid her. Had she not learnt her lesson?

Deciding counting to a hundred would help to banish thoughts of the enigmatic Mr Chance, Isabella focused on the task. Indeed, her tense muscles relaxed by the time she reached ten, and the water felt decidedly warmer.

Her eyelids grew heavy, the stress of the last few weeks taking its toll. She had two hours before Mr Gibbs arrived to ferry her and Mr Chance to the shipping office. More than enough time for a nap.

Sleep brought little comfort.

Her unconscious mind tormented her with visions of the inscrutable Christian Chance. The dream was so realistic she could hear his voice as clearly as if he were standing in her bedchamber.

"You can't throw her out," he said, his stern tone revealing the dark, compelling side of his nature. "We had an agreement."

"I agreed she could stay the night, nothing more."

"You can see she's vulnerable. We should leave before she wakes to find two men gawping at her comely figure."

"You might be gawping at her figure," came a stranger's stony voice. "I'm assessing the situation to decide how I remove the woman from my premises."

Remove her? The dream had quickly turned into a nightmare.

Doubtless her fear of being homeless was the cause.

"I swear on my mother's grave," Mr Chance snapped, "you will show some compassion, or I shall find her suitable accommodation elsewhere."

"Have you lost your damn mind?" Anger coated every syllable. "This isn't any bit of skirt. This is Lawton's bloody daughter. The spawn of Satan."

The sheer vehemence in his words jolted Isabella to her senses. This was by no means a dream or a nightmare. It was a terrifying reality. She opened her eyes, shocked to meet the gazes of two strapping men.

A scream caught in her throat. She shot up in a mad panic, slipped and would have tumbled from the bathtub had Christian Chance not caught her. Isabella gripped the man around the neck to keep her balance, her sodden shift wetting his waistcoat.

"Forgive us, Miss Lawton." Warm hands settled on her hips, the heat seeping through the sheer material. "We should not have entered the room unannounced."

"It's my house," moaned the dark-haired man who refused to look in her direction. "Miss Lawton is trespassing. She's lucky I've not had her arrested."

"Trespassing?" Isabella prised herself out of Mr Chance's grasp and glanced around the room. No. This was her mother's old chamber. She faced the black-haired devil. "You're mistaken, sir. I spent the first ten years of my life in this house."

His dark gaze sent a shiver down her spine. There was an air of authority about him no one dared question. "Get dressed, madam, and pack your things. You're leaving."

She recognised the dimple in the stranger's proud chin, although Aaron Chance was nothing like the quiet, subdued boy she remembered. "You used to live next door, Mr Chance. Clearly, you've entered the wrong house by mistake."

Aaron Chance withdrew a letter from his coat pocket,

opened it and held it a few inches from her face. "I won this house in a card game. My solicitor's letter proves I own the title deeds."

Isabella scanned the legal document, the life draining from her body when she realised he spoke the truth. "I—I have nowhere else to go, sir."

"We had nowhere to go when your father dragged us from our beds and threw us into a cart. You are not my problem, madam."

Christian Chance intervened. "For the love of God, at least let her stay until she gets paid. I despise Lawton as much as you do but—"

"Evidently, you don't."

Isabella's knees almost buckled. The determined look in Aaron Chance's black eyes said nothing would alter his decision.

Resigned to her fate, she said, "I shall gather my belongings." Though her teeth chattered from fear and the chill in the room, she raised her chin and glared at both brothers. "Or do you mean to throw me out in my shift?" Only when uttering the last word did she consider her state of undress. "At least have the decency to leave while I change."

Aaron Chance turned on his heel and stormed from the room.

She met Christian's gaze and noted the conflict in his striking blue eyes. He wanted to despise her. He wanted to feel hatred, and he probably did, to an extent, but the compassionate boy was not dead. He lived beneath this powerful construct of a man. A man who felt abiding loyalty to his brother.

"I know a few places where you might reside." His eyes dipped briefly to her shift, his jaw firming in response. He avoided looking at her loose curls. "We'll discuss it once we've visited the shipping office."

Christian left the room.

Isabella rushed to lock the door so she might dress in peace, but the growl of warring voices reached her ears. This house bred ill will. The last thing she wanted was to cause a problem between the Chance brothers. There had to be a way for them to work separately on the same case.

Quickly dressing before the beastly brother returned, Isabella threw her meagre belongings into a valise, fashioned her hair in a simple knot and crept downstairs.

Tempers had cooled.

The men were talking, not shouting.

"Lawton wants nothing to do with her," Christian said, the truth of his words causing a small stab to her heart. The world and his dog wanted rid of her. "She's no threat."

"I'll never trust a woman again, let alone one related to that blackguard. When Lawton learns of her connection to you, he will manipulate the situation to his advantage."

"I can handle Lawton."

"Can you? It's taken sixteen years to bury the man."

"We should have stabbed him in the heart long ago." Christian spoke like a rogue from the rookeries, not the learned scholar who respected historical artefacts.

"Perhaps," Aaron Chance said, his tone carrying a hint of regret. "Still, Miss Lawton cannot live in a property either of us owns. It complicates matters."

Despite a period of silence, Isabella remained hidden in the hall. It paid to be abreast of the facts. Had it not been for her snooping, she would be married to Mr Griffin.

"What if I speak to Mrs Maloney? She always keeps an empty room at the bookshop. No one would know Miss Lawton there."

"Give Daventry the responsibility. As her employer, he can source accommodation."

Sensing tempers rising, Isabella gave a discreet cough before entering the drawing room. "I'm ready to leave. Mr Gibbs won't be here for another half an hour. Would you like me to wait on the street?"

"I'm sure my brother won't mind if we wait inside for Gibbs," Christian said before noting the folded white garment in her hand. "Stealing the bed linen, Miss Lawton?" His tone spoke of distrust and amusement.

"It's my wet shift. I cannot afford to replace it, nor can I afford to make my other clothes damp. I shall carry it with me to the shipping office."

"Allow me to take it home and have it laundered." He shot his brother an irate glare. "It's the least I can do under the circumstances."

Aaron Chance glanced at the shrouded furniture. Doubtless he'd like to make a bonfire and raze the place to the ground. "We'll continue this conversation later. There's no need to secure the door on the way out. I've someone coming to change the locks. He should arrive before you leave."

Without giving her a second glance, he strode out of the house, slamming the front door behind him.

His absence did little to ease the mounting tension.

Christian cursed under his breath, his frustration a tangible energy clawing at the air. "Do not mistake my generosity for weakness, Miss Lawton. I shall find you somewhere comfortable to stay, but after our meeting with Daventry later today, I mean to tell him our working relationship isn't viable."

Isabella spoke past the lump in her throat. "I agree, sir. This is an impossible situation. And I do not want to be the cause of any animosity between you and your brother."

"Aaron is not as uncaring as he seems. But when a man has saved his family from drowning, he does everything possible to ensure his ship is watertight." Christian sighed, his shoulders relaxing. "I have to respect that."

"Of course. You owe me nothing, sir."

His gaze journeyed over her face, his blue eyes softening. "If you were anyone else," he began wistfully but did not finish the sentence.

She spent the entire journey to the Limestone Basin wondering what he planned to say. If she were anyone else, would he want to work with her, spend hours discussing old artefacts in a bustling coffeehouse? Could they be friends? Enjoy a stroll in the park, maybe even a picnic?

It was just as well her mind kept her occupied because he spent the time staring out of the window, mumbling her father's name and cursing him to the infernal bowels of hell.

They reached Narrow Street, a lane running parallel to the river, and Mr Gibbs brought the carriage to a halt outside the Bunch of Grapes tavern.

"We should rehearse our story," she said, suddenly nervous at having to lie to Captain Snell. How did one determine if the man was a crook? Should she mention transporting ancient treasures?

"We'll say we're archaeologists looking to hire a ship to take us to Egypt. That we mean to bring heavy artefacts home and will pay handsomely for his services."

Isabella nodded, but a sudden sense of trepidation said they should not leave the vehicle, let alone question a man who lived amongst mudlarks and river pirates. "We'll baffle him with Egyptian references and hope he believes our story." She paused. "Mr Chance?"

He looked at her for the first time in almost an hour. "Yes?"

His eyes … Good Lord! A lady might lose herself in the sapphire depths. The fluttering in her chest returned, an intense case of attraction, not fear. "Do you feel at all apprehensive? What if the captain sees through our facade? Something tells me questioning him is a mistake."

"A mistake?" He laughed, confidence exuding from his powerful aura. "Snell must deal with ten enquiries a week. If anything, he'll think we're too inexperienced to take on such an ambitious project and send us away."

Perhaps he was right.

Besides, she would have to give Mr Daventry a recount of what happened, else she might not receive her wages. One did not lie to one's employer.

"There's nothing to fear," Mr Chance added.

No, the life of an enquiry agent was considerably less dangerous than that of a maid or governess. Whenever men discovered her mother was an opera singer, they took it as an invitation to take liberties.

"Happen the door handle is broken," Mr Gibbs called from atop his box. The gruff fellow was far too free with his opinions and the most impolite servant she had ever encountered. "That, or you missed the street sign."

"I think he means we should alight," she said.

Mr Chance managed a smile as he opened the carriage door. "Gibbs takes some getting used to, but I'd rather work with an outspoken man than a sly snake."

Having dealt with more than her share of serpents, Isabella agreed. "Does the same apply to women, sir?"

"Yes, and don't call me sir." He stood on the pavement and offered his hand. "It makes me uncomfortable."

"Your uncle is an earl. As a gentleman, people should address you with respect." She gripped his hand as she alighted, the mere contact making her heart race faster. Good grief. The sooner they parted ways, the better. These odd sensations were a terrible distraction.

"I'm no gentleman," he said, quick to correct her. "My father was a rotten scoundrel whose family paid him a considerable sum to change his name." He leant closer, his gaze dipping to her mouth. "You'd be wise to keep your distance, madam. Wickedness is in my blood."

Isabella stifled a gasp. Of all the things he could have said, he had to repeat a phrase that resonated. "Then you have met your match, Mr Chance. As the devil's own spawn, my blood is equally tainted."

He grinned, his smile barely reaching his eyes. "Despite your exotic looks, you have the manner of a governess. I doubt you've done anything wicked in your life."

Affronted, she released his hand. "Don't let my facade fool you. I can be wicked when the need arises. I once locked a man in a crypt and threw away the key." How else might she have escaped Mr Griffin? "And I drugged the Conte di Barasian by adding laudanum to his brandy." Escaping his guards had proved a little more taxing.

Mr Chance laughed. "They're hardly immoral pursuits."

Although she battled to remain virtuous, she found herself saying, "Sir, you've seen me bathing. Is that not immoral? I do not recall shooing you from the room."

Mischief danced in his eyes. "Had you been naked, Miss Lawton, I might agree. But only prim ladies and preachers' wives bathe in a shift."

"I'd have bathed naked if the water had been warm."

The air between them crackled. Mr Chance did not tease her or make light of her remark. He ran his tongue over his bottom lip and whispered, "You can always call on me to heat the water."

Not wanting him to notice the blush burning her cheeks,

she quickly said, "Perhaps I might were I not homeless." And then she marched away along Narrow Street in search of the shipping office.

Mr Daventry said to enquire at Napier & Woods, a broker who acted as a middleman for those wishing to hire private vessels. Mr Chance reached the door of the establishment first, opening it for her as any gentleman would.

Inside, a young woman with fiery red hair directed them to the wharf, explaining that Captain Snell was busy preparing his ship for an ice trip to Norway.

"The nobility pay a fortune for spring water ice," Mr Chance said as he escorted Isabella past the whippers hauling coal from a ship onto barges. "I doubt we can persuade Snell to set sail for Egypt."

Isabella might have replied, but the burly fellows working along the wharf glanced up in her direction. Hopefully, they were just curious. In these parts, thieves and ruffians mingled with honest men keen to gauge who best to rob.

She slipped her hand around Mr Chance's arm for reassurance.

Touching him only made her heart race faster.

He looked at her with a mix of surprise and an unreadable emotion. "I've fought with my brothers enough times not to fear these men," he said, anticipating the cause of her anxiety.

"Having me as a partner will be a hindrance." Thugs always preyed on the weakest member. Perhaps she should start carrying a weapon.

"From what I've heard, you're resourceful enough to escape volatile situations. And if all else fails, run."

"Are you not afraid of anything?" She had never met a man so strong and capable. "There must be something that sets you on edge. What is your worst fear?"

She expected an arrogant reply, but the corners of his

mouth curled into a doleful expression. "It's not something I wish to repeat aloud. Besides, two scenarios spring to mind. I'm unsure which one bothers me most."

"Perhaps you fear being lumbered with a woman as prim as a governess," she teased.

He smiled. "I thought we'd established you have wickedness in your blood, though I'm still waiting to see the evidence."

He would have a long wait, though something about him made her lower her guard. "It sounds like you're tempting me to sin, sir."

"If you were anyone else, I might tempt you to do many things, Miss Lawton. And don't call me sir."

They happened upon a man blocking the walkway, a surprisingly young man with a mane of dark hair and a full beard. He stood with his hands braced on his hips, watching the crew inspect the rigging of a white-sailed brig.

Isabella noted *The Marigold*'s name-board and then cleared her throat. "Captain Snell?"

The handsome fellow turned to them, annoyed at the distraction. He scanned Mr Chance's impeccable clothing and frowned. "If you've come to nag me about Norwegian ice, you'll have to log your interest at the shipping office. The next lot of cargo has been bought and paid for."

Mr Chance straightened to stand a head taller than the captain. "Do I look like a man who cares about frozen spring water?"

The captain shifted nervously. "Then state your business. As you can see, I've a ship leaving on the morning tide."

"We're archaeologists," Isabella said, finding her nerve, "and need to charter a ship and crew to take us to Egypt. We plan to bring treasures home and will pay a premium, perhaps even a percentage of the bounty if you agree."

Captain Snell took one look at her and chuckled. "I doubt you know the difference between sand and sawdust. I don't know who told you to come here, but I've never ventured farther than Algiers."

Mr Chance snorted. "And yet Mr Quigley chartered your ship to ferry men from the Society of Antiquaries to Egypt. The artefacts were sold to the British Museum four weeks ago."

The captain seemed surprised they were so well informed and fought to maintain his indifference. "That's nonsense. You've got my vessel confused with *The Mayweather*. It makes frequent trips to the Orient. Now, if you don't mind, I've work to do."

"We've seen the documentation," Mr Chance persisted, his tone sabre sharp. "And we've studied the artefacts. If it's a case of money, I can pay double what you charged Quigley and will pay half in advance."

Any normal man for hire would have jumped at the chance to line his purse. But Captain Snell merely shook his head. "It's a generous offer, but I can't take you to Egypt."

"We can wait until you return from Norway," Isabella added.

The captain firmed his jaw and glared at them both. "Are you hard of hearing? My ship ain't for hire. And I don't know anyone named Quigley. I suggest you leave before a footpad spots your tidy gold watch. You wouldn't want the lady getting hurt in a robbery."

A growl rumbled in Mr Chance's throat. He grabbed Captain Snell's coat lapels and lifted the man a few inches off the ground. "I don't take kindly to threats. Perhaps I'll throw you in the Thames and see if you float."

A few of Captain Snell's crew heard the commotion. One

man hurried down the gangplank, quick to come to his master's aid. "What's going on, 'ere?"

Mr Chance shook the captain. "I'm not done with you. You're hiding something. I can smell a rat from a hundred yards, and you stink like vermin."

"Put me down, fool!" The captain tried kicking Mr Chance's shins but merely dangled like a marionette.

"Call me a fool again and I'll knock those rotten teeth out."

"Mr Chance," Isabella interjected, the sudden panic making it hard to catch her breath. "Perhaps we should leave before matters get out of hand."

But it was too late. The hulking boatswain thumped Mr Chance's arm in a bid to set his master free. "Put him down and be on your way, else I'll ruin that pretty face."

A fight ensued.

Like the devil's prized brawler, Mr Chance smashed his fists into both men's faces. He knocked them down and warned them to remain on their *arses* else there'd be hell to pay. "I suggest you avoid dark alleys for the foreseeable future," he said, his gaze sharp, threatening.

Isabella sensed a hundred pairs of eyes focused on them. She tugged Mr Chance's arm, eager to pull him away and return to the safety of the carriage.

Sensing her anxiety, he cursed both men to Hades, grabbed her hand and marched back along the wharf.

Isabella jogged to keep up with his long strides. "Now I know why Mr Daventry warned me about you." He'd mentioned Mr Chance had a volatile temper, not that touching him would stimulate and soothe her in equal measure.

"What did the blackguard say?"

She clutched his hand, taking comfort in his firm grip, while the dock workers along the wharf looked like they were priming themselves to attack. "He said I must remember you're a little dangerous."

"A little?" he protested, clearly offended by Mr Daventry's assessment. "Don't let my angelic looks fool you. I can be downright savage."

Chapter Five

Christian's blood boiled. Not because Daventry had warned Miss Lawton about his character. Or because the man had made a grave error in his assessment. No, Christian always kept his temper in check, but the moment Snell threatened to hurt Miss Lawton, he had lost his wits.

Cursed saints!

Why should he care what happened to a stranger?

Not just any stranger, one he was supposed to despise?

The dilemma was like a civil war raging inside him, his conscience battling with logic. Yet something else drove him forward, an inner knowing fuelling the fire's flames. Perhaps once he'd found Miss Lawton lodgings, he might banish the woman from his mind.

The lady tugged his hand, forcing him to come to an abrupt halt as they entered Narrow Street. "I need to stop for a moment to catch my breath."

"We need to keep moving." Doubtless Snell was gathering reinforcements. They might be set upon by a gang of baton-wielding thugs. "A wise man picks his battles. Only a fool fights when outnumbered."

God, he sounded like a blasted hypocrite.

"You have a valid point, sir." Miss Lawton released him, hiked her skirts past her trim ankles and ran.

Christian glanced back over his shoulder before following the lady along Narrow Street. Gibbs was in their sights, sitting atop his box like a sullen bear.

Miss Lawton stopped at the door of the shipping office. "Wait for me in the carriage. I need to question the clerk. Warn Mr Gibbs we must be ready to leave."

The clerk? The woman behind the counter looked more like a serving wench than a person of business. "I don't know what sort of men you're accustomed to, Miss Lawton. But I'll not wait in a vehicle like an ageing spinster while you place yourself in danger."

He gestured for her to enter the office while he lingered in the open doorway, watching the street. Miss Lawton approached the crude counter, rang the handbell and waited for the *clerk*.

The woman appeared, chewing her food like a cow did cud. "Didn't I tell you the captain is down on the wharf?" She wiped crumbs from her lips with the back of her hand.

Miss Lawton smiled. "You did. But Captain Snell won't negotiate a price because he cannot recall what he charged Mr Quigley. He sent us here so you might inspect his diary. It would have been the time he sailed to Egypt to bring back historical artefacts."

The woman tutted. "Tell him to come and look himself."

"He said he would buy you a drink at the Grapes if you obliged."

The woman's eyes brightened. "Oh, did he now?" She turned to a large cabinet and rifled through the drawers, stopping to rub her aching back before rummaging through a pile of papers. "Here it is! Mr Quigley paid two thousand pounds to hire the vessel along with the crew. He paid an extra two thousand once it returned safely to shore. He's paid the same the last four times."

"Four times?" Miss Lawton did an excellent job of sounding unsurprised. "And all trips were bound for Egypt?"

The woman nodded. "Snell makes one journey every two years, weather permitting. If you're looking to sail, it won't be until next spring. Best offer him more than Mr Quigley if you mean to secure his services."

"Hiring a vessel is rather more expensive than I thought," Miss Lawton admitted. "But thank you for your time."

Christian stepped into the room and slapped two sovereigns on the counter. "In case Snell forgets to pay for your drink tonight."

The woman snatched the coins like the starving did bread. Christian didn't wait to hear her mumbled thanks. He ushered Miss Lawton to the carriage, assisted her ascent and told Gibbs to head to Mrs Maloney's bookshop in Lime Street.

Miss Lawton settled into the seat opposite and gripped the overhead strap as the vehicle picked up speed. "Well, now we know Captain Snell lied."

Christian took a moment to study Miss Lawton. She had her father's cunning, though used it in pursuit of justice, not to scheme and trick men out of their inheritance.

"Few people impress me, madam." It would be wrong not to offer her due praise. The compliment was by no means a prelude to seduction. Yet the need to see pleasure dance in her sad eyes was as compelling as drawing breath. "Daventry should offer you a permanent position. You have a talent for gathering information."

"I pray you're right and such skills are in high demand," she said, fussing with her skirts. "Else how am I meant to put food on the table?" Her practical reply did not disguise the tinge of fear in her voice.

Guilt surfaced. "I must apologise for my violent outburst at the wharf. There's nothing I detest more than a man who preys on a woman's vulnerability."

Though Christian had been a boy when his mother died, sometimes he woke in the dead of night, convinced he could hear her sorrowful wails.

Miss Lawton's gaze journeyed down the length of his body, her mouth quirking though he could not read her thoughts. "If you were a debutante, you might be considered an Original, Mr Chance. Men with your exceptional looks are rarely so considerate."

"You find my features exceptional?" The compliment did nothing to stem his growing attraction to her. "That's high praise indeed." If only she had more experience with men, they might indulge in a brief affair.

"I'd be lying if I said you weren't handsome. But you have other qualities a lady might admire."

"Such as?"

He shouldn't ask personal questions, but he was desperate to know.

"I've never met anyone capable of putting two men on their *arses*."

A laugh escaped him. "And I've never met a prim woman who could say *arses* without stuttering."

She laughed, too. "In your company, Mr Chance, I'm learning to embrace wickedness. And we should laugh more often. I'm told it's good for the soul."

He couldn't recall the last time he had a reason to smile, let alone chuckle. "Around you, madam, I find I'm more of a gentleman than I'd like. I've never made excuses for hitting a man."

"Under any other circumstances, we would make an excellent team."

Her comment reminded him this was the last time they would be alone together. Pressure gathered in his chest. An uncomfortable feeling, much worse than the restlessness he'd experienced of late.

He was thankful when the carriage entered Lime Street and stopped outside the quaint bookshop. Then he could focus on fixing the problem, not these confounding pangs of regret.

Miss Lawton peered out of the window and craned her neck to read the sign. "Mrs Maloney's Bookshop. What makes you think she'll have a room for rent?"

An unexpected lump formed in his throat. "Mrs Maloney always keeps our old room ready. Should we ever find ourselves destitute or in need, she said it's important to know we have a home here."

Miss Lawton laid her hand over her heart and looked at him. "After the life you've had, it must be wonderful to know someone cares."

Christian allowed a wave of love for Mrs Maloney to sweep through him. "She's like the mother we lost. I don't know where we would be without her. Aaron offered to support her financially, but she refuses to leave the bookshop."

"She's kind and independent. I like her already."

"You're bound to get on well."

Christian opened the carriage door and alighted. He took a moment to glance at the upper window. He'd often kept his nose pressed to the glass, waiting for Aaron to return home from a fight.

Don't die tonight.

We need you.

And how had he repaid his brother?

By entertaining their enemy's daughter.

Like the worst sort of Judas, he turned and helped Miss Lawton step down from the carriage. Touching her felt so natural it helped banish the guilt. "I'll check Mrs Maloney will let you stay before I fetch your valise."

She nodded and showed him her crossed fingers. "I'll be grateful for a bed, even for a few nights. Mr Daventry agreed to give me an advance on my wages, then I should be able to secure a hotel."

"Mrs Maloney won't turn you away."

The overhead bell tinkled as they entered the shop. Mrs Maloney sat in a wing chair behind the counter, engrossed in a book, her round spectacles perched on the end of her nose.

Christian coughed discreetly, his whole person lighting on the inside when the ageing woman looked up and smiled.

"Christian. You never mentioned calling today." She placed the book on the counter along with her spectacles. It took three attempts to haul herself out of the chair, but he knew better than to offer assistance. "We always take tea on Thursday. Good Lord! It's not Thursday, is it? One day seems to merge into the next."

He rounded the counter and took her soft, wrinkled hand in his. "It's not Thursday, but I'll gladly take tea. I have a dilemma, and you're the only person I can turn to for help."

Mrs Maloney reached up and cupped his cheek like she had in his youth. "You always were a kind boy. You know how to make an old lady feel special. But there's not a problem in this world Aaron can't solve."

"Aaron is the problem."

Mrs Maloney paled. "Oh! Is he ill?"

"No, he's angry."

She chuckled. "He's always angry."

"He's angry with me," Christian corrected. He gestured to the woman he couldn't shake from his mind. "Allow me to present Miss Lawton. We were neighbours as children. That should help to explain my dilemma."

Miss Lawton stepped forward. "Good morning, Mrs Maloney. I'm afraid I'm to blame for their disagreement."

The woman's tired eyes brightened as they scanned Miss Lawton's exotic features. "Is that so? I've never known the men argue over a lady. Not in all the years of our acquaintance."

Why the devil did she look so pleased?

Christian explained Miss Lawton's parentage and her dire circumstances. "Aaron cannot see past the fact she's Lawton's daughter. But I cannot leave her to fend for herself on the street."

"And so you want me to give her your room until she can afford a place of her own?"

"In a nutshell, yes."

"I'm willing to pay," Miss Lawton blurted, her desperation clear for all to see. "And I shall be no trouble. Perhaps I might help in the shop for a few hours a day. I've spent most of my life reading."

Christian pictured her alone in an Italian tower with nothing but books for company while her mother entertained her lover downstairs.

Mrs Maloney considered him through narrowed eyes. "You've a house in Ludgate Hill. I'm told it's empty."

Christian inwardly groaned. "It's unsuitable. I do not want people thinking ill of Miss Lawton." Gossip would spread faster than a fire in a hay barn. He'd not have people think he was paying her for services rendered. And Lawton had more chance of finding her there. "I need to know she's safe."

"Well, this is a turn-up for the books."

"Does that mean you'll let her stay?"

Mrs Maloney patted Christian's upper arm. "Yes, she can have your old room for the time being. There'll be no charge, but I need someone to climb the steps and dust the top shelves."

Miss Lawton gasped in relief. "I'll do anything to help, Mrs Maloney. I cannot tell you how grateful I am for your kindness."

"You'll tell me if you require a hot meal. Dinner is around eight, once I've closed the shop. And you can help yourself to anything from the pantry." Mrs Maloney leaned closer. "No gentlemen callers. No callers of any kind."

Miss Lawton shook her head. "I've no friends in town."

"That's not true, dear. Christian risks his brother's wrath by bringing you here. He must consider you a good friend indeed."

Mrs Maloney made him sound like a saint when his motives were downright sinful. He told himself he couldn't see Miss Lawton suffer. In truth, he couldn't shake this damnable attraction.

He'd take her as his mistress in a heartbeat.

Yet he'd not insult her by making the lewd suggestion.

"Christian will show you the way while I make us some tea. The room is clean. I'd not have those boys sleeping in a dusty bed." They weren't boys anymore, but Mrs Maloney liked to maintain the illusion.

Christian kissed the woman on the cheek. "There'll be a golden chaise waiting for you in heaven, with a host of angels ready to feed you grapes."

The woman smiled. "I'd rather a pokey room in Lime Street with five filthy scamps for company. Now, take Miss Lawton upstairs. I'll have the tea ready when you return."

Miss Lawton didn't speak as Christian led the way up the

narrow staircase. His mind was full of memories of the past, his heart too full of gratitude to make polite conversation.

He opened the door to the modest room and stepped back to allow Miss Lawton to enter. She glanced at the sparse furnishings, noticed a book beside the candlestick on the nightstand, and smiled.

"I cannot thank you enough, Mr Chance. This will be perfect for the time being. And Mrs Maloney is the kindest, gentlest soul. I'm sure to feel safe here."

Christian snorted. "Don't let that soft voice fool you. She can be a tyrant when the need arises."

Get me water and a needle and thread. If I don't stitch Aaron's wound tonight, he might not wake in the morning. Move! There's no time to dally.

Christian shook his head to clear his thoughts. He should offer Miss Lawton every reassurance, but he'd not been in this room for years, and the sudden deluge of voices and images squeezed the air from his lungs.

Feeling slightly dizzy, he sat on the edge of the bed. Nausea roiled in his stomach. This room had been his worst nightmare and the answer to his prayers.

Miss Lawton surely felt the same because she approached him and laid her light hand on his shoulder. "I can see it's all too much for you. Wait downstairs, and I'll be along in a moment."

Heat radiated from her palm to relax his tense muscles. People said he had the strength of Achilles. Yet the past was like an arrow he'd failed to see. A barbed tip piercing his heart, not his heel.

"I understand what it's like to be a child and have your world turned upside down." Miss Lawton brushed a lock of hair from his brow to comfort him, yet desire tugged deep in his abdomen. "As adults, we do our damnedest not to dwell on the past. Sometimes the memories catch us unawares and it's like we're ten years old again."

Christian looked up at her. He wasn't thinking of anything but the present moment and the undeniable urge to kiss her.

He stood slowly, his body brushing against hers as he pushed to his feet. Being a keen detective, she noticed the hitch in his breath, surely felt the energy around them thrumming with barely contained lust.

She laid a hand on his chest to stall him. "Desperate people do desperate things. Lonely people make foolish mistakes. You should return to the bookshop before you do something you'll regret."

It was sensible advice, but he'd not listened to reason since locking eyes with her in the museum's basement. "I could play the seducer, tell you I'm falling apart and need your help to banish the ghosts. But the bare truth of it remains. I've thought about kissing you since I tied a parcel of biscuits to the tree sixteen years ago."

She swallowed hard. "No good can come of it."

"You're right. When I leave here today, I doubt I'll see you again." Gibbs would take her to visit Daventry. Being in this room confirmed Christian could not betray his brother. "I'll always regret never knowing the taste of your lips." He dared to reach for a stray curl and tuck it behind her ear.

Water pooled in her eyes. Her throat worked tirelessly as she fought to muster a reply. Her reply was unexpected.

She stretched up and brushed her mouth against his. Soft. Gentle. "Thank you for the biscuits. Thank you for being kind enough to send food and risking your brother's wrath in letting me stay here. I'll never forget it. I'll never forget you."

So this was goodbye.

The thought wrought havoc with his insides.

Something stopped him from letting go.

"I don't want you to kiss me out of gratitude. I want you to kiss me because it's the only thing you're compelled to do. I want you to be yourself with me."

She shook her head. "I don't know who that is."

"Then let me kiss you as I want to. Let me see if I can find her."

She hesitated for a few seconds. "One kiss goodbye?"

"Yes. One kiss goodbye."

Perhaps they might meet again in sixteen years when life was less complicated. When he was free to make different choices. When guilt didn't wrap around his heart like a choking vine.

Miss Lawton closed her eyes and puckered her lips.

Christian stared at her and smiled. She was about to kiss the devil, not a choirboy. "Look at me. Say if you want me to stop."

Her eyes flew open when he cupped her cheeks and stroked his thumbs over her silken skin. He'd never met a woman whose gaze conveyed a sultry innocence. It did things to him he couldn't explain. Roused a need that superseded any other.

His mouth covered hers, their lips melding slowly in an age-old dance—yet her touch and taste were undoubtedly unique. When she didn't pull away, he traced the seam of her lips with his tongue, seeking entrance, longing to push deep inside her wetness.

The first slide into her warm mouth was divine.

That's when the tempo changed.

That's when the shackles of restraint fell away, when she wrapped her arms around his neck, anchoring him to her. Perhaps wickedness was contagious. One minute they were standing, their hands moving rampantly, touching, exploring. The next, she was on top of him on the bed, him massaging her buttocks, pulling her against the rigid length of his cock, mimicking what he'd do to her if only they were naked.

The need to pound hard left him panting. They were swallowing each other's moans. Drinking from each other's mouths like parched nomads in the desert.

In his arms, Miss Lawton was no prim governess.

She was wild, passionate and utterly wicked.

"Tea is ready and on the table." Mrs Maloney's call broke the spell.

Startled, Miss Lawton dragged her lips from his and scrambled off his body. With shaky hands, she patted her hair and brushed her skirts. She seemed confused that a chaste kiss had turned into a rampant devouring.

Christian swung his legs off the bed, dragged his hand down his face and breathed deeply to settle his racing heart.

"Perhaps it's just as well this is goodbye," she stuttered. "This is insanity. You'll be the ruin of me, sir."

Frustration surfaced. "It's lust, not insanity. And you'll be the ruin of me, madam. I suspected we were compatible, but this ..." He waved his hand back and forth between them. "This is …"

So damn near perfect I could cry!

"Foolish," she offered.

"Madness!"

"I quite agree."

He stood and had no choice but to fiddle with his hard cock so it wasn't obvious in his trousers. "It would be unwise to take tea. I'll speak to Mrs Maloney and make an excuse. I'll have Gibbs fetch your valise and ferry you to Daventry's office in Hart Street."

"You're not coming?"

Most likely in his trousers if he didn't place some distance between them. "Tell Daventry I'll investigate

Quigley while you study the paperwork. It's evident we cannot work together."

She glanced at crumpled sheets on the bed. "You're right. I'm not sure we can ignore what just happened." She stepped back and straightened her shoulders. "Goodbye, Mr Chance. It was a pleasure meeting you again."

"Goodbye, Miss Lawton." Hellfire! His throat tightened. "I suspect there's no real mystery to solve, and Snell is only guilty of shipping contraband. Still, I pray Daventry notices your skills and offers you permanent work."

"I pray so, too." She smiled. "Well, do I look presentable?"

"You look beautiful," he said before engaging his brain.

She didn't reply but hurried from the room, leaving him alone with his thoughts and a heart heavy with regret.

Chapter Six

The British Museum
Great Russell Street

For the third time in as many minutes, Isabella stared at the list of Egyptian items purchased by the museum. The words blurred on the page as her mind drifted from her studies to thoughts of the charismatic Mr Chance.

She glanced at the empty chair opposite the desk, the dreaded ache of loneliness filling her chest. The void left by his absence seemed huge. Working alone on the case proved less thrilling. But she understood the need to avoid each other, and what happened in the quaint room had complicated matters.

Five days had passed since he'd kissed her passionately. Five days since she'd behaved like a wanton and permitted him to take liberties. Her heart should weigh heavy with remorse. She should have spent hours repenting, yet she couldn't rouse a flicker of shame.

Who would have thought the touch of a man's lips could

be so exhilarating? The memory caused the same tingling she'd experienced when locked in his embrace. The desire to kiss him again plagued her waking hours and invaded her dreams.

Isabella shook her head.

Perhaps a love of illicit liaisons was in the blood.

The thought that she might be anything like her mother proved sobering, so she returned to her questions about Captain Snell's shipment. Eight large crates of artefacts were listed on the docket Mr Daventry had obtained. And yet the museum had purchased so small a number they would fill one crate.

What had happened to the other artefacts?

It seemed odd that Mr Chance couldn't find the elusive Mr Quigley. Who was the man who acted as a broker? No one seemed to know.

Perhaps he was part of the criminal fraternity and had taken receipt of the other crates. If the real crime was avoiding paying duty, whatever was inside must be expensive. Was it gold or opium or something simple, like silk or tea?

The thought of tea had her thinking about Mr Chance.

He had sent a note explaining he could not take tea with Mrs Maloney last night. The lady said it was the first Thursday he'd missed in eight years. Although, knowing Isabella would be at the museum this morning, he had promised to call at the bookshop.

Hearing the curator's footsteps echoing along the corridor and somewhat annoyed that her mind had wandered again, Isabella quickly tidied the documents away.

She snatched her notebook and pencil and blew out the candle. But when she opened the door, she met the gaze of the stern-looking Mr Purton, not the custodian.

"Who the devil are you?" The man stared down his bulbous nose. The broken capillaries in his puffy cheeks said he drank to excess. "Higgins, fetch a constable," he shouted, though the corridor was deserted.

Isabella inhaled deeply and gathered her wits. "I'm studying here on behalf of the women's antiquaries group. I'm writing a thesis on Ancient Egyptian artefacts. Mr Brown has been assisting me. You must be Mr Purton." The curator had pointed out his assistant a few days ago.

Though he accepted her story without question, suspicion swam in his beady eyes. "Mr Brown said something about helping a female scholar with her notes."

"Excellent. Then you won't mind directing me to the Treasures of the Nile exhibition. I'd like to sketch the recent haul of rare objects."

"Mr Brown has been called away to Bath. I'm not sure he'd want you snooping around the museum in his absence."

Bath? He'd not mentioned a trip when greeting her this morning.

She offered her best smile, the sort her mother once used to make men fall at her feet. "I'm to leave London myself tomorrow to attend a lecture in York. My notes will be useless without the sketches, sir. I assure you, I'll be but half an hour."

"I'm a busy man, Miss …"

"Reeves."

Mr Purton's sinister gaze journeyed slowly down to her toes. He appreciated her figure, that much was evident, though he definitely disapproved of a woman out to educate the masses.

"As I said, Miss Reeves, I don't have time to waste."

Isabella persevered. "Never mind. I shall return with my patron Lord Oldman. I believe his funding helps to pay your wages." She uttered a silent prayer, hoping the blackguard wasn't on friendly terms with the peer.

"Lord Oldman?" Failing to suppress his frustration, Mr Purton mumbled to himself before conceding. "I suppose I can spare half an hour. Follow me. I'll show you to the exhibit. You'll go nowhere else, mind."

He didn't wait for her or hold the doors open.

She scuttled behind and raced up the vast marble staircase to keep his fast pace. "You'll find everything you need here." He left her standing beside the Rosetta Stone, a captivating attraction in its own right, and moved to walk away.

"Sir, might I ask how much you paid for your recent purchases? It would give our members an idea of how precious the most basic objects are."

Mr Purton came to an abrupt halt. "I don't know offhand, but I secured them for a reasonable price. Lord Oldman funds trips to the Orient and keeps some pieces. Best you ask him." And with that, he left her alone on the upper floor while he went about his business.

After taking a moment to appreciate the colossal bust of Rameses II, Isabella made quick sketches of papyri and a few antiquities in case Mr Purton demanded to see them.

She had left the Egyptian Gallery and was about to descend the stairs when she saw the horrid fellow greeting two gentlemen in the hall. In itself, it was nothing unusual. But like felons planning their next robbery, their shifty gazes said something was amiss.

Isabella approached the attendant, who was busy polishing the oak bannister. "I have business with Mr Purton but don't want to disturb him if he's with important gentlemen."

The attendant's nose wrinkled as he glanced at the men in

the hall. "Mr Purton doesn't take kindly to interruptions when he's with his friends from the Society of Antiquaries."

The Society of Antiquaries?

Isabella suppressed a gasp. How strange they should visit when Mr Brown was out of town. "Ah, it's Mr Clarke and Mr Woodrow." It was a wild guess, but their names were recorded on *The Marigold*'s passenger list. "They were on the recent expedition to the Orient."

The attendant nodded. "Mr Purton likes to keep abreast of new discoveries. The men often bring goods for sale. They sometimes meet in the private room at the Horse and Groom tavern."

He said *goods*, not historical artefacts. Was Mr Purton conspiring to sell something other than antiquities? And only devious men met in taverns.

"I imagine they find many trinkets on digs, ones that might interest a collector." Isabella caught herself. In an effort to establish if a crime had been committed, her imagination ran riot. But Mr Daventry thought the matter was worth pursuing, and a penniless lady didn't argue.

She thanked the attendant and waited until Mr Purton escorted his friends to his office before quickly descending the stairs.

Mr Gibbs would curse her tardiness if she dallied a moment longer, and so she kept the exit in her sights. For the past few days, she had been knocking on doors along Great Russell Street, looking for the ghostly woman in white. Sadly, there was no time to pursue her enquiries today.

She hurried through the vestibule and spotted Mr Gibbs atop his box, glaring beneath heavy brows. She raised her hand by way of an apology and crashed into a man about to enter the museum.

Her notebook and drawings tumbled to the ground, but the fellow did not offer an apology or crouch to gather her things.

No! He gripped her firmly by the upper arms, shook her and snapped, "Watch where you're going. You stepped on my new boots."

Isabella glanced up only to meet the cold, dark eyes of a man she knew. He was much older than she remembered, grey peppering his wavy brown locks, the creases around his eyes deeper now. Still, one never forgot the face of the devil.

Father!

Her heart missed a beat.

Her whole body shook violently.

"Forgive me, sir." She averted her gaze, pretended she didn't know him as she tugged her arms free. "The fault is mine." She needed to collect her drawings and make a dash for the carriage, but he uttered a word that filled her with dread.

"Isabella?"

No! No! No!

"You mistake me for someone else, sir."

"I think I know my own damn daughter. The conte wrote to me and told me your mother was dead. That you'd packed a valise and fled."

Panic choked her throat.

Mr Gibbs would intervene at any moment, and then her father would learn she worked for Mr Daventry and know of her connection to Mr Chance.

She bent to retrieve the papers off the pavement, but her father stamped on them and cried, "Look at me, girl! You know I despise insolence."

There was only one thing left to do.

What she'd done the night Mr Griffin attacked her in the seminary's chapel. What she'd done the night the Conte di Barasian tried to force her into bed.

She took to her heels and ran.

Fortune's Den
Aldgate Street

"They say Kingsley's vowels aren't worth the paper they're written on." Christian found the reprobate's name in the ledger. "He lost a substantial sum to Lord Brookhurst last night. We should bar him from the club until he settles his debts."

From his seat behind his mahogany desk, Aaron stared over his steepled fingers. "When punters cannot pay, it's bad for business. I'll tell Sigmund to turn Kingsley away tonight. We'll allow him back once his finances are in order."

Christian nodded before moving to the next item on an ever-growing list. The quicker this meeting was over with, the better. It took immense effort not to drag his brother over the desk and throttle him with his cravat. "Profits increased five per cent last month despite losing the revenue from renting the upstairs rooms."

Aaron remained silent, the tension in the air thick. He leant forward and narrowed his gaze. "How long do you mean to punish me for ruining your friendship with Miss Lawton?"

As long as I've breath in my lungs.

"I'm not sure what you mean," Christian said, but the thought of never seeing Miss Lawton again brought the sting of bile to his throat.

"You know damn well what I mean. You've been glum for days. Dragging your chin on the floor. Barely saying a word to anyone."

A veil of melancholy had fallen over him, darkening his mood. "That has nothing to do with Miss Lawton and everything to do with your lack of faith in me. I'm quite capable of managing my own affairs."

"Yet I find your judgement flawed."

Said the man who'd based his opinion on nothing more than the woman's name. "Miss Lawton is nothing like her father and despises the man. But rest assured, I shall fulfil my obligations to this family."

Aaron's brow quirked. "I suppose those large brown eyes and sumptuous lips helped to convince you of her good character."

Christian inwardly groaned. Damn his brother for noticing. "I can bed any woman of my choosing. It takes more than a pretty face to entice me."

It took a kind gesture, a selfless act, the brush of dainty fingers through his hair, gratitude for a pokey room above a bookshop.

"You'd be a fool to trust her."

"That's no longer of any concern."

Was he a fool to believe a stranger's word?

Was the timing anything but a coincidence?

"There are other intelligent women in the world," Aaron said.

"Yet you sit here night after night, refusing female company."

Aaron sneered. "I've seen what a vindictive woman can do. I'd rather cut out my heart with a rusty blade than place my faith in one again."

One day, a lady might force Aaron to question his beliefs. Until then, Christian had to live with his brother's cynical attitude.

"Can we hurry things along?" Christian said, tiring of the conversation. He planned to return to the shipping office and harass the *clerk* for a better description of Quigley. "I have somewhere else I need to be. We should discuss the next item on the list."

"I don't know why you're pursuing this business with Daventry. There's more than enough work here to keep you occupied."

Because few things grew beneath an oak tree. Aaron was such a powerful force in their family, Christian had to find a means of stepping out of his brother's shadow.

Thankfully, Sigmund's arrival provided the perfect distraction. "Sorry for disturbing your meeting," said their man-of-all-work, a frightening fellow in his own right, "but Daventry is here looking flustered. If that ain't worrying, I don't know what is."

Aaron cursed. "That man is the bane of my bloody existence."

Sigmund grimaced. "He's come about Miss Lawton."

"Miss Lawton?" Christian's heart lurched. Daventry would not call unless there was a problem. But Mrs Maloney hadn't sent a note. All seemed well when Christian spied on the bookshop last night. "Send him in."

Aaron huffed but made no objection.

As he burst into the room, Daventry did indeed look

panicked. He didn't bother passing pleasantries. "Has Miss Lawton called here?"

"I imagine this is the last place she'd come," Aaron replied.

Christian stood abruptly. "Why? Did Gibbs not collect her from the museum? She's supposed to be working in Mrs Maloney's bookshop this afternoon. As payment for food and lodgings."

Aaron cast him a sidelong glance but did not ask how Christian was party to the information.

"A man accosted Miss Lawton outside the museum. Gibbs was about to intervene when the lady took to her heels and ran." Daventry glanced at the mantel clock. "That was six hours ago, and no one has seen hide nor hair of her since."

"What do you mean, accosted her?" Christian couldn't catch his breath.

"Manhandled her and tried to prevent her leaving."

Christian shot his brother an irate glare. This wouldn't have happened had they not been forced to work alone. "Was it Captain Snell? The bastard as good as threatened her while we were at the wharf."

"Based on Gibbs' description, I suspect it was her father. To make matters worse, he has all the notes she dropped during the struggle. It will be nigh on impossible to crack the smuggling ring now they know we're on to them."

Christian wasn't convinced the men were smugglers. Still, that was of no importance now. "How the devil did he know she was in London?"

Daventry reached into his coat pocket, withdrew a folded piece of paper and gave it to Christian. "This might explain how Lawton knew where to look. It was written a few days ago."

It was an article torn from the *Scandal Sheet*.
Gossip, which happened to be true.

"It would seem the most unlikely pair were spotted in Narrow Street yesterday. Miss Isabella Lawton was seen holding the arm of Mr Christian Chance. The pair looked to be on extremely friendly terms. A little bird tells me they're regular visitors at the British Museum."

"That's absurd." Christian had no choice but to give his brother the note. "No one saw us enter the museum, and I doubt dock workers write for the *Scandal Sheet*."

Was this some vile conspiracy?

Perhaps realising there was no case of fraud to answer, the curator had sold the story.

"Someone did!" Aaron roared. "Did I not say this friendship would cause no end of trouble? Lawton will think we're using his daughter to conspire against him."

"You are conspiring against him."

"Yes, but when he's found dead in a ditch, I'll not have the authorities point the finger at us." Aaron tossed the paper on the desk and dragged his hand through his hair. "We need to find Miss Lawton as a matter of urgency."

"Damn right we do."

Aaron thumped the desk with his clenched fist. "Lawton is capable of anything. He'd kill his own daughter to see one of us hang."

"Miss Lawton isn't dead." Christian wasn't sure how he knew, but the lady was too clever to fall into her father's trap.

"You had better pray she's still breathing, else one of us is for the noose."

"Can you think where she might go?" Daventry said, bringing an element of logic to the conversation. "Did she mention friends or acquaintances?"

Christian swallowed past the boulder-sized lump in his throat. "She has no friends that I know of. She has no one." No one but him, and he'd abandoned her to appease his brother.

"Then all we can do is scour the streets."

"It will be like looking for a needle in a haystack," Aaron snapped.

"What choice do we have?" Christian pulled his watch from his pocket. "We'll reconvene here at eight o'clock. And don't stop me from leaving." With his temper hanging by a flimsy thread, Christian left the gaming hell and marched across the road to the mews.

He would cover more ground on horseback. It was three miles to the museum. Three miles to the Limestone Basin. Yet every instinct said she would not linger in dangerous places.

He rode to Hill Street and checked she wasn't hiding in the basement of Lawton's old house. He visited Daventry's office in Hart Street, all to no avail. She wasn't hiding in Green Park. Had not remained close to the museum and sought refuge in the Foundling Hospital or Gray's Inn Gardens.

She was so fearful of her father, had she stowed away on a ship bound for France? In London, she had a roof over her head and a means of earning a living. She'd be a fool to risk what little security she had.

It was nearing eight o'clock when Christian returned to Aldgate, his heart heavy in his chest. An inner voice told him to visit the bookshop before returning to Fortune's Den.

He handed his horse to his groom and covered the short

journey to Lime Street on foot. Mrs Maloney was outside, locking the bookshop door when he approached and scared the woman out of her wits.

"Bless the Lord, you gave me a fright." Mrs Maloney took a moment to settle her breathing. "I was just on my way to Aldgate Street. Miss Lawton returned twenty minutes ago. Heaven help her. She's in a terrible state."

Relief had Christian gasping aloud.

He scanned the street to make sure Miss Lawton had not been followed. "Did she say where she'd been?"

"Come inside. You look like you need a stiff brandy." She unlocked the door and beckoned him into the shop. The tinkling of the overhead bell was always comforting, as was the musty smell of old books.

It was dark inside, and she directed him to the small sitting room.

Miss Lawton was asleep in the chair, her bare feet immersed in a basin of water. Mud covered the hem of her dress, and her wild curls resembled a bird's nest.

Mrs Maloney lit the lamp. "She's been walking for hours. The poor mite was too afraid to return here in case her father followed her. When I opened the door, I found her shaking to the marrow of her bones. She downed three glasses of that expensive sherry you bought me last Christmas."

Christian picked up Miss Lawton's boot and turned it over in his hand. The sole was almost worn through. Doubtless it was the only pair she owned. He would rectify the problem in the morning.

While Mrs Maloney pulled a blanket over Miss Lawton's lap, he stared at the woman who'd kissed him so passionately. Why did he feel an overwhelming need to protect her? Was it nothing but a desire to help someone down on their luck? Her eyes held the same sadness as his sister

Delphine's. Yet these primal stirrings were by no means brotherly.

"It's not safe for Miss Lawton to remain here," he said, aware he was running out of options and Aaron would not permit her to reside at Fortune's Den. Perhaps Daventry would find her suitable accommodation. "And I'll not place you in danger. Until this matter is resolved, you must move to Fortune's Den."

"Move?" Mrs Maloney sounded flabbergasted. "I'm not leaving my books. I've lived here for nigh on thirty years. The King himself would have to drag me out kicking and screaming."

Christian knew better than to argue with the stubborn woman. "Let me stay here. Just until we've dealt with Geoffrey Lawton. We'll read together at night like we used to," he added to sweeten the deal. "Discuss the ancient world and Greek mythology."

Mrs Maloney's eyes brightened. "You scamp. You know how to bend a woman to your will. You can stay but only for a few nights, mind. A lady should never become too dependent on a man. Even if he is like her own son."

The last comment melted his heart. "I'll return to Fortune's Den and inform Aaron." There was also the matter of Miss Lawton's welfare to discuss, though it would be wrong to do so in her absence.

"I'll have a piece of currant cake waiting when you return." Mrs Maloney glanced at the sleeping Miss Lawton. "Be a dear and carry Miss Lawton to bed. Bless her soul. The poor thing hasn't an ounce of strength left. She can explain what happened when we take breakfast in the morning. Oh, best you dry her feet first. There's a towel on the chair. I need to check on a few things."

Mrs Maloney left him alone with Miss Lawton.

His traitorous gaze moved to her bare calves and trim ankles. It seemed wrong to tend to her ablutions without her permission, but where was the harm in dabbing her feet with a towel?

Christian knelt on the floor, slipped his hand into the water and captured Miss Lawton's dainty foot. Despite the small blister on her tiny toe, her skin was smooth. He'd never washed a woman. Who would have thought such a simple gesture would play havoc with his insides?

But that was nothing compared to how it felt to hold her in his arms. Taking slow, measured steps so as not to wake her, he held her tight to his body and mounted the stairs.

He tried not to think of Natasha orchestrating events from her throne in hell. His father's wife—the woman who had turfed them all out onto the streets—would love the irony of Christian's current predicament. What a shame she'd choked on a bone and not dangled from the gallows.

Christian kicked the door open and strode to the bed. He looked down at the woman huddled against his chest, possessiveness burning through him. Obsessed with the idea of kissing Miss Lawton again, he told himself it was an impossible situation. This infatuation would pass, but Aaron would always be his brother. And a boy who'd once lost everything didn't risk losing his only family.

If she were anyone else ...

The thought entered his mind for the umpteenth time as he laid her gently on the bed. He took the plaid blanket off the chair and draped it over her. Stole one last glance at the sleeping angel before creeping to the door.

"Mr Chance?" Her low, husky voice slipped over him like a soothing caress. "Stay a while."

It was the most tempting invitation of his life. But he

knew what would happen if they spent any time alone together.

"You need to rest, Miss Lawton," he said, keeping his back to her. Those large brown eyes had the power to bring him to his knees. "We can talk in the morning. Good night."

It took a saint's resolve to leave the room. It took the Lord's determination to close the door behind him.

Chapter Seven

The rich, aromatic smell of coffee teased Isabella awake. The distant strains of a woman singing a country tune slipped into her mind. She caught a whiff of smoked ham, her stomach growling for her to open her eyes and seek out the source.

She blinked and gazed at the ceiling, her vision blurring into a grotesque image of her father, the whites of his eyes red and veiny, the hard angles of his face twisting in outrage.

Your mother doesn't want you.

You're a noose around her neck.

That's the reason she left.

Heart pounding, Isabella shot out of bed.

No one blamed her mother for running. It merely hurt that Isabella had been left behind to suffer in the devil's den. Indeed, she had inherited the same trait and had spent her life seeking a means of escape.

But she couldn't run forever.

How did a young woman make a stand against a tyrant?

Pestered into action by her rumbling stomach, she washed her hands and face in the china bowl on the table, then tidied her hair. Her dress needed washing, but the sky looked grey and dreary, so it would have to do for another day.

She met Mrs Maloney at the bottom of the stairs. "Good morning, Mrs Maloney. Something smells good."

The woman's eyes brightened. "You're up. Bless you, dear. You slept so soundly, I feared it would take the kiss of a prince to stir you from slumber."

Heat rose to Isabella's cheeks at the memory of sharing a passionate kiss with Mr Chance. He wasn't royalty, and she doubted any woman would sleep when lying next to such a charismatic man in bed.

Isabella raised the hem of her gown to reveal her stocking feet. "Have you seen my boots? I recall you yanking them off last night." She had been too tired to argue.

"They're at the cobblers, dear. They were almost worn through."

"The cobblers! I haven't another pair."

Mrs Maloney gave a cheery smile and gestured to the sitting room. "Christian bought you new kid boots. He's waiting for you to join him for breakfast. Best hurry, else there'll be nothing left. That boy has a beast of an appetite."

Isabella's pulse soared. "Mr Chance is here?" They'd agreed not to see each other again. Flustered, she patted her hair and tried to brush the creases from her dress.

"Yes, dear. He spent the night."

"Spent the night?" She almost choked on the words. Where had he slept? She vaguely recalled him carrying her upstairs but presumed fatigue had played havoc with her imagination. Had he sat watching her until dawn? Had she dribbled and mumbled in her sleep?

"Yes, he'll remain here for the time being. I'll let him explain." And with that, she headed for the door leading to the bookshop.

"Are you not eating with us this morning?"

"Heavens, no. I woke with the larks and ate hours ago."

Isabella took a moment to gather herself before greeting Mr Chance.

As soon as she stepped into the room, the musky scent of his cologne assaulted her senses. He was dressed impeccably in a dark blue coat moulded to his muscular torso. Many years had passed since she'd watched him in the garden, but he was still the only person who made her heart flutter.

He glanced up, pushing a golden lock of hair from his brow before standing. "Miss Lawton. I trust your spirits are revived after your traumatic experience yesterday."

"Yesterday?" Every muscle ached. A tribute to how far she'd run. Yet she could think of nothing but how he'd spent his time while she dozed.

Mr Chance frowned. "Your father accosted you. At least that's what Mrs Maloney said last night."

"Yes. Forgive me. I'm just a little surprised to see you here."

He rounded the table and pulled out her chair. "I'll explain while you eat. I'm told you've eaten nothing since breakfast yesterday."

She found herself smiling as she moved to take her seat. "I thought you disliked playing the gentleman."

His fingers brushed against her shoulder, the merest touch sending shivers to her toes. "Perhaps you'd feel more comfortable if I did something wicked."

"Like put salt in my tea?"

"Maybe something a little more daring." He resumed his seat, his magnificent blue gaze pinning her to the chair, rendering her immobile.

"Does your brother know you're here?" she asked,

desperate to find a topic that didn't send her wits scattering like leaves in the wind.

He poured coffee into her cup. "He knows."

"From your tone, I presume he's still angry."

"His worst fears have been realised. Now Lawton knows of our connection, he will use it against us. None of us are safe until your father's body is rotting in a shallow grave."

Isabella inhaled sharply. Not because she felt a sliver of pity for the man who'd given her life—but because she felt nothing. Her heart was like a solid stone in her chest, except when she remembered the boy who'd given her biscuits.

"Does your brother have a plan, or are you sworn to secrecy?" She doubted he'd have permission to enlighten the enemy.

Mr Chance took two pieces of toast from the rack. "Daventry persuaded him to wait before making any rash decisions. He seems to think your father is smuggling goods from the Orient and selling them to the highest bidder. Lawton is on the verge of bankruptcy. It would explain why he'd take the risk."

She sipped her coffee, the warmth relaxing her a little. "Mr Purton met with the men from the antiquaries yesterday. They arrived as soon as the curator left for Bath. I'm certain my father was on his way to meet them."

"For what purpose?"

She shrugged. "To share the proceeds from their ill-gotten gains."

"Daventry thinks your father may have been looking for you." Mr Chance produced a piece of paper from his coat pocket—the latest gossip from the *Scandal Sheet*.

Isabella almost expired when she saw her name mentioned. "Who wrote this? There wasn't a soul at the museum while we were in attendance."

Mr Chance snorted. "It hardly matters who. Now our connection is public knowledge, Aaron fears your father might get rid of you and lay the blame at my door."

"Get rid of me?" She was too old for the seminary and would rather die than marry a stranger. But then recognition dawned. "Geoffrey Lawton is many things, but he would not murder his own daughter."

"Then why run?"

The question stumped her.

Why had she bolted? Heavens, she'd run so fast her lungs burned. She'd hidden amid the shrubbery in the park like an escaped Bedlamite. All because she feared what her father would do.

"He's not the sort of man one crosses."

"Precisely. We would have dealt with him years ago, but he'd made it clear Aaron would get the blame if he turned up dead."

Isabella bit into a piece of toast while contemplating the dilemma. "So, Mr Daventry wants us to prove my father is guilty of a crime. That way, it would solve everyone's problems."

Mr Chance searched her face. "Us?"

"I'll not remain here, waiting like a sitting duck. We'll continue as before. I have a few lines of enquiry we might pursue." Surely Aaron Chance could see the sense in them uncovering the mystery of the forged artefacts. Although she was not convinced the ushabti was fake.

Mrs Maloney entered the parlour, though the hairs on Isabella's nape prickled to attention when she saw Mr Daventry marching behind.

The man, whose powerful aura rivalled that of Mr Chance, did not greet them or offer an apology for the interruption. "It's good to see you looking so well, Miss Lawton. Sadly, I'm about to deliver shocking news."

Mrs Maloney ushered the man into a seat and poured him coffee.

Mr Daventry swallowed it down and sighed like it had the soothing effects of laudanum. "I've spent the last two hours at the mortuary."

Isabella jerked so violently she spilled coffee on the table. "If you're here to tell me my father is dead, sir, I assure you it will be the best news I've had in sixteen years."

He gave an apologetic smile. "They hauled a body from the river this morning. A young woman fitting the curator's description of the ghostly figure he met at the museum. Luckily, I'd asked to be informed of every suspicious death, else she would have been buried in a pauper's grave come noon."

An icy chill swept over Isabella.

In her notebook, she had sketched the woman's likeness. She had detailed the houses she had visited in a bid to locate her. Her father had that notebook. Now, the poor woman was dead.

She explained her fears to Mr Daventry. "My father has all my notes, my theories, my suspicions. If he has smuggled treasures into the country, he will most certainly cover his tracks."

Mr Chance did not mince words. "Do you think Lawton killed her?"

"I don't deal in coincidences. Which means someone involved in the sale of the artefacts did." Mr Daventry pinched the last piece of toast from the rack.

They fell into a heavy silence.

Isabella cradled her coffee cup, her thoughts turning to the investigation. The original crime must be serious for a man to resort to murder. The time for dallying and worrying about Aaron Chance was over.

"Sir, I understand the need to tread cautiously, but I believe we should interview the men from the Society of Antiquaries. They can explain what happened to the other seven crates listed in *The Marigold*'s log."

Mr Chance agreed. "The woman's death changes everything. We cannot tiptoe around the curator. In our efforts to keep the investigation a secret, we're getting nowhere. And we need to interview his assistant."

"The coroner believes the woman was dead before she entered the water. There were bruises on her neck and defensive wounds on her arms." Daventry paused and smiled at Mrs Maloney when she returned with more toast for the rack. "I've spoken to the Home Secretary. You have his permission to conduct a murder investigation, though I'm required to share your findings with Bow Street."

Mr Chance grinned as if he welcomed the challenge. The dangerous glint in his eye said he would love nothing more than to threaten and intimidate the suspects.

"What role am I to play?" she asked.

"As my agent, you'll lead the investigation. Regardless of outside objections, you're more likely to solve the case if you work together. You can begin this morning. I've made an appointment for you to visit Somerset House."

"We're to interview learned antiquaries?" Like a rowboat washed out to sea, she was more than out of her depth.

Daventry nodded. "You're to meet Mr Woodrow at one o'clock. I told the coroner you'd visit the mortuary this morning. Once you've seen the body, you'll have a better idea of what you're dealing with."

She was to study the corpse?

Mr Chance inhaled sharply. "Perhaps I should go alone. I'm not sure a mortuary is a suitable place for a woman."

"No, not for an ordinary woman," Mr Daventry replied before Isabella could protest. "But I think we both agree Miss Lawton is unique."

Mr Chance looked at her, his gaze falling to her lips. The corners of his mouth curled into a satisfied smile. "Indeed. I suppose you want me to support her where necessary."

"Will that be a problem?"

"Not at all."

"Excellent." Mr Daventry stood. "I shall leave you to pursue new lines of enquiry. I'm taking my wife to the theatre tonight. Leave a note at the Hart Street office if you encounter a problem at Somerset House."

The gentleman bid them good day and left.

Mr Chance resumed his breakfast and poured them both fresh coffee.

A relaxed intimacy flowed between them. Isabella was used to eating alone, used to her mother waking at noon and spending the next two hours bathing. That she should feel so at ease with a man proved an interesting development.

"I bought you new boots," he suddenly said. "You cannot navigate the treacherous road ahead with flimsy soles."

No one had ever considered her welfare. His generosity left her floundering. "That's very kind, but you must let me reimburse you once I'm settled."

He raised a hand in protest, the diamond in his signet ring sparkling amid the morning sunlight. "I'll not hear of it. They're a gift. You wouldn't have had to walk the streets for hours if we'd been working together on the case."

"I hid amongst the shrubbery for two hours," she admitted.

"That explains why I had to pick leaves and spiders out of your hair before putting you to bed."

Isabella almost choked on her coffee. She had not imagined it after all. "So you did carry me upstairs."

"You were so tired, Mrs Maloney didn't want to wake you." He offered a devilish grin. "I dried your feet, too. I'd have stripped you down to your shift, but I'd not remove your clothes without your permission."

"A rogue would have taken every advantage," she teased.

He was more of a gentleman than he cared to admit.

"If you want my hands on your body, you must say so." His compelling blue eyes caressed her across the table. "I don't take anything that doesn't belong to me. I'll not touch anything that isn't mine."

Oh, she'd had a glimpse of what it was like to be owned by this man. To be at the mercy of his wicked tongue. To feel the imprint of his hands on her buttocks. To be branded with the heat from every hard muscle.

"Then be assured, I cannot give you the permission you seek." How could she? She had not escaped Mr Griffin and the Conte di Barasian just to fall at the last hurdle. "You won't ever own me, Mr Chance. No man will."

His confident smile said he didn't believe her. "Yet you haven't stopped thinking about our kiss. You forget I own a gaming hell. I'm skilled at reading signs. You've looked at my mouth many times during breakfast, madam."

She'd thought about kissing him more times than she should. Indeed, she enjoyed this man's company so much he was dangerous on every level.

"You have crumbs on your lips. I wasn't quite sure how to tell you." She took her napkin, reached across the table and dabbed the corners of his sensual mouth. "Now, there should be no more confusion."

Mr Chance captured her wrist, his thumb stroking the delicate skin. "At the club, I'm known as the King of Diamonds. Although I'm cunning when it comes to decision making, I move slowly towards my goal. I'm an excellent negotiator and know how to make a woman want me."

Isabella didn't doubt him for a second. She could outwit the best seducer, but she was powerless against him.

Still, she arched a brow. "I've lived with a master game player. I've seen every trick, every device known to man." And yet she wanted his hands on her body, wanted to feel close to him in ways she could not explain. "I value honesty, not falsehoods. I'll take the truth over deception. It's why you'll never win, no matter how tempting the bait."

The wild glint in his eyes said she'd just challenged the devil. Doubtless he could feel the rapid beat of her pulse. That's why he exuded such confidence in his ability to get his own way.

He released her and relaxed back in the chair, a figure of masculine dominance. "If you've finished eating, shall we visit the mortuary?"

She raised her hem a fraction and wiggled her stocking-clad toes. "I cannot go anywhere without my new boots."

Mr Chance inhaled sharply, his gaze hot and intense as it drifted over her ankles. "I shall enjoy this challenge, Miss Lawton. I shall enjoy it immensely."

Though loathe to admit it, she relished his attention. "And yet you don't strike me as a man who enjoys bending to a woman's will."

"Where you're concerned, madam, I find I'm quite flexible."

Chapter Eight

Christian had visited the mortuary on three occasions. Once, when Aaron failed to come home after a bare-knuckle fight at the Dog and Gun. Once, when they found a man dead in the doorway after a bitterly cold night and Mrs Maloney feared a local surgeon might steal the body. Once, when he was five and he'd gone looking for his mother because he refused to believe she was dead.

Nothing had changed.

The room was cold and clinical; the body presented on a slab as if it were an artefact at the museum. A sheet protected the deceased woman's modesty, though one could not help but note the slimy texture of her skin and imagine her floating face-down in the water.

The scene was hardly conducive to his current aim—to make Miss Lawton want him so badly she would kiss him again. Still, he just needed the lady to faint, and he'd have every reason to haul her into an embrace.

"Has anyone come forward to identify the woman?" Miss Lawton asked, quickly covering her mouth and nose with her lace handkerchief to ward off the foul smell.

"No." Mr Paisley's skin was so thin and grey, he looked to have one foot in the grave. "And no one's reported her missing, though I believe she's of Mediterranean descent and came to London seeking employment."

"What makes you so sure?" Christian said.

He lifted a dull lock. "There's a certain coarseness to her hair."

Christian glanced at Miss Lawton, whose hair was as soft as silk, but did not suggest the coroner's theory had flaws. "The curator said she spoke in riddles. Perhaps English is not her first language."

Miss Lawton uncovered her mouth to comment. "We must assume she lives in the vicinity of the museum. We should have a constable knock on every door and enquire about a missing person."

He doubted the magistrate would waste manpower on a woman of modest means. Most would presume it was a case of *felo-de-se*.

"I'd guess she worked as a scullery maid." Paisley pulled back the sheet and pointed to the woman's knees. "There may be a record of her at one of the servants' registries."

"How long was she in the water?"

"Days, I'd say."

"Mr Daventry said drowning may not be the cause of death." Miss Lawton avoided looking at the bloated corpse.

Paisley drew attention to the other marks on the body. "Some people treat their servants like dogs. From the state of her nails, the bruising and defensive wounds, I'd say her employer assaulted her on a regular basis. It's a common occurrence. The blight of the lower classes."

"And you will write that in your report?" Miss Lawton asked.

Paisley shifted uncomfortably. "It will probably be

recorded as an accidental drowning, miss. These things are complicated. There's not much we can do for the poor soul now."

She made to object, but Christian interjected, "Thank you for your time. We'll be in touch if we need any further information."

"But I'm not finished," she whispered.

"Yes, you are." He cupped her elbow and escorted her out of the mortuary and onto the street. "We may need to ask more questions. If you challenge him, he'll avoid speaking to us in future."

Clearly frustrated, Miss Lawton tugged her arm free. "But if he records it as drowning, how can we prosecute the culprit?"

"Without witnesses to the crime, securing a conviction will be impossible. That's why Daventry is inundated with work. Finding evidence elsewhere must be our main focus. We need a confession."

Miss Lawton sighed. Water gathered in her eyes. "What if it's my fault she's dead? What if she knew about the smuggling operation and my notes helped my father identify her?"

Seeking any opportunity to touch her, Christian clasped Miss Lawton's upper arm. "While you're skilled with a pencil, I doubt you had any influence over what happened to her. As Paisley said, servants are abused on a regular basis. It's nothing new. Besides, we don't even know it's the same woman."

He noted her frown deepening, sensed her battling against his logical statement. He had a hard time believing it himself.

"I suppose you're right." She managed a weak smile before glancing over her shoulder. "Being outdoors has set my nerves on edge. Why do I get the sense we're being followed? Tell me, am I losing my mind, Mr Chance?"

In a bid to reassure her, he fought against his own inner trepidation. Danger lurked in the shadows. Every muscle in his body was primed to attack. Yet the enemy refused to show themselves.

"Whatever happens during this investigation, I will protect you. You can count on me, madam. I'll not leave you to work alone again."

She clasped his hand as it rested on her arm and squeezed gently. "I've never been able to depend on anyone. Forgive me if I ever seem disbelieving or ungrateful."

The merest touch of her hand heated his blood. This woman did things to him no other woman ever had. He should run a mile. But he wanted her. He wanted her more than he cared to admit.

Christian reached into his coat pocket and withdrew a small blade encased in a leather sheath. "Keep this in your reticule. Wield it with confidence, even if you have no intention of using it. Remember, the person you wish to portray to the outside world does not have to reflect who you are in private."

She stepped closer and took the knife, their fingers brushing so intimately his abdominal muscles hardened. "That explains it, then."

"Explains what?"

"Why people step aside for you and avoid meeting your gaze. They fail to notice you're the perfect gentleman."

"I'm different with you," he said, giving a mischievous wink. It was true. Despite everything he'd said when she laid down the gauntlet and challenged him to seduce her, with Miss Lawton, he didn't have to be anything but himself. "To his peers, a man's persona is the measure of his success."

"Did your brother tell you that?"

He laughed. "We've built an empire on that very philosophy."

She frowned while considering her reply. "As a woman who can barely afford her next meal, perhaps I should adopt the same strategy."

"On the contrary. I urge you to be yourself, Miss Lawton. I find I like *her* a great deal."

She tapped him playfully on the arm. "Is this a ploy to seduce me or settle my nerves, Mr Chance?"

"Both. Is it working?"

She gave a half-shrug. "A little."

Though they laughed, he kept his eyes secretly peeled. Something was wrong. Every instinct warned him to be on his guard.

"I fear Gibbs is growling at us again." Christian gestured to the ogre atop the box. Keen to relax amid the safety of the carriage, he cupped her elbow and escorted her across the street. "Somerset House, Gibbs."

"You're cutting it fine if you mean to make your one o'clock meeting. Happen you think this carriage has wings or it's being pulled by Arabian thoroughbreds."

"You underestimate your ability to get the job done, Gibbs."

"You overestimate my patience, Mr Chance."

Miss Lawton smiled. "We won't keep you waiting again."

Gibbs ushered them into the carriage and covered the mile to the Strand with minimal delays. They arrived at Mr Woodrow's office in the North Wing of Somerset House with less than a minute to spare. Indeed, the loud chime of a bell somewhere in the vicinity confirmed as much.

A well-dressed clerk made them wait ten minutes before escorting them into Woodrow's lavish office. "Your one o'clock appointment, sir. Mr Chance and Miss Lawton."

The gaunt, grey-haired man seated behind the walnut desk dragged his gaze from his ledger, quick to observe Miss Lawton's alluring countenance. "Any relation to Sir Geoffrey, madam?"

"He is my father, sir."

Daventry had urged them not to hide their identities when dealing with the Society's respected members. Based on the predatory way Woodrow looked at her, Christian wondered if they'd made a mistake.

Woodrow leant back in his chair and steepled his fingers. "I spent many months with your father in the Orient. He's an excellent cartographer with unrivalled attention to detail."

"I wouldn't know, sir. I've not seen him for sixteen years. Indeed, I'm here with my colleague in a professional capacity to discuss a recent incident at the British Museum."

Colleague?

One day soon, Christian hoped to be her lover.

Christian stepped forward and produced the letter from the Home Secretary, permitting them to investigate the death of a woman found in the Thames. "The lady in question had knowledge of stolen artefacts. Artefacts sold to the museum from your recent haul in Amarna."

That wasn't precisely true. According to the curator, the lady had spoken gibberish, but he meant to wring this snobbish oaf for every drop of information.

Woodrow scowled. "But this is outrageous. I negotiated the deal with the museum. I assure you, I unearthed those objects with my own hands."

Tired of waiting for Woodrow to offer them a seat, Christian moved two chairs and positioned them in front of the fellow's desk. He waited for Miss Lawton to sit before dropping into the chair beside her.

"Then let me tell you what we know, sir," Miss Lawton said calmly, but Woodrow raised a hand to object.

"I'll not discuss my personal affairs with a woman."

"For the purpose of this interview, consider me a sergeant at Bow Street, sir. This is a criminal investigation. You will answer any questions put to you."

Christian smiled to himself. His admiration for Miss Lawton grew by the hour. She wasn't ashamed to admit her fears. Despite being terrified of her father, her determination to uncover the truth was commendable. And he couldn't stop thinking about that heart-stopping kiss.

Woodrow stared at Christian down a long patrician nose. "Have you no shame? How can you sit there and let her ride roughshod over you?"

Christian took a moment to appreciate the mental image of her astride him in bed, sweat trickling between her breasts, her hair a cascade of wild curls. "With tremendous ease."

The lady turned to him, gratitude swimming in her sensual brown eyes. Hell. He'd lay on hot coals to earn a look like that again.

Christian hardened his tone. "Now, you'll tell her whatever she wants to know. Let me remind you, this is a murder enquiry. Miss Lawton has the Home Secretary's permission to arrest you and throw you into a cell with bawds and common thieves. I doubt the members would allow a man with a sullied reputation to hold a position here."

Woodrow realised he was out of his depth and minutes from drowning. His Adam's apple bobbed before he eventually said, "I'll be honest with you. The trip to Amarna failed to produce the results we hoped. Sources convinced us we would find a wealth of treasure in a buried temple, but we barely secured enough items to fill a crate."

"Your patrons must have been disappointed, sir."

A muscle in the man's cheek twitched. "We had to go cap in hand to the Grand Vizier and beg to purchase items from his private collection."

"How many of his treasures did you buy?" Christian said. Perhaps the Vizier's seal was genuine, though that didn't mean they'd brought original artefacts home.

Embarrassment coloured Woodrow's cheeks. "More than double what we recovered from the site. Probably twenty in total. Thankfully, they all came with provenance."

"And Lord Oldman sponsored your trip and claimed some treasures for his own collection?" Miss Lawton attempted to confirm.

Woodrow's brows quirked in response. Clearly, he wondered how Miss Lawton had learned the information. "A few select pieces: a ruby-encrusted scarab, a gold face mask and a lotus chalice. Again, with the provenance, they're considered rare. Rare indeed."

A brief silence ensued.

Christian could almost hear the cogs of Miss Lawton's inquisitive mind turning and decided to ask a question himself. "What reason would a woman have to accost the curator in the dead of night and warn him about fake treasures?" He pinned Woodrow to the seat with his stern gaze. "A woman found murdered and dumped in the Thames?"

Woodrow stuttered, stumbling over his own tongue. "I—I have no notion. But you have my word all the items purchased are genuine."

Items bought from a vizier who was desperate to raise funds?

It was doubtful.

Miss Lawton sat forward. "How many crates did you bring home, sir? We've seen the log and wish to account for all items brought ashore."

"I couldn't tell you how many crates came ashore." Woodrow scratched his temple. "But four were delivered here the night *The Marigold* docked. Captain Snell won't risk river pirates stealing his bounty and was quick to move his cargo."

Snell was probably worried about the River Police, not the damn pirates.

While Miss Lawton asked about the captain's character, Christian studied Woodrow, looking for the odd nuances that marked him a liar.

One thing was abundantly clear. For an arrogant man, Woodrow had developed a sudden case of nerves when speaking about the captain.

"Did the other crates belong to Captain Snell?"

Woodrow paled. He glanced about the room as if they were sitting in a dockside tavern surrounded by cutthroats and crooks. "Though we hired Snell to deliver us to Egypt, the captain had his own agenda."

"What does that mean, sir?" Miss Lawton sounded impatient.

"The man went missing for weeks on end. When we asked to catalogue the treasures during the long voyage home, he refused to let us have access to the hold. He said his crew feared bad omens. Said some of the pieces were cursed."

Miss Lawton straightened. "He could have tampered with your crates, and you'd be none the wiser. Therefore, you cannot attest to their authenticity."

A sudden flare of anger had Woodrow shooting out of his chair. "Of course they're genuine. We spent hours examining them before approaching the museum. I'm not an imbecile, madam."

"Sit down, Mr Woodrow," Christian said firmly.

A few questions sprang to mind, but Miss Lawton could read his thoughts and said exactly what he was thinking.

"I believe they're excellent forgeries, and Captain Snell swapped them for the original artefacts during the voyage. He may have smuggled contraband, too, hence his sudden absence."

From the look of resignation on Woodrow's face, he thought the same. "We've agreed not to hire Snell again. We sold the items to the museum for a ridiculously low price. I'm not sure what else we can do."

Christian doubted they had told Lord Oldman about the disastrous voyage but said nothing. He'd keep that under his hat for the time being. "How do you explain the woman's warning to the curator?"

The man thought for a moment, then shrugged. "Perhaps she's a sailor's wife or sister and knew of Snell's cunning operation. Perhaps she was hired by someone to cast doubt over the purchases."

"Or she is your mistress, sir," Miss Lawton said brazenly, "and knew of the problems you'd had with Captain Snell. Perhaps you cast her aside, and she sought revenge."

Woodrow's cheeks turned an unhealthy shade of purple. "That's outrageous. I'll not credit these slanderous remarks with a reply."

"Tell us where we might find Mr Quigley," she pressed, taking advantage of Woodrow's agitated state. "He chartered the ship on your behalf."

"I don't know anyone named Quigley. In the interest of historical study, Lord Oldman chartered the ship and paid the advance." He tugged on his waistcoat and called for his assistant. "Now, if you have any more questions about the voyage, I suggest you speak to my colleague Mr Clarke. He's away but will return to town sometime next week. Good day!"

Miss Lawton stood and offered a graceful smile. "Let us hope we uncover the truth soon, Mr Woodrow. How embarrassing it would be if the Society of Antiquaries became embroiled in a plot to smuggle opium. Good day."

God, she was incredible.

Overcome by a swell of pride, Christian was still smiling when he escorted Miss Lawton through the grand doors and into the vast courtyard.

"Why are you looking so pleased?" she said, frowning when she noticed his broad grin. "Mr Woodrow is clearly hiding something."

"I'm not so sure. Perhaps he's just a naive fool." He touched her lower back while rounding the huge bronze statue.

The lady's head shot in his direction. She felt it, too, the spark of attraction that accompanied every intimate gesture. "Such a learned gentleman should know better than to trust a man for hire."

Christian brought her to a halt and faced her. "Are you going to avoid discussing the real question burning in your mind?"

She arched a coy brow. "And what question would that be, Mr Chance? Why Mr Woodrow became defensive when I mentioned his mistress?"

"No." He cupped her elbow and drew her a little closer. "Why, whenever we touch, it's like the planets collide."

Her breath caught in her throat. She met his gaze, and his stomach flipped inside out. "Because you want what I cannot give. I'll never be any man's mistress, and it's evident that whatever lies between us is growing in intensity by the day."

"At least admit you want to kiss me."

She sighed and shook her head. "As you said this morning, I often look at your mouth. That's why it's better we keep ourselves busy trying to solve the case."

He refused to give up so easily. Something drove him to press his advances, and he feared it wasn't entirely lust. "What if I'm the only man you ever want to kiss? What if you never find anyone who stirs the same reaction? What if we were destined to meet again?"

Despite his experience, he had never met a woman whose mind he admired and whose body he craved. No one had ever made him question his loyalty to his kin. Why was she so different?

He had to know.

"Are you telling me this is fate, Mr Chance?"

It was as if events were being controlled by an other-worldly force. "I suspect this is a rare opportunity to feel something real. Be it a wild and passionate love affair." Be it something more profound.

Her breath quickened as she searched his face. "I run from everyone and will undoubtedly run from you. Despite outward appearances, we're both fragile beings and will probably cause each other a wealth of pain."

The burning need to have her forced him to say, "You don't know that. You shouldn't make presumptions."

"Your family hate me."

"What happens between us has nothing to do with them."

Her laugh held a wealth of cynicism. "They'll drive a wedge between us. You'll tire of me. Grow to despise me. It's like an old play I've seen too many times not to know how it ends."

So had *he*, but this was the first time he'd felt something more than a fleeting attraction. "Isabella," he dared to say, noting how her lips parted at the sound of her given name. "Do we not owe it to ourselves to—"

"Miss Lawton?" A deep masculine voice cut into their conversation. "It is you. Good Lord! What an uncanny coincidence."

Christian turned to meet the gaze of an extremely handsome man sporting a mop of greying black hair. He wore his collars high, his cravat fastened so tightly he continually gasped for air.

Miss Lawton turned ghostly pale. Her bottom lip trembled, but she straightened her spine and forced a smile. "Mr Griffin. Good heavens! How strange we might run into each other in such a busy metropolis. I'm surprised you recognised me after all these years."

"I'd know you anywhere, my dear," Griffin replied with smooth familiarity. His gaze searched her face like he'd been deprived of her company for far too long. "Though I never expected to find you on England's shores. Your father replied to my letters and told me you were living in Positano."

She floundered upon hearing the news. "He did?"

Christian was equally out of his depth. He had money and power and could have any woman of his choosing, but he'd never had to deal with jealousy's poison slithering in his veins.

Murderous thoughts consumed him.

He considered punching Griffin and breaking his perfect nose.

"I thought I saw you leaving the museum yesterday, thought I saw you again in my favourite bookshop. Well, if this isn't the most marvellous coincidence."

"How strange we should meet like this," she said, a tinge of fear evident. She gestured to Christian. "Allow me to introduce my husband, Mr Chance."

Her husband?

Who the devil was this fellow?

Griffin's countenance changed dramatically. His eyes darkened. His shoulders rose, hunching like a cat ready to pounce. "Your husband? Your father assured me you remained unmarried."

"He was mistaken. I've had no contact with my father since leaving the seminary." She reached for Christian's hand and gripped it tightly. "Mr Griffin made regular visits to Bramling. Being a keen theologist, he kindly devoted his time to the students' studies."

"How benevolent," Christian muttered.

"I still give the odd lecture on occasion," Griffin replied while observing the breadth of Christian's shoulders. "When I can spare the time, of course. I'm in London for a month, speaking at Mrs Gossman's School of Enlightenment in Covent Garden."

Miss Lawton feigned interest. "I'm certain they will appreciate the depth of your knowledge, sir."

An awkward silence ensued.

Griffin ignored the cue to leave.

One word from Miss Lawton and Christian would put his boot to the buffoon's arse. Indeed, the desire to beat this man to a pulp left his fists throbbing. It wasn't jealousy rousing these barbarous thoughts. It was a primal need to protect his friend and colleague.

Keen to escape the fellow, Miss Lawton said, "Well, we have an appointment across town and cannot be late. I pray you enjoy the rest of your day, Mr Griffin."

"I'm staying at Mivarts Hotel if you'd both care to join me for dinner. We might reminisce about your time at the seminary."

The lady looked like she would rather gouge out her eyes

with a blunt blade. "I'm afraid we're away to Bath this afternoon and must make haste. Good day, sir." Miss Lawton was already moving, clutching Christian's hand and pulling him through the courtyard.

Christian did not need to glance over his shoulder. He could feel Griffin's penetrating stare boring into his back. Once seated safely inside the carriage, he would probe Miss Lawton for more information. If need be, he would visit Mivarts under cover of darkness. Ensure Griffin knew not to trouble her again.

But the lady was struggling to catch her breath.

"What is it?" he said, concern shadowing his anger. "Why are you so afraid?" Her hand shook in his, but she gripped him as if teetering on a steep precipice. "Who was that man?"

She managed to stop her chin from trembling to say, "That, Mr Chance, was the devil's disciple."

Chapter Nine

Isabella couldn't breathe.

Her heart pounded so hard in her chest it would likely crack a rib.

The last time she'd locked gazes with the villainous Mr Griffin was through the crypt's iron gate. The man had gripped the bars tightly, his knuckles white amid the blackness as he demanded she unlock the door.

She could still hear the clang of metal as he shook the gate violently while threatening to whip her with a birch. She could still picture saliva dripping down his chin as he shouted obscenities, could recall the mask of propriety falling to reveal the grotesque savage hiding beneath.

Her skin crawled as she remembered the way he'd touched her.

Too intimately.

Too forceful.

Her stomach churned, needing to cast up the horrid memory along with her morning meal.

"Forgive me, Mr Chance." She brought him to an abrupt halt in the vestibule leading to the Strand. She faced him, seeking solace in his heavenly blue eyes. "This is probably the strangest request any woman has made, but would you mind holding me for a moment?"

He blinked in surprise but made no complaint about the task or the public setting. "It's not the strangest thing a woman has asked me to do, but without doubt, it's the most endearing."

It usually took hours to banish the memories. Like an army of ants, they found their way through every nook and cranny. "A brief embrace should suffice." Just a moment to know she did not have to deal with this alone.

Mr Chance drew her towards the tall Doric columns and wrapped both arms around her, a muscular barricade against outside forces.

"Breathe," he whispered. "Your whole body is tense."

She did breathe, inhaling Mr Chance's alluring scent in the process—an aroma more arousing than soothing. Pressing her cheek to his hard chest, she closed her eyes and thought of their passionate kiss. Mr Chance hadn't hurt her. He had not forced his attentions or taken anything she'd not wanted to give freely.

"Griffin is staring at us. Do you want me to speak to him?"

"Ignore him. Talk about something else."

He understood her meaning and quickly provided the perfect distraction. "I have Mrs Maloney to thank for my love of the ancient world. She'd purchased a pile of books from a merchant who'd fallen on hard times. Among them was one detailing the rise of the Roman Empire, another about Ancient Egyptian landmarks, sketches of Abu Simbel."

Isabella looked up at him. "Does she still have them?"

"No. I keep the books amongst my personal collection in my bedchamber at home." A slow smile touched his lips.

"Perhaps you might like to see them, touch them, examine them closely."

Isabella found herself grinning. Mr Chance was charming and amusing and downright mischievous. "I'm not sure your brother would approve. He'll not tolerate a Lawton under his roof."

He captured her chin between his long fingers and brushed her bottom lip gently with his thumb. "I could sneak you upstairs, but you'd have to remain there indefinitely. No one need know. You'd be my special secret." A sensual hum rumbled in his throat. "We'd dine together. Sleep together. Find adventurous ways to occupy our time."

Mr Chance made the clandestine sound tempting.

For a month, it would be perfect.

But soon cracks would appear.

"What sort of adventurous things would we do?" she said, desperate to ignore her doubts and keep hope alive.

He arched a brow. "Things no gentleman should repeat."

"You're no gentleman."

"No," he mused. "I'm not."

"If we were wicked, it would be no fault of our own. We could blame our parents for corrupting our poor souls."

Mr Chance narrowed his gaze. "Miss Lawton, are you attempting to seduce me? If so, I must tell you it will be as easy as eating cherry pie."

Her equilibrium restored, she raised her chin. "What a terrible pity. I'm a woman who thrives on a challenge."

"Do you want me to make it hard for you?" he uttered, his voice low and husky. "Trust me, it won't be a problem."

For the first time, she faced a romantic dilemma.

She'd sworn never to suffer her mother's fate, yet the need to strip this man out of his clothes and press her body close to his was too powerful to resist.

He must have sensed her inner struggle, the desire to do the opposite of what she'd professed. "You need to stop hiding and be honest with yourself. You're an intelligent woman. Surely you can see what's happening here."

Yes, she knew.

Their attraction was a palpable energy vibrating between them.

"What is happening?" she whispered.

Mr Chance leant closer. "We're going to kiss again. All this dallying is delaying the inevitable. When we do, it will be explosive. You'll beg me not to stop until you find your release."

He must have seen the glazed look of surrender in her eyes. Thank heavens they were in a public place or their mouths would have collided.

"I see you understand my meaning," he said, his gaze hot and intense. "You've already experienced such pleasure. Tell me. Who earned the right to touch you?"

Isabella shook her head. "No one." Sadly, she'd borne witness to the experience. People had probably heard her mother's moans in Milan. "I'm chaste, Mr Chance. That might be somewhat of a problem for you."

"If you're trying to deter me, you're doing a dreadful job."

"I'm not trying to deter you." Like the Earth's magnetic pull, she was drawn to him in inexplicable ways.

"Good. Because at this present moment, nothing could stop me from wanting you." He released her, the chill of loneliness quickly finding its way back into her bones. "But I'm not the one wavering between piousness and wickedness. You must think on the matter. If you want to dabble with danger, you'll need to let me know."

Her mind skipped to their impending carriage ride, to

those quiet hours after dinner tonight when she'd be alone in her room craving his company. He was right. The more time they spent together, the more she dreaded the time apart.

Mr Chance offered his arm. "You'll be glad to know Mr Griffin has left. Later, you'll tell me what he did to make you so fearful."

"It's an age-old story. A case of unrequited lust. A tale of a wolf in sheep's clothing." But she couldn't bear to think about Mr Griffin, and so she gripped his arm tightly and walked towards the Strand.

"Did he hurt you?" he said as if preparing to wreak vengeance on Satan's minions.

Fearing what he might do, she avoided the question. "I owe you an apology. I shouldn't have called you my husband without asking your permission."

"Pay it no mind. I've been called worse things."

"All of them undeserved, I'm sure."

"Unrepeatable, yet wholly deserved," he teased.

She chuckled, believing her troubles were behind her, but her gaze shot to the three men blocking their path, and she realised they'd only just begun.

She froze—stopping dead in her tracks. Fate was conspiring against her. Evil lurked on every street corner, waiting to put paid to these brief moments of happiness.

"Cursed saints," Mr Chance growled. "How in the Lord's name did your father know we were here?"

Isabella gulped. "I have no notion."

Her father stepped forward, his fists clenched and teeth bared. "Is this what it's come to, *Mr* Chance?" he mocked. "Playing an enquiry agent so you can manipulate my daughter and attempt to ruin me?"

Christian Chance did not cower as most men were wont to do. "Why would I need to manipulate her? From what I hear, you're practically bankrupt. You can't even pay your men."

In his outrage, her father's cheeks ballooned. "It's a temporary setback. Rest assured. I intend to make your brother pay for his devious scheming."

Mr Chance's laugh dripped with contempt. "We're not children anymore, and you're no longer in your prime. There's not a man in London capable of overthrowing my brother."

"Not legitimately, but I'm a man of cunning means, Mr Chance." Her father laughed with his cronies before turning his attention to her. "You're coming with me, Isabella. There's nowhere left to run."

Her heart sank. The image of what cruel fate awaited her proved blinding. She shook her head and closed her eyes "I'd rather die than leave with you."

The blackguard chuckled. "Where's your gratitude, girl? A life of splendour awaits. The Conte di Barasian will pay a fair price if I deliver you to his lavish abode." He snarled at Mr Chance, a victorious twinkle in his beady eyes. "Enough to restore my credit and keep the wolves at bay."

What? He meant to sell her to the conte?

Isabella's knees almost buckled.

"You're lying," she stuttered, convincing herself that time and distance made communication impossible. "You could not have corresponded with the conte during the brief weeks since my mother's death." Moreover, her father would not accompany her on a trip to Italy. She could easily evade one of his lackeys once they reached port.

The devil grinned. "The conte has been scheming since your mother took ill last year. He's grown tired of waiting for you to surrender your virtue. He arrived in London last night."

The conte was in London?

The news brought the sting of bile to her throat.

Mr Chance cracked his knuckles. Gone was the handsome man with the heart of an angel. The sinister twist of his mouth and his menacing gaze marked him as more than a little dangerous. "The conte will have to find his entertainment elsewhere. The lady is not for sale. She's accepted a proposal of marriage from me. As my betrothed, she has the full protection of my family."

Her father was undeterred. "Marriage? Marriage to you? Your brother would never allow it." Despite the frowns of numerous passersby, he lunged and grabbed her arm, his bony fingers pinching her skin. "Isabella is coming with me. Until you exchange vows, she's still my property."

"I'm no one's property!"

Mr Chance reached inside his coat and whipped out a blade. "I swear to God, release her, or I'll kill you where you stand."

No! No! No!

This was what her father wanted—to see one of the Chance brothers swinging from the gallows. "Wait! I'll go with him," she said, despite fear sinking its claws into her heart. No one deserved to die for her misfortune.

"Like hell you will."

"Put the weapon away, Christian," came a chilling voice from somewhere behind them. "You don't need to stoop to Sir Geoffrey's level. Vermin have a way of infecting all those in the vicinity."

Isabella turned to meet the cold gaze of Aaron Chance. He was not alone but with two other rugged men who looked just as terrifying. She had not seen Theodore and Aramis Chance since childhood, but they bore the countenance of men who'd learned hard lessons.

118

"Says the boy from the sewer," her father countered.

Aaron did not take the bait. "Ask him again to release her. Should Sir Geoffrey prove uncooperative, direct him to the men waiting across the street. I'm sure he's heard of Lucius Daventry and knows he has the King's favour."

Isabella glanced right to see Mr Daventry watching them intently. His agents were having difficulty keeping Mr Gibbs from charging across the road.

With a grumble of annoyance, her father released her arm. "You can't stop me from seeing my own daughter. This isn't the end of the matter, not by any means."

Aaron Chance's expression darkened. "Do what you must, but I'll be there in the shadows, ready to tear you to pieces."

Her father scowled at her. "I'll make you rue the day you chose them over me. You're just like your damn mother." He turned on his heel and marched away, his lackeys trailing behind like obedient pups.

The realisation that her father would not stop until he owned her, left Isabella trembling to her toes. She rubbed the tender spot on her arm that was surely bruised. But this fleeting pain was nothing compared to the horrors Sir Geoffrey Lawton could inflict if he sold her to the Conte di Barasian.

Christian released a deep sigh as he faced his brothers. "That man brings out the savage in me. I swear, I would have lost my head had you not arrived."

"Daventry warned me this would happen." Aaron Chance gripped Christian's shoulder. "It's my fault for keeping you in the dark, for not preparing you for the upcoming apocalypse. From now on, we remain united. It's the only way to bring that bastard to his knees."

"I'll not abandon Miss Lawton." Christian reached for

her, slipping a comforting arm around her waist and drawing her close. "I'm duty-bound to protect her. She needs our guidance and support."

"Duty-bound?" Aramis Chance snorted. "Did you eat a gentleman for breakfast, or have you always longed to play the gallant knight?"

"As the King of Diamonds, I have many facets."

While the brothers continued teasing each other, Isabella knew there was one option open to her. She had to leave London. Tonight. Travel far across the ocean, somewhere her father couldn't find her. Perhaps America. She just needed to find money for her passage.

Christian Chance had other ideas. "Miss Lawton should remain at Fortune's Den. It's not safe for her at the bookshop. You heard her father's vile threats." Thankfully, he did not mention Mr Griffin else Aaron Chance might think she attracted deranged men.

Good Lord!

Her life was a disaster.

None of it was of her own making.

"I agree," Aaron Chance said, shocking them all. "Though there are rules, Miss Lawton. Rules I expect you to follow. Of course, you're free to refuse, but if you think anything of my brother, you will see the sense in us all remaining under one roof."

Isabella looked at Christian, her mind torn. He had risked being disowned in order to help her. While every cell in her body urged her to run, her heart ached to remain close to him.

"You're right," she said, knowing her father would kill Christian should the opportunity arise. "Remaining united is the only way to avoid a tragedy. But what of Mrs Maloney? I'll not rest knowing she's alone at the bookshop."

"I shall make her see sense," Christian said, though his tone suggested it would be a thankless task. "Failing that, I'll throw her over my shoulder and lock her in the Den's basement."

Aaron Chance nodded. "Mrs Maloney will be your chaperone while you're under our roof, Miss Lawton. That should be incentive enough to make her shut the shop for a few days."

Christian looked at her, his frown revealing his frustration. There would be no time to explore a romantic relationship. No time to discover what destiny had planned. Perhaps they were only meant to be friends. Two lonely ships passing in the night.

The thought caused an inner tug of resistance.

A need to fight to prove fate wrong.

Having dismissed his agents, Mr Daventry approached them and demanded to know what had happened with her father. Isabella listened while Christian told the tale which had the makings of a Shakespearian tragedy.

"Are you both willing to continue the investigation?" Mr Daventry said. "I've no agents available, but I can hire protection."

"Protection?" Christian scoffed. "I don't need a nursemaid. Besides, based on the information we gathered today, we're closer to discovering the truth."

Whether aware of it or not, Mr Woodrow had provided new leads. Pursuing answers would be dangerous, but Isabella was too invested in the outcome to turn back now.

"I agree with Mr Chance," she said. "All I ask is that you do everything in your power to prevent my father taking me hostage."

It was Aaron Chance who answered. "He'll not take you, Miss Lawton. My family will provide the protection you need. In return, I hope you find enough evidence to bury Geoffrey Lawton."

"We will try our best, sir." Isabella had no option but to find a means of getting rid of her father. The alternative was a life spent looking over her shoulder or as a slave to the Conte di Barasian.

Aaron Chance spoke privately with Mr Daventry, during which time Isabella renewed her acquaintance with Aramis and Theodore Chance. They were amusing and intimidating in equal measure.

"We'll see you both for dinner this evening," Aaron said in his usual blunt tone. "Daventry has agreed to be your companion for the rest of the day."

The news was like a blow to Isabella's heart. There would be no more intimate conversations with Christian. No begging him to hold her and chase away the darkness.

Still, she smiled, keen to turn the situation to their advantage. "May I suggest we visit Lord Oldman, sir?" Being the illegitimate son of a duke, Mr Daventry could enter houses barred to them.

"On what grounds?"

"We should discuss the matter once safely inside the carriage," Christian interjected, sharpening his gaze as he peered along the Strand. "It would be unwise to linger here longer than necessary."

Mr Daventry agreed, and so they bid the Chance brothers farewell and crossed the road.

"It makes no sense," Mr Gibbs said, opening the carriage door. "We could have put an end to the matter, scared the blighters away for good instead of watching from the sidelines."

Isabella shared his frustration. "That's what my father wants, Mr Gibbs. A reason to put Mr Chance behind bars."

Removing a key player from the board would weaken the brothers' defences.

Christian slapped the coachman playfully on the back. "You'll have an opportunity to flex those fists. The devil's at work and will continue to cause havoc until someone pays his dues."

Appeased, Mr Gibbs waited for them to climb into the conveyance, but Mr Daventry raised a staying hand when the coachman moved to close the door. "I'll travel in my own vehicle. Give us a moment to speak privately."

Isabella fought to hide her elation. The prospect of spending time alone with Christian Chance had desire unfurling in her belly. Judging by the glint in his eyes, he seemed equally pleased.

"Tell me what you learned from Woodrow," Mr Daventry said from the opposite seat.

Isabella told him about Captain Snell's need for secrecy. "They weren't allowed to inspect the artefacts until the crates were delivered to Somerset House."

"I'd wager Snell stole the artefacts and swapped them for fakes," Christian said. "That, or with the surge in the need for opium, Snell has a lucrative business smuggling narcotic substances."

Mr Daventry cast doubt over the first theory. "To swap the artefacts, Snell would need prior knowledge of what the Vizier planned to sell. The operation would be too complicated for a simple man."

"He may have clever accomplices." Christian shook his head, his sigh heavy with frustration. "We've no hope of questioning Snell's crew now they've set sail for Norway."

"Sadly, Snell has been forced to postpone his trip until next week." Though Mr Daventry kept an indifferent expression, a flicker of amusement lit his dark eyes. "Some blackguard managed to sneak aboard his vessel and cause considerable damage to the mainsail."

"How fortunate, sir." She suspected the blackguard worked as an enquiry agent for the gentleman sitting opposite.

Christian laughed. "Remind me never to cross you."

Mr Daventry did an excellent job of looking innocent."I credit you with more intelligence, though I cannot imagine why you think I played a part in causing the damage."

"Like everything else about this case," Christian said with an edge of suspicion, "it must be an uncanny coincidence."

"Indeed. Now, with Snell marooned, you must find a way to question his crew. Might I suggest you secure a table at the Bunch of Grapes tavern? If you make it known you'll trade coin for the right information, someone will be forthcoming."

While there, they could find the clerk from the shipping office and get a good description of the elusive Mr Quigley.

Amongst other matters, Christian explained their need to question Lord Oldman. "His lordship might be behind the deception. We need to know who else purchased the artefacts and how many expeditions Oldman has funded."

After a brief silence, Mr Daventry nodded. "We'll use the murder to force his compliance. And I'll have a man follow Woodrow. See what we can uncover about his nightly habits. He wouldn't be the first to keep his gossiping mistress a prisoner at a secret location."

I could force you to stay here, Bella.

No one will look for you.

No one cares.

The conte's sinister words invaded her thoughts. She had gone to great lengths to put an ocean between them, but it wasn't enough. It would never be enough.

She tried to clear her throat, but her voice was hoarse and

croaky. "Could you attempt to discover what the Conte di Barasian is doing in London? I know he has a mansion house west of Tothill Fields." A mansion that may one day be her prison.

His expression unreadable, Mr Daventry inclined his head. "Whatever the reason, it must be important for the conte to travel a thousand miles."

Rich, titled men did not need to scour the world for a mate. The conte surely had business in town, and her father had distorted the facts to frighten her. Indeed, he had done an excellent job of leaving her terrified.

"I'm sure there is a simple explanation," she said before quickly returning to the matter at hand. "We should make haste and attempt to locate Lord Oldman. You're at the theatre tonight, as I recall."

Mr Daventry's black eyes brightened. "Yes, my wife is keen to see *Mary Queen of Scots* at the Olympic, and she's the last person I'd ever disappoint." He stepped down from the vehicle. "We'll head to Bloomsbury Square directly and see if Lord Oldman is home. I'll have Gibbs follow my carriage."

Bloomsbury Square?

But that was a stone's throw from the museum.

Perhaps the deceased woman worked for Lord Oldman.

Mr Daventry closed the carriage door, leaving her alone with Christian Chance. They both made to speak, both laughed when they interrupted each other again.

"I must thank you, Mr Chance." A swell of emotion filled her chest as she turned to face him. "No one has ever defended me. No one has ever considered my welfare a priority. I'm most grateful for your assistance today."

A mischievous smile touched his lips as he spread his legs wider, touching his thigh to hers. "You might reconsider your statement once you've spent a few days at Fortune's Den."

"Nothing could be worse than my final days at the seminary." Fearing he might mention Mr Griffin, and quite unable to dismiss the urge to fling herself into his lap, she said, "Would you mind drawing the blinds?"

He studied her for a second, a hopeful gleam in his blue eyes. "Sun too bright for you?"

"No." She tugged down the blind nearest to her before daring to place a shaky hand on his muscular thigh. She planned to seize the day and decide her own destiny. "I'd rather no outside interruptions when you devour my mouth."

Chapter Ten

Christian's blood charged through his veins. As a man confident in his ability to please, he knew Miss Lawton desired him. The moment their mouths met, he knew their passions would overwhelm them, and he might not stop until he was pushing deep inside her.

But was gratitude the impetus for her rash decision?

"You know I'd kiss you in a heartbeat." He was staring at her mouth, his cock hardening as he imagined the wild tangle of their tongues. "But I need to know you want *me*, Isabella, not a means of escaping the nightmares. Not a way of repaying a perceived debt."

Those seductive brown eyes remained fixed on his person. She reached over him, her breasts brushing his chest as she pulled down the open blind, plunging them into darkness. "I don't know what the future holds. I don't know where I'll be or what I'll be forced to do. And so, I mean to snatch every moment of freedom. I mean to follow my heart while I still can."

"Life is precarious," he agreed, but he'd be damned if he'd let her father steal her away under cover of darkness. He might have no choice but to pounce on Lawton in a dark alley and drive a blade into his chest. "But we've a mile until we reach Bloomsbury Square. Fifteen minutes until we must vacate the vehicle." No time to indulge their whims.

Her smile turned coy. "How long does it take to kiss a woman?"

Rising to the challenge, he captured her chin. "I fear a lifetime won't be long enough to satisfy my desire for you."

Everything about her fascinated him.

"You know how to boost a lady's confidence, sir."

"You have me bewitched, madam. I'm totally under your spell."

She leant closer, her mouth a mere inch from his. "Then let us put your theory to the test. Let's pray our passion doesn't wither and die too soon."

Time was against them. Still, he claimed her mouth in a slow, lingering kiss. He closed his eyes, inhaled the scent of exotic soap, and drew her essence into his body—a body tense and aching with need.

"Isabella." He cupped her nape, stroked the sensitive spot below her ear with his thumb, in the slow teasing way he would her sex.

Touch me, Isabella. Consume me.

"Christian." She held him rigid in the seat with the heat of her gaze. "Kiss me. Kiss me like you did in the bedchamber. Kiss me like I'm the air you need to breathe."

His heart thumped hard in his chest.

He was on her in a second. The kiss was rough, a frantic mating of mouths, a wild dance of tongues. They were grabbing each other's clothes. Touching. Panting. Writhing on the seat.

Lust burned in his veins.

Lust like he had never encountered.

The need to consummate this union left his cock solid, his ballocks heavy. Matters were already spiralling. He longed to part her legs and push inside her warmth. The urge to pump hard made it impossible to think.

He tore his mouth from hers while he still had an ounce of control. "Daventry was wrong about me. I'm more than a little dangerous. If we don't stop now, I'm going to have you right here on the damn carriage seat."

The lady touched her fingers to her lips, fingers that slid slowly down to her throat and breast as she gasped for breath. Every sensual movement said she wanted to feel him thrusting inside her, filling her, fucking her.

Mother of all saints!

He closed his eyes and tried to temper his arousal, but the minx put her hand on his thigh. "I've had to be strong all my life, but I cannot fight this, Christian. I'm told there are ways to ease a man's tension, a means of giving pleasure without giving my virtue. You'll have to tutor me. Hurry. We might not get a moment alone together again."

He thought of pinching himself to check he wasn't dreaming.

But Isabella kissed him, her tongue sliding over his as her hand slipped higher up his thigh. "I need you. But it has to be on my terms." Tentatively, she dared to touch the cockstand in his trousers. "You must give me some control over what's happening."

"Do with me what you will."

And so there, in a carriage rattling through the streets of London, Christian unbuttoned his trousers and let his erection spring free. He showed her how to hold him and pump in just the right way to give maximum pleasure.

"Is it normal to be so big?" she panted, her dainty hand moving nervously up and down his shaft, slowly building to an intoxicating rhythm. "Lovemaking almost seems impossible."

"Trust me. It's possible." He'd never made love, had only ever chased his release. Despite his current state of dishabille, this was different. "Let me touch you, Isabella. Kiss me. Don't worry if you lose your rhythm."

He waited for her nod of approval before claiming her mouth in a searing kiss. "That's it, love," he breathed as she worked him with ease. God, it felt so good. "Come a little closer. Let me hike up your skirts."

She did as he asked, her dark eyes fluttering closed as he slid his hand up her silky thigh and stroked his thumb over her sex. "Christian."

"Do you like me touching you, Isabella?"

Beneath lids heavy with desire, she looked at him, them both inhaling sharply when he slipped a long finger inside her.

"You're so wet, love."

"You say that like you find it arousing?"

"I'm on the verge of losing control." His shaft swelled beneath her novice fingers. Despite her lack of experience, she drove him wild. "I've never been so solid."

She took that as a cue to pump his cock.

Merciful Lord! He was going to come hard and fast in a bloody carriage. But he resisted the urge to relax against the squab and take his pleasure. He wanted to stroke her, ensure they came together.

She wasn't far from release. Not if her arched back and thrusting hips were any indication.

"Kiss me," he commanded, though he wanted to drag her onto his lap and impale her. Hell, he was losing his mind. "But whatever you do, love, don't stop touching me."

Don't ever stop touching me.

Their mouths met, their tongues dancing seductively, stoking lust's flames. She came first, moaning against his lips, shuddering and calling his name.

He covered her hand, moving it to the base of his shaft as his climax ripped through him, and he spurted over his own blasted fingers.

Saints and sinners!

He was shaking—the aftershocks of his release rocking him to his core. "That was so damn good, love."

"Yes," she panted.

But then they stilled, realising the vehicle was stationary and Daventry was outside talking to Gibbs.

"Damnation!" Christian whipped his hand from under Isabella's skirts and yanked a handkerchief from his coat pocket. He cleaned himself while she tucked loose curls into her bonnet and straightened her pelisse.

Then she did something other than panic.

A chuckle escaped her lips.

He might have laughed, too, had Daventry not been about to open the door and catch him dabbing his cock with a silk square.

"You won't be laughing if we're caught," he whispered.

"What can he do?"

"Relieve you of your position."

She covered her mouth with the hand that had gripped his erection mere moments ago. The minx inhaled. "Who'd have thought the musky smell of a man could be so arousing. Everything about you stirs such a profound reaction in me."

He tucked himself back into his trousers and quickly fastened the buttons. "We need to face facts, Isabella. These carnal cravings will consume us." He still hungered for her. How would he sleep tonight knowing she was in bed upstairs? "You'd do well to distance yourself from me before I ruin you for good."

"We've tried that. It doesn't work."

"Then we'll be lovers before the week is out."

She shrugged. "If I'm still in London."

Her answer caught him off guard.

What the devil did she mean?

Christian straightened. "You plan to leave town?" His heart clenched, hard, almost cutting off the blood supply. "Where would you go?"

"As far away as money will allow." Sensing his disappointment, she reached for his hand and gave a reassuring squeeze. "I cannot stay here, Christian. I'm powerless against my father and his wicked machinations."

If Aaron had his way, Lawton would be buried in the family crypt before the week was out. "There's nothing to fear. You'll have my full protection. I'll not let you out of my sight."

Her watery smile said she doubted him. "A moment ago, you said we should place some distance between us." She didn't give him a chance to explain why. "You're the only man I've ever desired. My only friend in the world. Let us enjoy each other's company while we can. Let's not think about tomorrow."

Christian found himself at odds.

When a boy was ripped from his home in the dead of night and forced to survive on the streets, he craved security. How long could he cope floundering in a wild sea of uncertainty? How would he fare when Aaron came to tell him she'd gone?

His chest tightened. Loss was a recurring theme in his life. The loss of his mother, his father, his home, to some extent, his independence. The latter was the reason he'd accepted Daventry's offer. A desperate attempt to find the boy he'd left behind.

"Isabella, if we mean to spend time together, you must promise me something." Every insecurity rose to the surface, leaving him teetering on unstable ground. "Promise me you will always speak honestly. Promise me you'll tell me before you disappear into the night."

A knock on the window made them both jump.

Ignoring it, she cupped his cheek and pressed a quick kiss to his lips. "I promise you will always know what I'm thinking. If I decide to leave, you'll be the only person I tell."

"Trust is everything to me."

"I'll never give you a reason to doubt me."

He reached for her, kissed her, tried not to make it feel like goodbye. Yet he knew one day soon he would be waving her away at the docks.

"Miss Lawton?" Daventry's impatient voice broke through the internal chaos. "Time is of the essence."

After a quick assessment, and agreeing they both looked presentable, she opened the carriage door. "Forgive the delay, sir. I needed a private word with Mr Chance and some things cannot be left unsaid."

Daventry assisted her descent, his assessing gaze shifting to Christian. "I trust all is well."

"Indeed." He'd just experienced the most powerful climax of his life, only to have his heart ripped from his chest moments later. One thing was certain. He'd need to take the brandy decanter to bed with him tonight.

"Good. Lord Oldman is home and has agreed to speak to us." Daventry gestured to the elegant townhouse. "We're here to find flaws in his story, to hunt for clues, not accuse the man of killing his mistress."

"So, you want him to think we're seeking his help to find the villain?" Isabella seemed keen to confirm.

"Yes. We cannot accuse a peer of a crime without solid evidence."

"We'll play enthusiasts of Egyptian history," she said.

"We must be clever about uncovering information."

Lord Oldman was in his library on the first floor, flicking through the pages of a leather-bound book with his meaty paws. With broad shoulders and a thick neck, he was built for a life in the rookeries, though his pompous tone marked him as a man of Mayfair.

"Ah, Daventry. I'd offer you a seat, but as you can see, I'm busy cataloguing my library." He motioned to the books stacked on the desk and chairs. "If I move them, it will just confuse matters."

"It's just a brief visit," Daventry said in his usual calm manner. "We won't keep you from your work for too long. The Home Secretary has asked us to investigate a serious matter. Consequently, we need your opinion on Woodrow and Clarke from the Society of Antiquaries. We're aware you've had some dealings with them recently."

"What sort of matter?" Lord Oldman placed a piece of paper inside the book he was holding and put it with the others on the desk.

"Deception and murder."

The peer almost sent the pile of books crashing to the floor. "Murder? Good grief. And you think Woodrow and Clarke are involved?"

"That's what we're attempting to establish. Hence our visit today."

Taking a moment to recover from his visible shock, Lord Oldman said, "I funded their last Egyptian expedition, though I'll not be quick to do so again."

Isabella cleared her throat. "Mr Woodrow claims he was misinformed and there were no real treasures to be found in Amarna."

Lord Oldman's narrowed gaze slid over Isabella's figure. "Another of your waifs and strays, Daventry? Have you not learnt your lesson? Why invest time training female agents? All of them seem to marry within a month."

"Miss Lawton is Sir Geoffrey's daughter. She has extensive knowledge of Egyptian artefacts and is working as my advisor, not my agent."

The fool blinked in surprise, though the slight hitch in his breath said he feared Sir Geoffrey. "Ah, yes. I see the likeness. Thankfully, your mother's exotic beauty shines through, my dear. So, you inherited your father's love of Egypt."

"My father has no real interest in Egypt, my lord. Power and wealth drive him to venture to distant shores."

A muscle in the lord's cheek twitched. He quickly turned his attention to Christian. "I thought your knowledge lay in pugilism and robbing men of their hard-earned coin."

Although Christian would love nothing more than to put this man on his arse, he merely smiled. "As you say, I'm an expert in pugilism and stripping fools of their inherited wealth. I also study the history of ancient civilisations while waiting for my opponents to bleed to death."

Lord Oldman laughed. "A man must find avenues to alleviate the anger he bears his family. It must grate that they forced your father to change his name, that your kin refuse to associate with you."

He was referring to Christian's uncle, the foppish Earl of Berridge—or the Earl of *Arsedom* as his brothers called him when cursing the man to Hades. "On the contrary, weak men turn my stomach."

Oldman chuckled again. "Quite right. Quite right. Now,

you want to know of my dealings with those men from the Society of Antiquaries. I can tell you they live for the study and preservation of historical treasures."

"And yet they purchased items from the Grand Vizier when their quota fell short," Isabella said, her tone quite critical. "Treasures that, one might argue, should remain in the country of origin."

Oldman hardened his gaze. "Treasures that would be destroyed or lost during times of war," he corrected. "Your father can attest to the volatile nature of matters abroad."

"We've been at war with France periodically for over a hundred years. And yet we continued to keep our treasures here."

Oldman ground his teeth. "Are you deliberately trying to provoke me, madam?"

Christian expected Daventry to intervene, but he didn't.

"Not at all, my lord. I merely use the example to highlight our desperation to own precious things. It is the reason Mr Woodrow was forced to approach the Vizier. The reason someone was able to swap real artefacts for forgeries and people were too blind to question it."

"Forgeries?" The lord struggled to contain his outrage. "What the devil are you talking about, girl?"

Jumping to her defence, Christian lied and said, "We suspect the treasures sold to the museum aren't genuine. We're concerned those sold to private collectors may be forgeries, too."

The man shook his head in disbelief. "But they come with provenance. Clarke and Woodrow are experts in their field. There must be some mistake."

"There's no mistake," Daventry said bluntly.

A tense silence ensued.

Oldman began pacing. "But I presented the gold mask to the King."

"We need a detailed list of all items brought ashore, sir." Isabella paused. "We need to know what you sold and to whom. It's clear you funded the expedition to profit from the sale of the treasures."

Oldman's head shot up. "You make me sound like a criminal."

Daventry raised a hand to bring an element of calm to the situation. "Miss Lawton is merely keen to protect your reputation. This is a murder enquiry. A woman found dead in the Thames warned the curator about the forged pieces. Which is why we need to confirm exactly what was in the eight crates."

"Eight? Woodrow said there were four."

So, Woodrow had spoken the truth.

What had Snell done with the other four crates?

"Snell brought eight ashore," Daventry said.

Oldman pushed papers aside and perched on the edge of his desk. He scrubbed his face with his hands, his shoulders sagging. "Snell strikes me as the sort who'd smuggle the odd bit of contraband, but he hasn't the intelligence or knowledge needed to fool the experts."

Christian had to agree. "How many times have you hired Snell?"

"This is the fourth trip I've funded, but the first time I've agreed to let Woodrow and Clarke come along. I have archaeologists working permanently along the Nile. They catalogue their findings, and Snell ships the items home."

Being astute, Miss Lawton asked the question burning in Christian's mind. "Have you ever had reason to question the authenticity of the archaeological finds?"

"Never!"

"Lawton rarely travels abroad," Christian said, his disdain for the man evident in his tone. But Lawton had gone missing for months on end. No one could confirm his whereabouts. "How did he come to work as the cartographer on this particular trip?"

Oldman gave a half-shrug. "I can't recall if he approached me or I approached him. I believe he wanted to escape London for a time. You'll need to speak to Woodrow." He gestured to Isabella. "Or surely Miss Lawton can ask him."

A light tap on the door brought the maid, a young slip of a girl with a pale face. After a clumsy curtsey, she asked if his lordship required refreshments.

"We'll have tea," the lord snapped. "Be quick about it, girl."

Anger flashed in Isabella's eyes as she watched the terrified maid scurry from the room. She turned to Lord Oldman and might have chastised him for his brusque manner had Daventry not intervened.

"We're trying to find Mr Quigley. He acts as a broker. Does he work for you, the shipping office, or Captain Snell?"

"Quigley? Quigley works for himself. I met him in a tavern years ago. He heard me discussing my desire for Egyptian artefacts and knew of a captain willing to sail to the Orient. I pay him to deal with Snell."

"Then you can tell us where to find him."

Lord Oldman was quick to disappoint them. "My secretary Mr Myers deals with all financial matters. He's in Bristol on business. I've not spoken to Quigley since that night in the tavern."

"Can you give us a description?" Isabella asked.

Perhaps it was Christian's imagination, but he sensed some hesitance before the lord said, "He was of average height and build. Perhaps thirty. But it was dark, and I'd consumed half a bottle of port."

Christian suppressed a sigh of frustration.

This pompous oaf cared about nothing other than accumulating treasures. Like Lawton, he was obsessed with power and wealth and wanted to own things other men couldn't. But his passion might be the bargaining chip they needed.

"The Home Secretary demands we confiscate all the relics brought ashore from *The Marigold* to check for forgeries." Christian noted the sudden panic in Oldman's beady eyes. "I'm told you exhibit your treasures in a makeshift museum in the basement." He wasn't sure how he knew. Perhaps it was gaming hell gossip.

Oldman jumped to his feet. "Now listen here. I'll not let a single item leave these premises. This could be some wicked conspiracy."

His ever quick-witted self, Daventry supported Christian's claim. "We're extremely busy and don't have much time. I could have my associates sketch and catalogue the treasures. You can make a list of the private collectors while they authenticate your artefacts. It will appease the Home Secretary, and you know how clumsy constables can be."

Oldman refused and gave a ream of excuses.

"Very well. I'll return for the list of collectors tonight." Daventry moved to leave. "I hope the magistrate in charge of collecting the goods will not be too quick to label the objects fake."

They'd reached the library door before Oldman called, "Wait. They can have thirty minutes to study the pieces, but they can't touch or open the display cases."

Christian hid the sudden rush of elation.

Instinct said Oldman would only keep genuine trophies,

but he felt compelled to examine them himself. Still, the lord was hiding something.

Yet as the butler led them down into the basement, it wasn't Lord Oldman peering at them from behind the door jamb.

It was the nervous-looking maid.

Chapter Eleven

The butler unlocked the sturdy iron door, one at odds with all the other doors in the basement. Though he carried himself with the usual aplomb, his hand shook as he turned the ornate key.

After beckoning a footman to fetch a lit lamp, he escorted Isabella and Christian into the windowless room and cautioned them not to touch the display cases.

In the gloom, and amid the dull pottery, the gold chalice caught Isabella's eye. "Good Lord!" Heart racing, she moved closer and gazed through the small glass pane. "It's magnificent. So beautiful it takes one's breath away."

"Indeed." Christian was looking at her, not the splendid vessel. "I find myself equally mesmerised."

She smiled, feeling lighter than she had in years. He had a way of making all her problems disappear, if only temporarily.

"Close your mouth before you choke on dust," she teased.

The room was spotlessly clean, a fact made clear when the footman arrived with the lamp and placed it on a plinth near the door. He remained in the corridor outside, keeping watch like a palace guard.

Christian crossed the room. As he observed the rows of cabinets, his hand snaked around her waist and came to rest on her hip. After their intimate encounter in the carriage, it felt natural to touch each other now.

"There must be fifty objects here."

"Yes, and all museum quality." Isabella lowered her voice. "Lord Oldman kept the best pieces for himself. If these aren't genuine, he will have lost a small fortune."

"We're not qualified to confirm their authenticity."

"No. It's likely he's sold the forgeries."

"Still, it's worth making a quick appraisal." He bent his head, his mouth an inch from her ear. "And it means we get to spend a moment alone. In the coming days, such things will be as rare as that gold chalice."

A vision of the lecherous conte invaded her mind. She didn't want to think beyond the next minute, let alone the next few days. Powerful men did not take no for an answer. Cunning men found ways to achieve their goals.

Panic rising, she faced Christian, wishing things were different and they were free of their burdens. "Like thieves, we must steal every second, make every precious moment count."

"I'll take anything you're willing to give," he drawled, his masculine confidence holding her spellbound. "If I were a thief, I'd slip into your chamber at night, touch you, make love to you, hold you close and watch you sleep."

The thought of his warm body covering hers had her shivering with need. "I'll be sure to leave the door unlocked. I'll leave a note telling you to take everything." Everything but her independence. She'd trust no one enough to give that.

Their gazes locked.

Their breath quickened.

Despite the footman watching from the corridor, they kissed. Slowly. So deeply her insides clenched. This raw carnal need left them ravenous. If they were anywhere else, lust would consume them.

Run away with me, Christian!

They could be gone tonight.

But he would never leave his brothers.

You're destined to be alone, Isabella.

Her mother said they'd carve the words on her headstone.

Fate conspired to make it so.

Eager to keep destiny at bay, she gripped his lapels, anchoring him to her mouth, silently begging him to chase away the demons.

A discreet cough from the doorway brought them both to their senses. Christian tore his mouth from hers, though the hazy look in his eyes said he was by no means finished.

Isabella forced herself to turn towards the door, expecting to find Mr Daventry standing like an angry Zeus, ready to bring the heavens hurtling down on top of them. She was shocked to find the distraught maid and no sign of the footman.

The woman checked the corridor before dashing into the dimly lit room. She grabbed Isabella's arm. "I need your help, miss," she pleaded, her face as white as her apron. "I need to leave this place but ain't got the means to pay for lodgings."

Isabella placed a calming hand on the young woman's shoulder. "I, too, am short of funds, but I know someone who can help you."

The maid jumped out of her skin when Christian spoke. "Why would you want to leave a perfectly good job? You've food and board. Comforts you'd miss if you found yourself on the streets."

The woman hurried to peer around the jamb before returning. "The maids don't stay here long, sir. Every two months, one runs away. It's only a matter of time before it's my turn to find out why."

Isabella's thoughts turned to the coroner's assessment of the corpse on the mortuary slab. The victim was of Mediterranean descent. Most likely a servant abused by her master. A maid fleeing Bloomsbury Square might easily find herself at the museum at night.

The ghost had mentioned the artefacts by name.

The ghost had blood spots on her nightgown.

"Have any maids left recently?" Isabella did not describe the ghostly figure. In her current state of mind, this servant might say anything for a few coins.

"Sarah left three months ago. One minute she was here. The next, she was gone. No one has heard from her since. Oh, you must help me, miss. People don't disappear."

Isabella tried to remain rational. "Perhaps she's gone to stay with family or taken another position." It happened all the time. Servants rarely gave notice of an intention to flee. "She might have married."

"She might be dead, miss."

Isabella exchanged glances with Christian.

The entire case was based on a dead woman's testimony. Had the person the curator spoke to mentioned Lord Oldman by name? Had she lied about the forgeries to gain the authorities' attention? Why not run to the nearest police office instead?

They needed to question the curator again.

"Does Sarah hail from London?"

"No, from somewhere up north near the coast. It might be Scotland judging by her accent. I've never seen skin so white. And hair as light as silver threads. It must be the sea air."

So, Sarah was not the woman in the mortuary.

"I heard her crying the night before she left, but the butler said the Egyptian ornaments are cursed." She trembled as she glanced at the cabinet of small ushabti figurines. "He said I'd heard spirits from the underworld. Desperate souls begging to be set free."

"What's your name?" Christian asked.

"Nancy, sir. Nancy Jones."

He reached into his pocket, then thrust a few sovereigns into the maid's chapped hand. "Should you decide to leave, Nancy, come to Fortune's Den in Aldgate Street and ask for Delphine. She will help you."

Nancy was not shy. She yanked the collar of her dress, shoved the coins between her breasts and removed a small pewter pendant. "This belonged to Sarah, sir." She pushed it into Christian's palm, sealing his fingers around the metal. "It was hidden under her bed. She'd never have left here without it. Maybe it might help you find her, sir."

The sudden slam of a door made Nancy jump. Before they could question her further, she darted from the room like a frightened doe.

Isabella clutched Christian's arm. "Do you think there's any truth to her claim? Maybe she needs money to send home, and we were foolish enough to fall for her tale?"

Christian ran his finger over the carvings on the pendant before tucking it away in his coat pocket. "Who can say? Lord Oldman's lust for power means he's capable of anything."

"You heard how he spoke to the maid. Perhaps Sarah couldn't tolerate his aggressive manner and decided to return home."

Christian looked her keenly in the eyes. "Is that not what

you do when faced with a monster, Isabella? Leave and put an ocean between you?"

Every horrid memory flashed before her eyes. "Sadly, my tactic has one major flaw. Monsters have a nasty habit of finding me."

"Then you agree it's pointless running?"

She heard the thread of hope in his voice. "Running has saved my life on more than one occasion. One does what one must in times of crisis. I have no qualms in doing so again."

From his woeful expression, it wasn't the answer he wanted. But she had sworn to be honest. Yes, when they fell into each other's arms, the rest of the world blurred into the background. Still, his family would not accept her. And men soon tired of opinionated women. She'd witnessed her mother's many mistakes and knew when it was time to leave.

Sensing a presence in the doorway, she turned to see Mr Daventry.

The man had a way of appearing at inconvenient moments.

"Have you examined the artefacts?"

No, they had kissed so deeply her toes had curled. Their lips would be locked now were it not for Nancy and her shocking claims. "We were interrupted by the maid." Isabella beckoned the gentleman into the candlelit room and relayed Nancy's tale.

Mr Daventry considered the information. "You'll tell Oldman you believe the relics are genuine. That you cannot make a more thorough assessment without removing them from the cases. Leave the rest to me."

They made to leave, but a sudden chill in the air stopped Isabella in her tracks. She stared into the room full of ancient treasures, wondering if the spirits of their owners did indeed haunt the small space.

She was still thinking about ghosts when they met Lord Oldman in the hall. Mr Daventry mentioned their findings, and she spoke when prompted.

"We would need to remove the items from the cabinets to be certain, my lord. Based on appearances, the pieces look genuine. We'll inform the magistrate of our findings."

Lord Oldman seemed elated. "I'll not forget this, Daventry. I cannot bear the thought of those blighters handling such delicate treasures. Should you require assistance in the future, feel free to call in the debt."

Mr Daventry smiled. "Well, you could do me a small kindness."

"Name it."

"I'm having a devil of a job finding a decent maid. I've exhausted Mrs Shaw's Registry on Old Kent Road. Do you know where I might find competent staff?"

Lord Oldman moaned about his current crop of servants. He believed times were changing, and those capable of hard graft were few and far between. "Speak to Winthrop in Stanhope Street. He weeds out the weak ones."

Mr Daventry thanked him, and they bid the lord good day.

Once outside, they were given their orders. "Visit Winthrop in the morning. If what Oldman says is true, and he hires his staff from that establishment, they will have a forwarding address for Sarah and any other maid who's left without notice."

"You think it's a matter worth pursuing?" Christian said.

"Every line of enquiry is worth pursuing."

Fortune's Den
Aldgate Street

Isabella was used to dining alone, not being the focus of five people's attention. She was used to a basic bill of fare, not the range of sumptuous dishes laid out on the long oak table.

Of the four men who studied her intently, two made her heart race but for very different reasons. Under the weight of Aaron Chance's unforgiving gaze, she was aware of every drawn breath. Christian's visual caresses had her fanning her cheeks to cool her heated blood.

Thank heavens for Delphine, the sister they'd adopted off the street. Relieved to have a female companion, she chatted constantly. "Christian has never brought a lady home. In fact, none of my brothers have."

"Christian has not brought Miss Lawton home," Aaron Chance corrected coldly. He took a long sip of wine. "Necessity calls for her to remain here until we've dealt with our current problem."

Delphine's wide mouth curled into a teasing grin. "Well, it's certainly no ordinary night. I'll not be surprised to find Miss Scrumptious enjoying supper with us tomorrow."

Aaron ground his teeth. "Her name is not Miss Scrumptious. And I'd rather eat my own eyeballs than entertain that woman."

Aware of Isabella's confusion, Christian said, "Delphine

is referring to Miss Lovelace. Her father owns the gaming establishment across the road. Aaron had a doll made in her likeness to which he adds pins daily."

"Perhaps you've been conspiring with Miss Lovelace, too," Aaron challenged. "Why not invite all our enemies to dine at our table?"

Aramis was keen to explain the reason for his brother's temper. "Aaron accosted Miss Scrumptious in the street this morning and demanded to know why she'd spent the night at her father's gaming hell. She stuck her nose in the air and said she refused to discuss business with her competitor."

"She made it sound like she owned the damn place," Aaron growled.

For the first time in an hour, Isabella's shoulders relaxed. At least she wasn't the only one to feel the depth of Aaron Chance's disdain.

Delphine laughed. "Miss Scrumptious is—"

Aaron thumped the table with his fist, the cutlery jumping to attention along with his kin. "She's not bloody scrumptious. She's an annoying bluestocking who's used to getting her own way. Now, change the damn subject before I flip this table on its head, and you're forced to eat off the floor."

Delphine seemed to find her brother's volatile reaction pleasing. She brushed a lock of ebony hair behind her ear. "Christian tells me you knew each other as children, Miss Lawton."

Before Isabella could answer, Aaron snapped, "We do not talk about the past, Delphine."

Delphine slammed her cutlery down on the china plate. "Can I talk about scones? Or did you almost choke on one in a previous life?"

Isabella bit back a chuckle and cleared her throat. "I must thank you, Mr Chance," she said, keen to bring an order of calm. "It can't be easy having me here, and I know you do so purely out of concern for your brother."

The tension in the air dissipated slightly.

Aaron Chance looked at Christian, the hard angles of his face softening. "I would die for my brother, Miss Lawton. He would do well to remember it."

That was the cue to stop talking and eat their meal.

Delphine filled the silence by asking Isabella questions about Italy. "I've always wondered if my mother was Italian," the dark-haired beauty said. "We have the same complexion, do we not, Miss Lawton?"

"You have no memory of your parents?" Isabella asked.

"None at all."

The men glanced nervously at each other, but it was Christian who spoke. "Delphine had a plum-sized lump on her head when she found us. She couldn't recall her name or address, and no one had reported her missing. Delphine was the name sewn into the back of her tatty dress."

Isabella stared in wonder.

Fortune's Den wasn't a gaming hell.

It was a house full of secrets.

"Are you not curious to know—"

"That's enough, Miss Lawton. Can a man not eat without suffering the scourge of indigestion?" Aaron Chance scrunched his napkin in his fist and threw it on the table. "Before we open for business tonight, I must collect Mrs Maloney. Why the woman insists on bringing boxes of books is beyond me." He fixed his impenetrable gaze on Christian. "You'll accompany me. I trust you have nowhere else to be tonight."

"No. We need to visit the Servants' Registry in the morning and a tavern near the Limestone Basin tomorrow night."

The news dragged a groan from Aaron's lips. "Aramis has been spoiling for a fight. He'll accompany you tomorrow evening. Along with Gibbs, that should suffice. Make sure you take blades and pistols."

Mischief flashed in Aramis' eyes. "I'll be only too glad to help. There's always trouble brewing near the docks."

"Perhaps I could go too," Delphine chirped. "Thanks to your skilled tutorage, I'm an expert shot with a pocket pistol."

"And have half the lords in the *ton* attempt to kidnap you and force me to tear up their debts? I think not."

"I'm not a child. I can take care of myself."

Despite the bonds of kinship, Isabella sensed the ties that held this family together were wearing thin.

Aaron Chance stood. "God, life was easier when you were all children." And without another word, he stormed from the room.

"Don't mind him," Christian said from the seat beside her, his hand moving to give hers a reassuring squeeze under the table. "The weight of responsibility weighs heavily on his shoulders. Too heavily sometimes."

"I understand. He's like a father to you all." Isabella considered her own father, and her mother's many lovers. "I'd rather suffer the sharp edge of his tongue than his neglect or indifference."

They drank their wine and finished their meal.

Though Aaron had left the room, she still sensed a thrum of hostility from Aramis. As the second oldest brother, he undoubtedly wished to appear loyal to his kin. It would make for an uncomfortable evening tomorrow.

Christian leaned closer and whispered, "We should find somewhere quiet to discuss the case. Once Sigmund opens the doors for business, we'll not hear ourselves think."

There was nowhere to go.

They'd sent Gibbs home for the night.

And they were being watched from all quarters.

He sensed her hesitance but seemed confident of her desire to be alone with him. "I shall show Miss Lawton to her room. So she might settle in before Mrs Maloney arrives." He pushed out of the chair and addressed a frowning Aramis. "I shall be sure to leave the bedchamber door open."

Heat rose to her cheeks, but she refused to be ashamed of her attraction to this man. "I'd like to see the sketches of Abu Simbel, if I may."

"We'll collect the book from my room en route."

All eyes were upon her when she stood. Delphine was the only one wearing a knowing grin. Theodore looked at Aaron's empty chair but said nothing. Aramis merely grunted his disapproval.

"We're not accountable for our father's sins," Christian said, speaking like the best barrister. "The same can be said for Miss Lawton. She was away at boarding school on that fateful night."

"Her being here puts us all at risk," Aramis countered.

"Our brother's need for vengeance leaves us vulnerable," he corrected. "Besides, the die is cast. It's pointless raising objections now."

They left the dining room and walked through the lavish red hall, a place designed to put a man in the mood for sin. Christian was quiet as they mounted the stairs. When they reached his room on the second floor, he'd managed to cast aside his disagreement with his brother.

"Come in, but leave the door open," he said, his mood restored.

Isabella lingered on the threshold before finding the courage to enter. Her hesitance had nothing to do with his brother's comment. Something about the intimate setting deepened her attraction to Mr Chance.

A potent masculine smell hung in the air, tugging at her stomach muscles, much like the rich, musky scent of his skin. The solid mahogany bed looked as sturdy as the man. Like every muscle, the posts were carved to perfection.

"It's extremely tidy." She wanted to touch everything, slip into his shirt, hug his pillow, wrap herself in his sheets. She wanted to lock the door and shut the world out.

"I always take care of what's mine."

She didn't doubt him for a second. He was strong, fearless, passionate, yet kind. Qualities that would make any woman fall hopelessly in love with him.

Experiencing a twinge of jealousy, Isabella made for the bookcase. "When you've had nothing, you appreciate the small things."

He watched her as she searched the spines and drew the book she wanted. His gaze remained fixed on every movement as she flicked through the pages.

She stopped at no place in particular. *He* was the focus of her attention, not the expert engravings. "I've always wanted to visit Egypt."

"Because it's the farthest place you know?"

His insight left her feeling a little exposed. "And because there's something mystical about foreign lands. It must be easy to lose oneself in a place full of hidden meaning."

"I wouldn't know. I cannot leave London, not after everything my brother sacrificed to give us the life we deserved." He gestured to his rugged physique, a body that made her heart race and sex pulse. "I have no desire to hide. This is who I am. I agreed to help Daventry to gain a modicum of independence, but my loyalties will always be with my family."

Sadness shrouded her. Only a fool would try to compete. "It must feel good to have people you can depend upon."

He closed the gap between them, drew the book from her hands and placed it back on the bookshelf. "You'll never know unless you stop running. You'll never know until you learn to trust someone, Isabella."

Lust's dynamic energy pulsed in the air between them. It took command of her heartbeat, of her breathing, heightened her senses.

"You make trust sound easy."

He didn't reinforce his point but asked a question that left her floundering. "What do you want from me, Isabella?"

I want you to talk to me like my opinions matter.

I want you to touch me so I don't feel so alone.

When it's time, I want you to save yourself and set me free.

She swallowed past a lump in her throat. "I thought we agreed to pursue our romantic connection. To steal every moment of pleasure."

"Oh, I can do pleasure." He drew the backs of his fingers across her cheek. "I can do pleasure extremely well. I can be the best lover you've ever had."

"You'll be the only lover I've ever had." That's what she wanted. Beautiful memories to cling to in the darkness. "But we barely have time to discuss the case, let alone steal a moment alone together."

Christian glanced at the open door, a slow smile teasing the corners of his mouth. "As the King of Diamonds, I know how to take advantage of every situation. Will you permit me to take liberties, Isabella?"

Intrigued to know what he planned to do, she nodded.

He captured her hand and led her behind the open door, out of view. "We'll discuss the case tomorrow. For now, I want you to describe life in Egypt." He moved closer, his breath hot against her ear. "Anyone coming upstairs must believe there's nothing erotic about our conversation."

He pressed her to the wall and claimed her mouth, the kiss wild and wicked and over too quickly. "As a man who has never left London, help me see the mystical world through your dazzling eyes. Begin aboard ship."

With his body so close, she couldn't rouse a coherent thought. But he stared at her like he might eat her alive, his breath warm against her cheek.

"The j-journey across the sea is long," she stuttered. Lord, her pulse thumped a rapid beat in her throat. She was so hot she might swoon.

"How long, love?" He captured her hand and smoothed her fingers over the hard ridge in his trousers. His lips parted on a silent gasp, his eyes closing briefly.

"Longer than one might imagine." He was so big, making love seemed an impossible concept.

"I'm told the beds aboard ship are hard." His impressive manhood thickened beneath her fingers, and he mouthed, "Hell, yes."

"Soft sheets cover a base of steel."

He cocked his head and listened for a moment before gathering up her skirts and sliding his fingers through her damp folds. "All that swaying must play havoc with your balance. You must become accustomed to your legs trembling and shaking without notice."

"Yes," she breathed as his wicked fingers moved in a tantalising rhythm, stroking in just the right spot. *Yes!*

"The back-and-forth motion must make you dizzy," he said, building a steady rhythm. "The relentless movements must leave you quite wet when on deck." He pushed two fingers inside her, filling the emptiness temporarily.

"Soaking." Heavens, she could hear every moist movement.

He used his knee to nudge her legs wider apart. "Does it not ease as you move deeper into the sea?" He pressed his mouth to her ear and whispered, "I'm deep now, love. So deep, I'd give anything to be inside you, pumping so damn hard we'd come together."

She could feel the inner coil tightening, the tension building within. "I want you," she whispered when his gaze locked with hers.

"Enjoy the journey. Soon, you'll be basking in all the pleasures of Egypt. I'm told it's so hot one can barely breathe." He lowered his voice as he brought her to a climax, the sudden clenching in her core leaving her knees weak. "We'll continue this ride tomorrow."

He said nothing more but claimed her mouth to smother every sensual cry. And for the first time in her life, Isabella knew exactly where she would be in the morning.

Chapter Twelve

*The Servants' Registry
Stanhope Street*

"Should we pretend we're married or tell Mr Winthrop why we're really here?" Isabella worried her bottom lip. "I think we should show him the letter from the Home Secretary or he's unlikely to reveal a servant's private details."

"Hmm." Since their interlude last night, Christian could not stop staring at her mouth. He had never seen lips so naturally red. Might the colour be claret or deep rose? They were as intoxicating as wine. Certainly as soft as flower petals. And they tasted like—

"Christian, you're not listening." She gripped his arm and guided him from the agency's front door to the entrance of the adjacent alley. "What's wrong? You've been preoccupied since we left Fortune's Den."

"Can a man not take time to think before deciding on the

best course of action? We have a lot of leads to consider at present."

How did he tell her what he was really thinking?

The urgency to bed her grew more intense by the hour. Lust with the right woman was more potent than laudanum. It went beyond a mere physical need. It played havoc with his mind, toyed with his emotions. It made him lower his guard and dream the impossible.

"Oh," she said, placated. "I thought it had something to do with Delphine's comment at breakfast this morning."

He's never looked at a woman the way he looks at you.

I sense there's more to it than meets the eye.

It had left them both shifting uncomfortably in their seats, quick to lie and confirm they were merely friends and associates, not lovers who could not keep their hands off each other.

But despite everything, that's not what bothered him.

He needed to stop wanting a woman who was one ticket away from leaving. Had he learned nothing about survival and self-preservation?

"Delphine is hoping one of us will break the bonds of brotherhood. It would give her an excuse to follow her own heart and—" He stopped abruptly, unable to finish the sentence.

What if Delphine had a better life awaiting her elsewhere?

What if she left and never came back?

It would kill Aaron.

It would kill them all.

"Delphine wants to find her family?" Isabella said, drawing the obvious conclusion.

"Yes, though she's not as strong as she appears." The same might be said for them all. "The truth might enslave her, not set her free."

Isabella laid her hand on his arm, the simple touch firing his blood. "Or you might lose her, and I doubt any of you could cope with that."

This woman could read his mind, access his thoughts.

Did she see he wore two masks?

The mask of a cold, arrogant man who would never trust anyone with his heart. The mask of a lonely man seeking security. One willing to give everything of himself, hoping someone might love him enough not to leave.

Gibbs suddenly appeared, his nostrils flaring. "Men die when they don't follow Mr Daventry's orders. I can't protect you if you're going to disappear to canoodle in the alley."

"Canoodle?" Isabella's cheeks flamed. "We were discussing the case, Mr Gibbs. Deciding how best to proceed."

"And I'm heir to the throne of Persia. I'm paid to see you safely to the Servants' Registry. You'll thank me for my rudeness if it means you live to see another day." He glared at Christian. "I credit *you* with more sense, Mr Chance."

Christian laughed. If he wanted to canoodle with Isabella, the King of Persia couldn't stop him. Aaron was the only one who could sentence him to die a lonely death.

"Next time, we'll make a plan of action before leaving the safety of the carriage." He turned to Isabella. "We'll use the Home Secretary's letter to force Winthrop to show us his records."

She nodded. "I shall follow your lead."

While a disgruntled Gibbs climbed atop his box, they entered the Servants' Registry, though the place was more like Leadenhall Market than somewhere one hired help.

Desperate women of all ages stood against the far wall. Some stern with robust figures. Some meek and gaunt and in desperate need of a decent meal. A fellow sat on a stool

159

behind a lectern, waving a cane and urging prospective buyers to survey the goods.

A lady carrying a small pug examined three men through her eye glass before calling, "I'll take the dark-haired one, Mr Pike. He looks sturdier than the rest, and I've had a run of rotten luck of late."

"Excellent choice, Mrs Coombs. Excellent choice." He scribbled in his ledger and summoned an attendant to complete the transaction. "As God is my witness, this one won't give you any trouble."

Christian marched over to the lectern but before he could speak, Pike pointed his cane at the far wall. "You'll have to wait your turn, sir. It's always busy the first week of the month."

"We're here to see Mr Winthrop."

Pike glanced up from his ledger and stared down his beak-like nose. "Mr Winthrop is busy interviewing new candidates." He happened to gesture to the door behind him. "If you've come to hire servants, you'll have to join the queue like the rest."

Ordinarily, Christian would have dragged the clerk over the lectern by his flimsy cravat, but he was on official business. "We're here on behalf of the Home Secretary and demand to see Winthrop immediately."

"The H-Home Secretary?" Pike nearly fell off his stool. "Still, you can't interrupt Mr Winthrop halfway through an interview. Wait here. I'll direct you to the office as soon as he's finished with the current candidate."

Christian gripped the edge of the lectern and leant forward. "Don't trouble yourself. We shall find our own way."

Pike jumped off his stool as if he'd singed his backside.

He charged at Christian and tugged his coat sleeve. "Wait. You can't go in there."

The room fell silent.

All eyes were upon them.

"Remove your hand at once, sir," Isabella said, echoing Christian's thoughts. She was the only person who could touch him. "Else I shall call a constable and have you arrested for hindering a murder investigation."

"Murder!" someone cried behind them.

"What sort of place is this?" said another.

Prospective servants and employers alike gathered their belongings and hurried out through the front door, escaping onto Stanhope Street.

"No! Wait!" Pike charged after them, begging them to return. "I assure you, no one has been murdered. There's been a dreadful mistake."

Christian took it as his cue to find Winthrop. Alerted by a woman's squeal, he knocked on the door at the end of the corridor before barging inside.

If the fellow with a paunch the size of a barrel was Winthrop, he had an odd way of interviewing maids. The poor girl on his lap struggled and squirmed. She took one look at them, her frantic eyes pleading for help.

"Who the devil are you? This is my private office."

"Agents acting on behalf of the Home Secretary," Christian said, relishing the sudden flash of panic in the buffoon's eye. He decided to toy with the lecherous oaf. "Questions have been raised about your business practices, and I see our timing couldn't be better."

He shoved the woman off his lap as if she had the pox and waved her away. "Tell Mr Pike to share your details with our clients. He'll help you secure a permanent position."

The girl fled the room while Winthrop tried his best to

disguise his guilt by being efficient. He gestured to the chairs flanking his cluttered desk and invited them to sit as he rustled a few papers.

Christian introduced himself and flashed the letter bearing the Home Secretary's signature and seal. "And this is Miss Lawton. She's here to question the female servants, those hoping to secure positions."

Winthrop gulped, his wobbling jowls revealing an inner panic. "I don't know who made the complaint, but I can assure you, everything that happens on these premises is above board."

Isabella snorted. "The poor woman forced to sit on your lap didn't seem to think so."

Winthrop hardened his gaze. "Madam, these girls may have to work in households where disreputable men are regular visitors. The meek ones won't survive. I provide a valuable service."

Was that what Lord Oldman meant when he said this fellow would weed out the weak ones?

"So what we witnessed is a means of ensuring the women are fit for work?" Christian mocked. "And you were acting a role, playing a rakish bounder as part of the interview process?"

"Indeed." Winthrop slapped his hand on the desk. "I place the right servant in the right household. I have a reputation to uphold. It's bad for business if they last no more than a week."

Deciding to stretch the truth to his advantage, Christian said, "A maid was murdered, Mr Winthrop. A maid carrying your card. She left a note detailing your unconventional practices. We may be forced to arrest you if you cannot provide an alibi."

Winthrop's eyes widened, and he leaned on the desk for

support. "Murder! But that's outrageous! I'm trying to help these girls, not hurt them. Do you know what life is like for homeless women on the streets?"

Christian shook off a host of horrid images. "Terrifying."

"I toughen them up," he said as if proud he'd been caught groping the girl. "It's that, or they end up as fodder in a bawdy house." He looked at Isabella. "Forgive my crudeness, madam, but the truth is not all sunshine and roses."

"You do not have to tell me, sir, but you make light of the horrors women in wealthy homes face. You should be striving for the better treatment of the working classes, not encouraging lewd behaviour."

While Christian found her comment inspiring, Winthrop looked at her as if she had lost her marbles. "I'd be out of business within the week, and be forced to sell brick dust from a barrow."

"Someone has to make a stand, sir."

"Well, it won't be me."

"Then let us return to the topic of murder," Christian said, keen to make this fellow squirm. "You keep a record of all the servants on your books and which households employ them."

"Yes, though the files are listed under the employers' names. Servants often use an alias. Some are running from a bad situation. Some were tossed out without a reference."

Winthrop spoke like he was a disciple of God, out to help the meek and needy. In truth, he was guilty of abusing his position. When the case was solved, Christian would return to make him see the error of his ways.

"We want to see the records relating to Lord Oldman." Christian fixed the man with a hard stare. "If you can't find them, we will take you into custody and rip this office apart."

Winthrop froze. "Lord Oldman? You suspect he is involved?"

"Fetch the file, Winthrop."

The man hauled himself out of the seat and waddled across the room. His hands shook as he searched a drawer in the oak cabinet. He returned with a portfolio of papers and flicked through them until he found the relevant document.

"What is it you want to know?"

"Start with the maids he's employed via the agency this year."

Winthrop cast his beady eyes over the paper. "I've received commission for two maids and a footman. He hired two maids last year."

Christian met Isabella's confused gaze.

It was hardly the number Nancy Jones mentioned.

"Does he hire staff elsewhere?" Isabella said.

"Not that I'm aware."

"Were any of the women Spanish or Italian?"

Winthrop shrugged and read out the English-sounding names—none named Sarah and one being Nancy Jones. The latter went to work for him in February.

Isabella described the woman in the mortuary and the maid who owned the pewter pendant. "Are they at all familiar to you?"

Winthrop relaxed back in the chair and splayed his hands over his paunch. "Hundreds of people pass through here."

Christian had grown tired of Winthrop's waffling. "Pike said you interview all the maids. Are you telling me you don't remember the pretty ones?" He described Sarah again. "Think, man! It's important. Has Oldman hired a woman of that description?"

"No! As you said, I'd remember."

Christian showed him the pendant, but it failed to jog his memory. "Are you aware Lord Oldman mistreats his staff?"

The twitch of Winthrop's cheek confirmed Christian's theory. "I think *mistreat* is too harsh a word."

"Then how would you describe it?"

"Men of his ilk are hard taskmasters, too stern for some girls." He scoffed. "There's silly talk about his house being haunted by the ghosts of previous maids. Some are too scared to accept a position there."

Christian sat back in the chair. This was supposed to be an enquiry into Oldman's character to prove he was capable of fraud. They were being led down a different path, one that had little to do with historical artefacts. One involving missing maids and ghosts.

He should return to the matter at hand, but he knew Isabella cared more about saving the innocent than uncovering fake artefacts. Moreover, this was a murder enquiry. "I need to speak to a maid who's refused to work for Lord Oldman. You must have her direction. It will save us remaining here to question all who walk through the front door."

Aware his back was to the wall, Winthrop huffed and puffed and crossed the room to rifle in the cabinet.

"Ethel Cartwright." He mumbled a curse and moaned like the woman was the bane of his existence. "She's the one who rallied the others. Said Oldman only hires meek girls because he enjoys frightening them to death."

"And where is Miss Cartwright now?" Isabella asked.

"The workhouse, most likely." He pulled out a piece of paper. "Try St Margaret's on Dean Street. That was her last known abode."

They left Winthrop quaking in his boots, Christian threatening to bind the man naked and let the injured maids wallop him with sticks.

Isabella decided on a more respectable approach. "I shall write a piece for the *Weekly Times*, warning all young women to avoid the agency."

He smiled as he helped her into the carriage.

They complemented each other in many ways. She was the calm to his storm. The light to his darkness. The order to his chaos. But he'd been wrong to warn her away. Whenever their lips met, he realised *he* was out of his depth, and *she* was more than a little dangerous.

"Prevention is better than a cure, my mother used to say." Christian glanced at Gibbs. "St Margaret's Workhouse. We're chasing a lead." He climbed inside the vehicle and slammed the door shut. "There are more than enough agencies in town. Women seeking employment should not have to deal with the likes of Winthrop."

She narrowed her gaze. "Your mother must have been a sensible woman. It's nice you can recall her wise sayings after all these years."

Every muscle in his body stiffened. The day his mother died was a pivotal point in the family's downward spiral.

"Only a fool would have married my father. She paid a heavy price for trusting a man with a devil's smooth tongue."

Isabella shifted nervously in the seat. "Are the rumours true?"

Few dared to ask such a question.

She referred to the fact his father's first two wives had died in the same manner. Both were found with twisted necks at the bottom of a dark staircase. No one dared speak of it at Fortune's Den. No one dared remind Aaron they did not all share the same mother.

"Murder is a difficult thing to prove," he said.

Isabella did not appear shocked. Gossip was rife. Lawton must have mentioned it on numerous occasions. "It's hard to imagine your father could be guilty of such a heinous crime."

"I prefer not to think about it." His father was the sort of man who forced his eldest son to fight in a tavern basement just to settle a debt. He was the sort who moved his mistress into the house while his wife's body was still warm. "If you heard the gossip, then you know there's another theory."

Isabella sighed. "Yes, but I'm sure your mother loved you and would never have intentionally taken her life."

"Perhaps. Sadly, we will never know." As this was a confessional of sorts, he asked his own probing question. "Did your mother love you, Isabella?"

She averted her gaze and took to staring at the passing houses. "Some people don't understand what love is. My mother was an orphan and had no guidance. I take solace in the fact she did her best while battling her demons."

"We often resort to anger when we feel neglected." God, he'd have lived in a permanent rage had it not been for Mrs Maloney. "A wise woman once told me we should strive to do the opposite. To give without expectation. To give to those we consider undeserving."

Isabella looked at him, her eager eyes wide. "Was it Socrates who said those who are the hardest to love need it most?"

"I believe it was." He watched her, the need to have her, possess her, like a living thing growing inside him. "Based on your upbringing, do you think you're capable of loving someone?"

She shrugged. "Do you?"

"All the odds are against us."

"I've never met anyone who professes to feel true love."

Christian snorted as an image of a powerful man came to

mind. "Daventry is hopelessly in love with his wife. He's still besotted after all these years."

Isabella laughed. The sound stirred something warm and deep in his chest. "But he's not a mortal man and therefore doesn't count."

"Yes, he's certainly unlike anyone I've ever met." She was unlike anyone he had ever met. He found himself transfixed by her smile, by her depthless brown eyes and clever mouth. "While romantic love may be a questionable emotion, one cannot deny the power of lust."

She touched her fingers to her throat. "Worldly people understand that's all there is. They don't set their expectations too high."

"You consider me worldly?" he teased.

"You may not have ventured far, but make up for it in experience."

"I learnt a little more about the journey to Egypt last night."

A pretty blush stained her cheeks. "I suppose you want to know what happens when you enter port."

He laughed. "I know what happens when I enter port, love."

"Not an Egyptian port. You may find it a totally new experience."

"It's fair to say that's probable." There was no question this woman was unique. "Do let me know when you're ready to continue with my education."

Her eyes met his, and he saw his own desire shimmering there. "Is there somewhere we could go? Somewhere quiet where we won't be disturbed?"

With Gibbs playing nursemaid, it would be impossible to escape him. And with Lawton out for their blood, he couldn't take her to his house in Ludgate Hill. Mrs Maloney had given him the key to the bookshop. With it being a stone's throw from Fortune's Den, help would be on hand.

"I told Mrs Maloney I would visit the bookshop and check all is well," he said, dismissing the faint flicker of guilt. "She promised Aaron she wouldn't leave Fortune's Den, and she never breaks a vow."

Isabella remained silent while contemplating his proposition. "I do need to collect the receipt for the cobblers."

"Then we'll call at the shop once we've spoken to Ethel Cartwright." It was the only opportunity they'd get to explore their deepening connection. And their work at the docks tonight came with certain risks. There's every chance he would wake tomorrow to find her gone.

They sat in companionable silence, the thrum of nervous excitement palpable in the air. Every few seconds, they looked at each other. He was debating whether there was time to kiss her when Gibbs brought the carriage to a halt in Dean Street.

The walk past the chapel to the warden's office took longer than their meeting with the balding guardian. After explaining the purpose of their visit, he checked his ledger, quickly finding the necessary information.

"Yes, Ethel Cartwright was here for a time. She caused no end of trouble and earned the moniker The Revolutionist."

"Do you know where she went?"

"Yes, she got a job at the docks near the Limestone Basin. Don't ask me how. But some poor fellow saw fit to employ her at the shipping office." He checked his notes. "Yes, she went to work at Napier & Woods on Narrow Street."

Chapter Thirteen

"Wait here, Gibbs." Christian's tone was firm as he issued the command. "We promised Mrs Maloney we'd perform a few duties at the shop. We should be no longer than an hour."

Isabella stood on the pavement, doing her utmost to look nonchalant when nerves had her trembling and guilt made her restless. Not that she had any reservations about giving herself to Christian.

Every illicit encounter brought them closer together. Every meaningful conversation made her value his friendship all the more. Just thinking about kissing him robbed her of rational thought. Soon, they would be lovers. *He* would take her virtue, not Mr Griffin, not the Conte di Barasian, not some other wicked fellow.

Christian glanced at her, his gaze dropping to her lips. "Maybe a little longer than an hour, Gibbs."

Mr Gibbs considered them both but made no protest. He looked resigned to his fate and dug deep into his greatcoat pocket, found a silver flask and a small bible.

"You'll be sure to keep watch?" Christian asked, scanning the narrow street like a hawk searching for prey.

"I'm paid to deliver you to Fortune's Den. I'm on duty until you walk through the gaming hell door."

Thankfully, Mr Gibbs didn't stare at them with a knowing eye. He pulled the stopper from his flask and took a hearty swig before flicking to a page in his bible.

Isabella prayed it wasn't a parable about sinners.

Christian retrieved a key from his pocket and let them into the musty bookshop. The overhead bell tinkled. Today, it seemed so loud Aaron Chance could probably hear it from the depths of Fortune's Den.

Locking the door behind them, Christian moved through the shop, his steps strong and purposeful. He scanned the bookshelves, poked his head around the parlour door, and looked pleased everything was in order.

Then he turned to her, his intention clear in his slow, sensual smile. "Finally, we're alone."

"Yes." Her pulse galloped faster than an Arabian thoroughbred.

His gaze devoured her. "God, Isabella. I could never tire of looking at you. You're so beautiful you steal my breath."

She'd heard the same flattering words countless times. This time, her heart fluttered like a caged bird. "What? Even in this dowdy dress?"

"I'd prefer you out of it, but you could wear a grain sack and still look appealing. To me, at any rate."

Though she knew he wasn't lying, she found compliments hard to swallow. "Why don't you say what's really on your mind?"

He drew his thumb over his bottom lip, his gaze roaming over her body. "Do you want to go upstairs, Isabella?" He must have sensed her slight hesitance. "You're allowed to change your mind. We can fetch the things Mrs Maloney wanted and leave. You won't have to suffer my mood as punishment. I know some men use it to get their own way."

Her mother's lovers were master manipulators. "The conte withdrew funds if my mother refused to make the weekly quota."

"But we're not doing this for mere gratification."

She stepped closer, keen to know his thoughts, eager to understand his motives. "Why are we doing this?"

He closed the gap between them, captured her hand, and kissed the inside of her wrist. "Because the connection between us is too strong to ignore. Because we can't fight it and are both desperate to know why. Because neither of us believe in love and wonder if friendship and lust make a formidable combination."

They were standing inches apart, yet in this intimate moment, she felt like they were one. Joined in heart and mind. About to join bodies.

"I always take what I want, Isabella. I've never made love to a woman." He stroked her cheek softly. "Yet I want to make love to you. Desperately so."

The powerful beat of blood in her veins was like an incessant drum, a call to sate a physical need. "What's the difference?"

"I'll be damned if I know."

She smiled. "You're supposed to be my tutor."

"Yet I can't help but feel it's the other way around." He looked at her with such intensity it stole her breath. "I'm different when I'm with you. I'm the best version of myself."

She was different, too. She'd imagined dying a virgin, yet craved everything this man could give. "Promise me nothing will change."

He laughed. "If I take your virtue, it's gone forever."

"No, promise me things won't be awkward between us."

She placed her hand on his chest, though touching him intensified the inner ache. "Promise me our friendship will survive."

"Of course our friendship will survive. I'm a man, not a child."

Oh, there was no denying his potent masculinity.

It was there in the deep timbre of his voice, in his seductive smile. His clothes hid a body of steel. She felt it now, had felt it the moment his erection had slipped through her tight fingers.

"I'd like to see the man," she said, finding the courage to be bold. "I'd like to see what you look like naked, without these fine clothes."

He hissed a breath and seemed suddenly fixated on her lips. "From you, words are a potent aphrodisiac. Perhaps you'd like to strip me, Isabella. I'll try not to come when you do."

Her pulse rose more than a notch.

"I was told you're a master of restraint, Mr Chance."

"Not around you, Miss Lawton."

Aware time was of the essence, she glanced at the shop window. "Mr Gibbs will be pleased. He may only have a ten-minute wait."

His gaze turned dark and predatory. "I can entertain us both for a damn sight longer than an hour. Come. Let me take you to bed."

Never in her wildest dreams had she imagined seeing Christian Chance again, let alone engaging in flirtatious banter or holding his hand as they mounted the stairs to make love.

He led her past the door to the first-floor bedchamber, heading towards the flight of steps to the attic.

"Wait." She tugged his hand, pulling him back to the

room she'd used while staying with Mrs Maloney. "The bed here is comfortable." And it was where they'd shared their first kiss. Not that she had ever been sentimental.

Christian hesitated. He looked at the door as if it were the gateway to hell. "When I'm in that room, I have to fight to banish the bad memories."

"All the more reason to make new ones."

He kissed her tenderly on the forehead. "Please, Isabella. I want nothing to spoil this moment."

Neither did she. "I understand. The attic it is."

He remained rooted to the spot, then sighed and muttered a curse. "The desire to make you happy leaves me questioning my own logic."

"Then why don't we let fate decide?"

"Do you want me to flip a coin?"

"No. I want you to kiss me."

Fearing Mr Gibbs might lose the will to live and fetch Aaron Chance, Isabella fell into Christian's arms.

They kissed. Slowly. Deeply.

Every muscle relaxed as she bathed in the wonder of their beautiful connection. But, as was always the way with them, the simmering hunger boiled over into an explosion of unbridled passion.

Soon, his hands were on her buttocks, his tongue thrusting against hers in a primal dance. She tugged his hair, moaned into his mouth and stroked the ever-growing bulge in his trousers.

"You're so hard," she breathed against his lips.

"I need out of my damn clothes," he growled, practically tearing his coat off his back. "I should have told Gibbs we'd be two hours." He was panting, staring at her mouth. "I need you naked. I need you naked now."

Before she'd finished unbuttoning her pelisse, he was

pushing the garment off her shoulders. His arm snaked around her back, drawing her closer. He was so ravenous he bent his head and sucked her breast through layers of fabric.

Despite the obvious barrier, her nipples pushed hard against the material. Her breasts were so heavy they ached.

"Christian!" She pushed her hands into his hair, anchoring him to her. "Touch me. Touch me like you did in the carriage." She was losing control. The pressure to find her release was overwhelming.

He reached under her skirts, his long fingers sliding through her sex. "You're so wet, love. So wet you'll take me with ease." He pushed his fingers inside her channel and pumped slowly.

"Oh, yes!"

"Be patient, minx," he whispered, his hot breath tickling her ear. "When you come this time, it will be against my mouth, then around my cock. Do you like the sound of that, Isabella?"

She gulped. "You'll remember I've not done this before."

"Trust me. We'll be perfect together. I knew it sixteen years ago, and I know it now. You thought the boy was kind. You'll love what the man has to give you."

His husky voice made her sex clench. The way he worked his fingers deep inside her tore a whimper from her throat. The lewd words he used had her reaching to stroke his erection through his trousers.

"Unbutton me, love."

She managed to undo a button securing the placket and slip her hand inside. His member was hot and hard and jerked against her cold fingers.

"Mother of all saints," he uttered. "Love, I'm going to have you here unless you open the damn door."

Amid the haze of desire, Isabella reached behind her and

fumbled with the handle. The door flew open, and they fell inside like tavern drunkards. They stumbled over each other's feet and tumbled to the floor.

A laugh escaped her, one that quickly turned into a sweet moan when Christian pushed her skirts to her waist and kneeled between her parted legs.

He moistened his lips and fixed his gaze on her sex. "Let me show you I'm still as kind as you remember. I'm the King of Diamonds, and I'm going to own this little jewel."

His mouth was hot and wet on her sex, his grip firm on her thighs. He lavished her with attention, sucking and flicking her bud with his tongue.

"You taste like heaven, love," he murmured.

Every part of her tingled.

The tightening in her abdomen grew more profound.

Yet she wanted to feel the heat of his skin, the weight of him crushing her. Him pushing into her so deeply she'd lack the strength to leave.

"Christian! Hurry! I need you."

She gripped his hair and rolled her hips against the wicked onslaught of his tongue. Then their eyes met, the desire in those blue pools sending her hurtling over the edge into oblivion.

Stars danced in her eyes. She arched her back, the muscles in her core clenching at too fast a pace. The sound of her ragged breathing filled the room. Despite the rush of euphoria, she wanted him out of his clothes.

"I need to touch you. I need to feel you."

"Hellfire!" He undid his trousers and shoved them down past his hips. "Do you want to stop, Isabella? Tell me now. I want you so badly, I'll lose my mind if I wait. Tell me."

"Don't stop," she urged, loving how he lost control with her. "Take me now. Take me here on the floor. Hurry."

He glanced at their surroundings and muttered a curse as he gripped his solid shaft. "This wasn't how I planned it."

She reached for him. "This is what fate decreed."

A sinful smile lit his handsome features. "Do you know how incredible you are? You're the most incredible person I've ever met."

A rush of emotion almost choked her. She'd been called many things. Useless. Annoying. A pest. A burden. Never anything as beautiful as the word he had just uttered.

Don't cry!

Let him love you!

If only this once!

"Make love to me. Don't wait."

She would never forget the moment he nudged slowly into her body. Not because she felt the slight burn as he stretched her wide. Not because she lay on the hard floor, half-dressed.

It was the tender look on his face that stole the air from her lungs. It was the hot flash of desire in his eyes. The way he reassured her before groaning in ecstasy and pushing deeper.

"I swear it will get easier." Christian held himself up on muscular arms, angled his hips and moved against her sex with each short thrust.

Pleasurable sensations rippled to her toes. It wasn't long before she grabbed his buttocks and urged him to push deeper.

"It's not too late to stop," he growled, the muscles in his jaw clenched tightly. "With the next thrust, there's no going back."

There wasn't a shred of doubt in her mind.

Christian Chance was her only friend.

He would be her only lover.

She rocked her hips in answer, but he demanded to hear the words aloud. "You're the only man I want. Do it now." Him filling her full was the only thought on her mind.

In one sleek movement, he thrust hard and buried himself deep.

The sudden intrusion tore a gasp from her lips.

He stilled, looked to be waiting for reassurance.

But she did not feel pain.

She felt an instant outpouring of love.

Was it a fleeting love that would fade when they tired of each other? Was it a love that might deepen over time? It was impossible to know.

He seemed in awe of her body, of the undeniable pleasure they experienced together. And so she focused on enjoying this perfect moment. She inhaled the scent of his skin. She closed her eyes as he withdrew and then entered her fully again.

Emptiness. Utter completion.

Nothing. Everything.

Loneliness. Love.

"Kiss me, Christian."

He lay on top of her and claimed her mouth in fierce possession. The man was the King of Lovemaking. With every stroke of his tongue, he entered her. Pleasure radiated. An intense beating in her blood.

"Christian."

He tore his mouth from hers, concentrating on every measured stroke. "That's it, love. You're almost there."

She shuddered hard, her sex clenching around his manhood, hugging him, holding him, staking her claim.

He withdrew, pumping his seed over her thigh.

He looked heavenward, his chest heaving as he struggled

to catch his breath. Then a smile curled his lips, and he hit her with the full force of his gaze.

"We need to do that again and soon," he panted.

She looked at him. His hair was mussed, his cravat askew, his trousers halfway down his muscular legs, the head of his manhood red and glistening.

A laugh escaped her. She was on the floor, something wet trickling down her thigh, her sex a little sore, her skirts bunched to her waist.

And she'd never been happier.

"Perhaps next time we might remove our clothes and lie together in bed. I'd like nothing more than the heat of your skin warming me."

He glanced at the scene and laughed, too. "I've never lost control like that. I've never been so aroused." His smile faded as guilt assailed him. "I should have been more mindful of your comfort."

An idea formed in her mind.

"You might afford me one kindness before we leave."

"Anything," he growled, and she knew he meant it.

"Undress me. Lie next to me and hold me."

Mischief twinkled in his eyes. "By my estimation, we have half an hour before Gibbs comes knocking." He reached into his waistcoat pocket, removed a handkerchief and wiped her sex and thigh. "Let me fetch some water and wash you properly."

"I'll bathe when we're home." Except Fortune's Den wasn't her home, a fact Aaron Chance had made abundantly clear. A silly thought entered her head. Them finding lodgings, a cosy room they could call their own. Conducting investigations for Mr Daventry, dining together and making love every night.

It sounded idyllic.

Beyond impossible.

She wasn't the only one questioning what this meant. Christian watched her intently as he undressed. His body was magnificent, all hard planes and rippling muscles. But needing to savour this moment, she tempered the incessant stirrings of arousal.

Despite her embarrassment, she let him undress her.

He stroked the backs of his fingers over her arm, marvelling at the softness of her skin. "You're so delicate, so smooth." He knew this was not about sexual gratification. Hence, he merely exhaled deeply as he gazed upon her breasts. "I wish we had more time."

His sentiment echoed her own.

And yet she was the one who must leave.

They climbed into bed, the touch of their naked bodies making them both gasp aloud. He drew the bedsheets over them and pulled her close.

"Whatever we do, we cannot fall asleep," she said, not wanting to wake to find Aaron Chance looming over them. "Talk to me. Tell me something about you. Something I don't know."

He was quiet for a time. Perhaps he was sifting through the memories, trying to find one that didn't cause him pain.

"Do you want to know a secret?" he whispered against her hair.

She snuggled into him. "Yes."

"There's nothing but plain glass in my spectacles. I use them as a tool when I wish to appear intelligent."

"You are intelligent."

He pressed his finger to her lips. "Hush! You're the only one who knows. Everyone else thinks I'm a dangerous bastard."

She smiled. "Like a diamond, you have many facets."

"But few people take the time to study them."

They fell into a companionable silence, their tender touches the only language needed. Minutes passed before she spoke again.

"Christian?" she whispered as she lay naked in his arms.

He smoothed her hair off her brow. "Yes?"

"Whatever happens, I'm glad I met you."

Chapter Fourteen

The Bunch of Grapes Tavern
Narrow Street

Aramis Chance sat on the wooden bench opposite Isabella and Christian, filling the seat with his broad, muscular frame. He was handsome, like his brothers. His devil-may-care attitude added a ruggedness to his character that captured every woman's eye.

"To what shall we drink?" Aramis raised his tankard, though his stern tone said there was nothing to celebrate. "To blossoming friendships or tough choices?"

The man's sarcasm knew no bounds.

Isabella tempered her nerves. "To solving the case."

But the thought brought a shadow of sorrow. The end would soon be nigh. Christian would return to his life at Fortune's Den. Lord knows where she would be. Her father's prisoner. The slave of a deranged conte. A stowaway hoping to hide in the vast wilds of America.

Christian lifted his tankard in salute. "To breaking old habits."

It was aimed at her—an effort to prevent her from running.

If only life were that simple.

Isabella sipped her watery ale and scanned the crowded taproom. They were the focus of attention. Two unkempt men stood at the crude oak counter, watching them and whispering as they drank. A sinister fellow on the adjacent table kept them in his sights, too, the meagre candlelight highlighting his jagged facial scar.

Christian noticed the perceived threat. "Should a fight erupt, you'll return to the carriage, Isabella, and alert Gibbs."

He'd not realised he'd spoken her given name until Aramis said, "Isabella? Not Miss Lawton?"

Christian straightened. "What of it?"

Aramis raised his hands in mock surrender, yet his hard eyes were full of scorn. "It was just an observation. No need to be so tetchy, brother."

"We're all on edge, Mr Chance." Isabella could feel the simmering hostility in the room. "We must keep our eyes peeled for Ethel Cartwright. She is instrumental in helping us gain a better understanding of the case."

Christian stood, his chair scraping the boards. "I'll order more drinks. See if the landlord can point us in the right direction."

Nausea roiled in her stomach. She wanted to grab his hand, urge him to be careful and not to take risks—but could do nothing other than nod and smile and pretend they were colleagues, not lovers.

Perhaps he'd intended to leave her alone with his brother.

Aramis watched Christian push through the crowd before

engaging her in conversation. "Unlike your father, you seem like an honest woman, Miss Lawton."

"I shall take that as a compliment, sir."

"A sensible woman, too."

"Hardships make us stronger." Why did he not get to the point?

He sipped his ale. "Then you know Christian will never turn his back on his family. Whatever is going on between you won't last. It can't last."

Sadly, his opinion echoed her own thoughts.

She was resigned to the fact they were lovers, nothing more. The intense need for him was a fleeting thing, not permanent. And yet, when he held her in his arms, she could stay there forever. When he moved deep inside her body and kissed her tenderly, she felt like she was finally home.

Isabella swallowed past the lump in her throat. "Christian is honest and loyal and a dear friend." Her only friend. "I have never met a kinder man and would never hurt him. Besides, he needs his family more than he needs me."

Aramis relaxed back in his seat, his brow arching in surprise. "Most women I know would see my comments as a challenge. They would hiss their objection, stake their claim, swear to prove me wrong."

"Then perhaps you need to move in different circles, Mr Chance. I would never hurt Christian for my own selfish gain." She stared into her tankard, gathering the strength to reveal her true plans. "Once the case is solved and I receive my full pay, I shall run, sir. It's the only way to escape my father and his dastardly schemes."

At all costs, she had to remain one step ahead of the conte.

He stared at her, his dark gaze unnerving. "Aaron seems

to think Lawton is guilty of a crime. That our efforts will ensure we get rid of him for good."

Her father had nine lives. She knew better than to pin her hopes on the impossible. "And I often dream of a life free from worry. But I'm old enough to know fantasies rarely come true."

Aramis frowned. "Why wait? Why not run now while you have the chance? You risk all our lives by remaining here."

Knots of unease tightened in her chest. She looked across the sea of heads, searching for Christian. Despite everything she'd said, the thought of leaving him hurt. She was afraid to admit why. It meant using words like *happiness* and *love* and *forever*.

Tears gathered behind her eyes. "I need money, Mr Chance."

"I'll give you whatever you need."

"You're that desperate to get rid of me?" She laughed, else she would cry. It was the story of her life. Perhaps Christian was right. Perhaps it was time to finish the chapter, close the book and start anew.

"I'd do anything to stop my brother suffering. It's obvious your affair will end in tears, and he'll be left with another hole in his chest that books cannot fill."

Despite his stern personae, Aramis Chance loved his brother.

And by God, Christian deserved everyone's adoration.

She might have considered his proposal, but a feminine shriek punctuated the loud chatter and the clink of tankards.

Christian pushed through the crowd, the clerk from the shipping office clinging to him like ivy, touching his chest, giggling and whispering in his ear.

Jealousy slithered like a serpent in Isabella's veins as she watched him grin and whisper something amusing.

Christian approached the table. "Miss Cartwright wishes to join us." He helped the woman into the seat he'd recently vacated. "The landlord is bringing four tankards of ale."

Ethel stumbled into the chair, hiccuped, burped and gripped Isabella's arm. "It ain't what it looks like," she whispered. "I need them to think I'm drunk and keen to bed one of these fine fellows."

Christian sat beside his brother on the bench. "She heard we would pay for information regarding Snell's shipments and accosted me at the bar."

"Ain't you a handsome one?" Ethel leant forward and gazed adoringly at Aramis, her large breasts almost spilling from her dress onto the table. "I like them mean, and you've the look of the devil about you."

Aramis observed Ethel's impressive breasts. "And you have much to recommend you, madam."

Ethel giggled. "Too much for you to handle, I'll wager."

"Too much for an ordinary man, not for me."

Isabella listened to their bawdy banter—to the meaningless flirtation she had heard countless times before. Her mother knew how to hold a man's attention. Her passing had been a long, painful journey from a graceful opera singer capable of attracting every man's eye to a bag of bones in an overly large bed.

Christian found Aramis' witty retorts amusing. "We're acting on behalf of the Home Secretary," he said, nudging his brother. "You cannot bed a witness."

"You know me. I rise to every challenge."

Ethel laughed like a deranged fool at the fair. Then her voice turned serious as she whispered, "I hear you're investigating Captain Snell and his mysterious shipments."

"Specifically, the most recent one," Isabella muttered, hugging the woman's arm as an excuse to move closer. "From the eight crates brought ashore, only four were delivered to the Society of Antiquaries."

They all remained silent when the serving wench came and deposited their drinks on the table. She knocked over an empty tankard while gawping at the handsome Chance brothers, started patting Christian's chest with a stained towel.

"He's importing contraband," Ethel said once they'd shooed the wench away. "Most likely opium from the Far East. I know he's got connections in Italy and Egypt. I've seen him loading a crate onto a barge that disappeared along the Regent's Canal."

Isabella considered the information.

Captain Snell would swing from the gallows if caught. The threat was enough to force him to murder a witness. And yet, the deceased woman had only mentioned artefacts. She must have had no knowledge of opium smuggling.

Moreover, the prickle of hairs on Isabella's nape said they were missing the vital clue that bound all threads together.

"Another ship docked two nights ago." Ethel wagged her brows. "An Italian vessel. Snell's men loaded a crate onto the ship from a warehouse down by Rope Walk."

Isabella suppressed a gasp. She'd lay odds it had something to do with the conte. So, he was in London on business, albeit nefarious, not to broker a deal with her father.

The sick feeling in her gut warned her not to be complacent. They should seek confirmation from one of Snell's men. For now, she was eager to broach the subject of Lord Oldman.

"There are twenty warehouses in that area," Aramis said. "Which one does Snell own?"

"None. That's the problem. No one seems to know who owns it."

"Might it be Mr Quigley?" Isabella asked.

The woman's smile died. She glanced over her shoulder. "I can't see how a man of Quigley's means could afford to keep a warehouse."

Christian sat forward, a cloud of suspicion dimming his vibrant blue eyes. "Why do you say that?"

"Because I was told he works at the museum."

"The British Museum?"

Ethel shrugged.

"Can you describe him?" Christian said with some urgency.

As if suddenly aware all eyes were upon them, Ethel grabbed Isabella's hand and exposed her palm. "You can tell a lot from these fine lines," she said, tracing her finger over the ridges. "He's of average height and build." She pointed to the diagonal line cutting across Isabella's palm. "This here is the heart line."

Isabella stared intently as the woman tilted her hand beneath the candlelight. The line forked, one groove growing faint and disappearing, one veering in a different direction. "What does that mean?"

"That you should expect a heavy loss. The deeper the line, the deeper the feelings. This one will hurt."

Isabella met Christian's gaze across the table. He was the only person she had ever cared about. Her need for him grew deeper by the day. When they said goodbye, it would be a moment of profound sorrow. One she would likely live to regret.

"I'd say Quigley is thirty or so," Ethel added quietly. "I'm sure his hair is brown, but he always wears a broad-brimmed hat."

Perhaps Quigley was an alias. Based on those working at the museum, the description matched the curator more than his assistant. That said, there must be many men working behind the scenes. It made sense why one would encourage Lord Oldman to hire a ship to bring back historical antiquities.

It would be fair to assume Captain Snell was dealing in contraband and Lord Oldman was dealing in fake artefacts. The question was, which one killed the woman found in the Thames? And was Isabella's father involved?

It was looking unlikely.

"We spoke to Mr Winthrop," Christian said curiously. "He said you had a gripe with Lord Oldman and warned other women about accepting a job in his household. It seems rather a coincidence to find you working at the shipping office close to where Snell docked *The Marigold*."

Ethel pointed to a line on Isabella's palm. "This is the lifeline. It's what I gave those girls when I warned them about Oldman." She quickly changed tack when two men passed, eyeing everyone at their table. "This here says you're independent. A lover of liberty."

"I'd say that's accurate," Christian muttered.

Aramis watched the men keenly while keeping his hand close to his coat pocket. They left the premises, though Aramis' gaze remained fixed on the paint-chipped door.

Isabella snatched back her hand. "If you've never worked for his lordship, where did you get your information?"

"And what were you warning them about?" Christian added.

Ethel shuffled closer. "I knew someone what worked for him once. If the tea was too cold, he'd tie her up in the basement as punishment. He starts by intimidating them. Sometimes, he lashes out in a rage, blames their crying on Egyptian curses."

Isabella's blood ran cold.

She couldn't bear to think about what happened in

wealthy households. Her arm was still bruised where her father had grabbed her too tightly. It bore no comparison, but she knew how it felt to live in fear.

They needed to free Nancy Jones before it was too late.

But they could hardly take the word of this woman over a peer.

"Is this person willing to make a statement?" she said.

Ethel shook her head. "She was last seen boarding the stage to Brighton. No one has seen or heard from her since."

And so they were back to believing Lord Oldman was guilty of selling forged or stolen artefacts. That the woman who'd accosted the curator was a fleeing servant, keen to warn others about her devious master.

The only other question related to the missing women, but Ethel looked blankly when Isabella gave a brief description.

"I heard Oldman keeps the plain ones. The ones who don't complain and are down on their luck. The pretty ones soon find better opportunities elsewhere."

Christian produced the pewter pendant and handed it to Ethel. "Does this look at all familiar?"

The woman studied it, turning it over in her rough hands. "It looks like something you can buy from a hawker at Farringdon Market."

"May I look at the pendant?" Aramis said.

Ethel passed it to him, gripping his long fingers. "One of you gents will have to take me outside and kiss me. Else it will look mighty suspicious."

Christian turned to Aramis. "I'm afraid the onus falls on you."

"Why me?"

"Because my affections are engaged elsewhere."

Isabella's heart flipped. Were his affections engaged? Did

their romantic interludes mean more to him than she'd suspected?

Aramis frowned. He scanned the taproom then pinned Ethel to the chair with his intense gaze. "Is this where your friends rob my purse while you're stroking my cock?" He inclined his head to Isabella. "Forgive my crude language, but I'm not one to mince words."

"Pay it no mind, Mr Chance. I heard worse during my recent voyage to England, and my mother often spoke in the devil's own tongue."

Christian smiled. His eyes conveyed a need to get rid of present company and indulge in private pleasures. Sadly, they wouldn't get a moment alone tonight. Not unless she risked her neck and stole into his bedchamber.

"Happen you'd rather we found a room." Ethel gestured to the wooden stairs. "I can get a good rate."

Aramis gave a sinful grin. "Tempting as it may be, my brother is right. I cannot bed a witness. You'd best have another drink to dim your disappointment. I would have been the best fuck you've ever had."

Christian chuckled. In his brother's company, he looked free of all burdens. His rightful place was with the formidable men of Fortune's Den, not miles away with no one but her for company.

A sensible woman would avoid all physical contact. It would make their parting easier in the end. But logic abandoned her whenever their eyes met.

"More's the pity. I can do things with my tongue you've only dreamed of," Ethel countered. "Still, one of you gents will have to kiss me."

Aramis stood and straightened his coat. "What a man must do in the name of justice." He beckoned Miss Cartwright. That's when Isabella noticed the thickened skin and scarring just above his wrist. "We'll remain indoors, madam, in full view of the punters."

Miss Cartwright gave a coy grin before accepting his proffered hand. "At least make it look like we want a little privacy."

Like Lucifer leading an unsuspecting victim to the bowels of hell, Aramis led Ethel to the darkened corner beneath the stairs.

"What happened to his arm?" Isabella asked, curiosity getting the better of her. If she felt an ounce of compassion for the man, it might make accepting his money easier to bear.

Christian recoiled at the question. He glanced at his brother, who currently had his tongue down Ethel's throat. "In his youth, a lady tricked him into believing they were in love. She was married, and her husband held his arm over a lit brazier as punishment."

"Good Lord!" No wonder Aramis Chance was cold and unfeeling to the opposite sex. No wonder he thought affairs of the heart always ended in disaster.

"Aaron would have killed the man had Aramis not demanded the right to seek vengeance. He's never said what happened afterwards, and none of us have asked."

Isabella peeked at Ethel. The woman clung to Aramis as if desperate to prolong the kiss. "Well, it hasn't prevented him from pursuing romantic relationships."

Christian laughed. "There's nothing romantic about the way Aramis takes his pleasure. Unlike me, Isabella, he has yet to find a woman who gives him the incentive to change."

And there it was—as constant as ever—the hope they would survive her father's schemes. The desire for her to stop running and give their friendship a chance. The need to explore their undeniable connection.

She reached across the table and clutched his hand. "How might I escape Mrs Maloney's watchful eye to visit you in your chamber tonight?"

He moistened his lips, his breath quickening like he was already pushing inside her. "Be honest. Tell her everything. Listen to her advice. If she's the woman I think she is, you will find my door unlocked and me waiting naked beneath the bedsheets."

Her sex clenched in anticipation. "Now we've questioned Miss Cartwright, I see little point remaining here."

She wanted to hold him close in the darkness.

Never let go.

"We must speak to at least one of Snell's men," he said with obvious regret. "It will be the first question Daventry asks tomorrow. Any insight into who's buying his contraband will be invaluable."

A sigh escaped her. "Yes, you're right."

His gaze dipped to her mouth. "Don't look so down-hearted. I'll be inside you before the night is through. Even if I have to bind and gag Mrs Maloney."

Her temperature soaring, Isabella fanned her face with her hand. "What about Aaron?" She would risk his wrath for one night of heavenly bliss.

Christian shrugged. "He's hot-headed but will calm down eventually. I'll not let his fears stop me from pursuing you." He stood. "Come. Let's return to the carriage and see if Gibbs has learnt anything new. If one of Snell's men means to spill his guts, he'll want to do so where there are no witnesses."

All heads turned in their direction as they stood.

There was no need to alert Aramis of their intention to leave. His eyes were open as he kissed Ethel Cartwright. He moved his hands from her buttocks to her shoulders and held her upright as he tore his mouth away.

Aramis crossed the room, Ethel staring at his retreating figure as if he were the Messiah. The man was no one's saviour. He flayed people alive with his intense eyes and brooding temperament.

"Are you quite finished?" Christian teased.

Aramis wiped his mouth with the back of his hand and grinned. "Miss Cartwright wasn't lying. She knows how to kiss. A mortal man would have been tripping over his feet to take her upstairs."

Isabella studied him. His eyes were like dull black marbles. His pulse wasn't beating so hard in his throat it left him breathless. He was entirely unaffected.

"I beg to differ," she said, feeling a little more confident around the man now she knew his weaknesses. "A passionless kiss is no kiss at all."

Aramis arched a brow. "Who said it was passionless?"

"It was mechanical. A staged act."

Christian cleared his throat. "Miss Lawton is trying to say passion makes for a more enlightening experience."

"Like you'd know," Aramis scoffed. He looked at Isabella as heat rose to her cheeks, then uttered something inaudible.

She suggested they step outside into the cool night air before Aramis demanded to know the exact nature of their relationship.

How could she explain what Christian meant to her when she hardly understood it herself? Yes, she had praised his character. Made it clear she would put his needs before her own. How could she make a cold-hearted man understand that loving Christian was like craving a drug?

A drug she couldn't live without.

Chapter Fifteen

"We've company, Mr Chance." Gibbs remained atop his box but nodded at the unmarked vehicle parked further along the dim street. "Two men left the tavern and disappeared into the alley leading to the warehouses near Rope Walk. They returned to wait on the street until the carriage arrived."

Christian glanced at the vehicle, an ominous black shadow in the darkness. "How many men are inside?"

"There's no telling. Only four, I'd say."

Aramis stepped forward, looking pleased to have an opportunity to flex his fists. "We're more than equipped to deal with them, though it depends how many men they have waiting in the tavern."

Christian glanced at Isabella. He'd not risk her getting hurt in a brawl or shot by a stray lead ball. "Get inside the carriage, Isabella." It was a command, not a suggestion. "Gibbs, take her somewhere safe, then return for us. There's the chapel for the alms' houses by the foundry."

The lady jerked in response. "I'm not leaving you."

If only she meant it.

If only she didn't have her sights set on distant shores.

But as long as she was in London, her father posed a threat.

"You're a liability, Miss Lawton," Aramis snapped.

Although compelled to defend her, Christian knew Aramis was right. "I can't protect you like this. There aren't enough of us to hold back an army and prevent you from being taken hostage."

Gibbs tutted. "A wise man knows when to retreat. I'd have told you all to climb into the carriage if I thought we were outnumbered." He gestured to the vehicle. "It's intimidation. That's what this is." Handing Isabella his riding crop, Gibbs added, "If some devil comes near you, miss, hit 'em hard. Take no prisoners."

Isabella nodded. "Thank you, Mr Gibbs." She turned to Christian, her brown eyes pleading to remain at his side. "I can protect myself. There's no need to worry."

But he did worry.

The deep ache in his heart warned of two things. He was in love with her. He'd likely been in love with her since watching her steal biscuits from the tree and hug the small parcels to her chest. Yet he knew he was going to lose her. He just didn't know how or when.

"Please, Isabella." He was not averse to begging.

But the decision was taken out of their hands.

Four men stepped out of the unmarked vehicle, their intention evident in their determined strides.

Isabella gasped. "Merciful Lord. It's my father." Her hand shot to her throat. "And ... and the Conte di Barasian."

Christian hissed a breath, his anger firing into a blistering rage. The foppish gentleman bore the King's arrogance. Dressed impeccably in a mustard velvet coat, he walked with

196

a silver-topped cane, a means to beat back peasants, not help steady his gait.

Lawton glared at Christian with reproachful eyes. "I've come for my damned daughter," he growled, coming to an abrupt halt ten feet away.

"You can't have her." Christian would rather die than hand Isabella to this devil. "She's of an age to make her own decisions. You have no claim."

The conte couldn't take his lecherous eyes off Isabella. "Bella, *cara mia*. We had an agreement." He clicked his fingers to the fellow behind, who promptly handed the conte a scroll. "This is our marriage contract. The one you signed before fleeing Positano."

"Marriage contract?" Isabella gripped the crop and pointed it at the conte. "If you're referring to the paper you forced me to sign, I did so under duress. It's in Italian. You said it related to me remaining in the villa."

Unable to hide his shock, Christian's head shot in her direction. Who signed something they couldn't read? He wanted to whip her with his tongue for being so damn foolish. But Aaron had taught him to remain calm under pressure.

"Then prosecute her for breach of contract," he snapped, convinced he could trust this woman. "I'm quite certain she has no intention of marrying you."

To reinforce the point, Aramis stabbed his finger at the flamboyant conte. "I suggest you take your pampered arse back to Positano. Miss Lawton has been granted our protection. We've no qualms in thumping that crooked nose straight."

Isabella touched Aramis briefly on the arm, a gesture of gratitude, but he firmed his jaw and whispered, "If you want to thank me, buy me a Cuban cigar, but never touch my arm again. I defended you for Christian's sake. That doesn't mean I trust you."

Christian scowled at his brother.

But Isabella proved she could defend herself. "I've no money to buy you a cigar, sir, so you'll take what you're given." She faced the conte. "The document is a means to frighten and intimidate me. You have a wife. You want a mistress. A puppet who does your bidding."

The conte's dark eyes turned sinister. "I want what is mine. One way or another, you will be on my ship when we sail, madam."

Lawton laughed. "You'll have to let her go. The conte's brothers will come to his aid. Aaron isn't strong enough to defend you against an Italian invasion."

"Then you don't know my brother," Christian said with a deep sense of pride. Aaron had a backbone of steel. "He'd die for his cause."

"His cause is guarding his family." Lawton's arrogant grin grated. "Without you, he's nothing. You're the chink in his armour. He loses a brother, he loses everything."

There was truth to Lawton's claim.

They were strong together. Nothing when torn apart. Aaron lived to protect them, as he had done long before they were dragged from their home in the dead of night. He'd fought bare-knuckle brawls, suffered many beatings, not to pay their father's debts, but to prevent Aramis being a target.

"You underestimate our skill in battle," Aramis growled. "We control a hidden army. Half the *ton* would join us in a war if we agreed to wipe their debts."

From the flicker of uncertainty in Lawton's eyes, he'd overlooked the desperation of men destined for the Marshalsea. "Hand my daughter over, and we can avoid any conflict."

Lawton's disregard for his family reminded Christian of his own father. The reprobate hadn't given a damn about his children either.

"I told you. We're betrothed. I am marrying Miss Lawton." Christian ignored his brother's muttered curse. "I'm as loyal as my brothers. Nothing you could say or do would convince me to betray her."

The conte signalled to the man behind, who whipped out a pistol. Before he could cock the hammer, Gibbs had the muzzle of his own weapon pointed at the conte's head.

"I've no qualms pulling the trigger." Gibbs' nose wrinkled while observing the conte's lace cravat. "I'm paid to see my clients safely home. Even if it means shooting a canary."

The Conte di Barasian froze. "One click of my fingers, and I can have twenty men here ready to fight."

"I've never seen a dead man click his fingers," Gibbs mocked. "And if you mean those drinking in the Grapes, you should know I grew up on this street. Everyone supping ale here tonight knows which side to choose."

As if to prove the point, the man with the scarred face appeared in the tavern doorway. The steel blade in his hand glinted in the darkness.

Lawton's cheeks ballooned as he struggled to contain his fury. "This isn't the end of the matter. We'll continue this conversation soon."

Christian considered pulling his own weapon and finishing this fool for good. But Aaron had stressed the need to attack only when one could prove self-defence. Unless, of course, there were no witnesses. Still, he couldn't help but feel Aaron was watching from the shadows.

"I suggest you return to the carriage, Lawton, and take your pompous friend with you." Christian felt a brief rush of satisfaction as he watched the men retreat. He kept them in his sights while praising his coachman. "Remind me to pay you a bonus, Gibbs."

"I've my own reasons for threatening blackguards. Watching a nabob squirm is payment enough." Gibbs beckoned his scarred accomplice forward. "This is Pretty Pete. I used to dunk his head in a water trough to see how long he could last without breathing. He has news about Snell and the warehouse."

Christian watched Lawton's unmarked vehicle drive past and disappear along Narrow Lane. Still seething, he prompted Pete to continue.

"Lord Oldman owns a warehouse near Rope Walk," Pete said, his gritty voice as menacing as his scar. He returned the blade to the leather sheath fastened around his waist. "Captain Snell rents it for a small fee."

Recovering after the conte's threat, Isabella was quick to make a suggestion. "We need to look inside the warehouse. Hopefully, we will find clues to explain what's going on there."

Pete looked over his shoulder before saying, "I'm told the place is empty. That they've moved the crates. Snell's focusing on getting his ship seaworthy for the voyage to Norway."

Christian frowned—a pang in his gut said they were missing a vital clue. "So what were the Conte di Barasian and Geoffrey Lawton doing near Rope Walk? Their prompt arrival suggests they had business inside one warehouse."

Pretty Pete shrugged.

"The men who warned them ain't from around here," Gibbs said. He looked Christian in the eye. "Daventry said I must take orders from you tonight. If you want to check the warehouses, I can gather a few men."

This was exactly what Christian had signed up for when

he'd agreed to help Lucius Daventry. A means of proving himself. A means of convincing Aaron to slacken the reins.

Aramis put his hand on Christian's shoulder. "I'm at your beck and call, brother. I'll do whatever you ask."

Christian grinned. "Then be nice to Miss Lawton. Once we enter the warehouse, I need to know you'll protect her."

Aramis inclined his head. "I can see she's important to you."

A fool couldn't miss how this woman made him feel. Despite longing for an opportunity to prove himself worthy of his brother's respect, his only thoughts were of Isabella.

The sooner they dealt with this matter, the sooner she would be in his bed. Mrs Maloney wasn't stupid or blind and would not deprive them of time alone together.

Christian stepped closer to the carriage and addressed Gibbs. "We'll walk to the warehouse. Pete will come with us while you gather a few friends in case we need reinforcements."

Gibbs had a stern word with Pete, reminding him to take every precaution. "I'll be a few minutes behind, no more."

As they readied to leave, Christian drew Aramis aside. He lowered his voice, casting a glance Miss Lawton's way. "She's everything to me. Do you understand?"

Aramis sighed. "As regrettable as the situation may be, I understand."

Pete directed them past the cramped terraced houses occupied by seafaring men, to a row of warehouses opposite the fields near Rope Walk.

It was dark but for the soft glow of light from one window. They passed a group of men drinking on the street, taking turns to swig from a bottle. One nodded to Pete but made no comment.

Aramis seemed disappointed they'd avoided an altercation.

Christian's fears had nothing to do with their current predicament and everything to do with the conte's ugly threat. He reached for Isabella's hand. "There's no need to run. I'll not let the conte take you."

She looked up at him, her wide brown eyes conveying an inner sadness. "The conte is more than a little dangerous. He would have killed my mother if she'd left him. I've seen how ruthless he can be."

"On his own, he's nothing."

The same was true of all men.

"Perhaps." Her sigh sounded like it came from the soul. "Let's pray Mr Daventry is right, and we find a means to charge my father with a crime. It might encourage the conte to flee."

The lack of conviction in her voice was unmistakable.

Days ago, she had asked him to name his worst fear. There were two, but he'd been unable to choose or repeat them aloud. He feared loving a woman. It made a man weak. Vulnerable. Gave him the sense he was standing on unstable ground. He feared loving someone so deeply he couldn't cope when they left—be it a journey to an otherworldly plane or far across a volatile sea.

Now, both of their fears had been realised.

And all they could do was place their faith in the Lord.

"This is it." Pretty Pete's hoarse voice dragged Christian from his reverie. The scarred man pointed to a brick building. A brass and steel combination lock secured the large wooden doors, one requiring the correct six letters to spring the latch. "Norway. That's the code. I heard one of Snell's men mention it in the tavern."

Christian smiled to himself.

If only collecting evidence had been this easy.

Pete gestured to Aramis. "You'll have to open it. I can't read or write. I could have a wild guess, but happen we'll be here for hours."

Aramis obliged, but the lock remained steadfast. He twirled the brass barrels, spelling the word backwards. The lock sprang open. Aramis removed it and slipped it into his pocket before insisting they all step back as he yanked open the heavy door. It creaked and groaned.

The stale smell of tobacco and rum assailed Christian's nostrils. "I think we have a rough idea what Snell is smuggling."

"Let me enter first." Aramis peered into the dark depths of the cavernous room. "Follow when I say it's safe to do so." He disappeared into the shadows, as eager as Christian to bring the investigation to a swift conclusion.

A minute passed. A minute of clattering and banging before Aramis assured them it was safe to enter.

Christian kept Isabella close and told Pete to stand guard at the door until Gibbs arrived.

"There's nothing here but empty crates." Aramis gestured to the rows of wooden containers lining the wall. "I've inspected the ones with lids to ensure no one was hiding inside."

Once his eyes grew accustomed to the gloom, Christian moved to examine the crates. Some slats were broken. Some had dents and score marks littering the panels.

He glanced at Aramis. "Did you find anything of interest?"

Aramis pointed to a crate near the crude desk in the corner of the vast room. "There's a soiled ream of silk in that one. Blood spots on the floor and broken pottery."

"Pottery?" Isabella hurried to look.

"It's scattered at the bottom." Aramis reached into the large box. He retrieved a sizeable fragment and handed it to her without recoiling.

Isabella hurried to the opposite side of the room and studied it beneath the moonlight filtering through the window. "Christian! It's part of an ushabti figurine. It's not faience but possibly mud with a small metal weight added to make it appear heavy."

"What the devil is she talking about?" Aramis muttered.

"A fake Egyptian artefact. You wouldn't understand." Christian crossed the room and studied the piece for himself, though it was Isabella's smile that held him captivated. "So, Snell did load his ship with fake artefacts. The question is, does Lord Oldman know he's sold worthless trinkets?"

"Perhaps we should tell him." She touched his arm. "It's not too late to visit him in Bloomsbury Square."

He suspected she had another motive for visiting the lord late at night. A motive that had more to do with the welfare of Nancy Jones.

"Do you want me to retrieve all the broken pieces?" Aramis called. "There's a strange jar with a jackal's head and what looks like the remnants of a bronze cat."

In her excitement, Isabella replied, "Yes. Gather everything you can find, Mr Chance."

Christian didn't want her to raise her hopes. "We don't know your father is involved. At best, Snell and Oldman will argue the Vizier duped them." He cupped her cheek and couldn't help but brush his lips gently over hers. God, his addiction was killing him. "Especially if the items come with provenance."

She placed her palm on his chest. "Then we've no hope of seeing him locked in Newgate, where he can do no harm."

He didn't want her to think she had no option but to run.

"We'll find a reason to be rid of him. Even if we have to stalk him night and day." Getting rid of a man like the Conte di Barasian was a different matter.

The need to kiss away their troubles had them looking at each other's mouths, fighting back the urge to lock lips.

"I wish there was no one in the world but us," she whispered. "I wish we didn't have to worry about what tomorrow will bring."

He wasn't sure how to explain that he came as a package. That as badly as he wanted her, he would not wish to be without his kin. He couldn't lose her, and he couldn't lose them. The situation was untenable.

In the gloom, Aramis watched them, his gaze more curious than hostile. When he approached, he was more like the man who put pine cones on Delphine's seat for a lark. The man whose countenance was not always as dark as the devil's.

"Gibbs warned me I might find you canoodling in the corner."

Unable to hide his feelings from those he trusted most, Christian hit his brother with the truth. "We'd be canoodling in the privacy of my bedchamber were it not for this blasted case. The need to be alone is often overwhelming."

Isabella's eyes widened in shock.

She straightened as if expecting a verbal attack, but Aramis snorted. "Then tell me what you want me to do. All this fawning makes me heave."

Christian turned to Isabella. "You're Daventry's agent. Shall we determine what your father is doing here and break into the other warehouses? Or visit Oldman and present him with the fake ushabti?"

She nibbled her cheek while considering the matter.

Christian imagined sucking her plump bottom lip, antici-pated the first glide of their tongues.

"My father is too clever to leave clues behind. I think we have a better chance of forcing Lord Oldman to confess. Mr Daventry might disagree, but we should accuse his lordship of abusing his staff. We'll tell him the dead woman named him as her tormentor."

Christian looked at Aramis. "We could frighten Oldman into believing anything, especially if we catch him unawares."

Aramis grinned. "Then what are we waiting for?"

Gibbs arrived with an entourage of brutes from the tavern. "Lawton removed two crates from Snell's warehouse while you were supping ale in the tavern. They were heavy." Gibbs glanced at the toothless fellow leading the gang.

"It took two men to lift 'em onto a cart," the fellow mumbled. "The foreign nabob warned 'em not to drop the crates, said he wanted nothing broken."

"No doubt he was moving the evidence," Isabella said, all hope restored. "Perhaps he's delivering the items to Lord Oldman."

"Or loading them aboard the conte's ship." Christian made a mental note to discover where it was docked. "Either way, we'll deal with Oldman first."

Oldman's snooty butler would get a medal for sheer stubbornness. Despite Christian shoving the letter from the Home Secretary in the servant's face, he insisted his master wasn't home.

"His lordship is dining at his club."

The butler was lying. Christian had spent enough time with gamblers and cheats to know the signs. "We've been watching the house for two hours and saw your master at the window."

The manservant's indifferent mask slipped. His bottom lip trembled, and he lowered his voice. "Trust me, sir. Leave now. Take the lady with you. Come back in an hour, if you must. If I let you into this house, we'll all be out of work."

With courage abound, Isabella stepped forward. "You don't need to welcome us over the threshold." She pushed past the servant before he had time to stop her. "We're forcing our way inside. Follow me, gentlemen."

The butler's eyes widened, the brief look of terror giving way to a flash of relief. "We've been powerless to stop him," the man said cryptically before hanging his head in shame.

"Nancy!" A sudden panic had Isabella darting through the dimly lit house, heading for the basement stairs.

Fearing what Oldman would do if she reached him first, Christian sprinted ahead, vaulting down the stone staircase and landing with a thud on the tiled floor.

The corridor was deserted.

All the doors to the servants' rooms were closed.

The faint whimpering came from Lord Oldman's treasure vault.

"The door's closed," Isabella whispered.

The butler appeared behind them, still trembling in fear. "He locks it from the inside when he's in one of his moods. There's no getting in."

Aramis joined Christian at the bottom of the stairs. "He'll have left the key in the door. If we want inside, we need to lure him out."

A muffled string of obscenities reached their ears.

Oldman was angry and needed someone weak to blame.

Isabella wrapped her arms around Christian's waist and hugged him tightly. "Please, Christian. Make him stop. I cannot bear it."

Christian stroked Isabella's hair while glaring at the butler. "Tell your master that Daventry is here and won't leave until he's been granted an audience."

The servant found every excuse not to disturb the lord, but Aramis grabbed him and dragged him to the sturdy iron door.

"He'll kill me if he knows I've betrayed him."

"I'll kill you if you don't comply with my brother's request."

The butler gathered himself. After three failed attempts, he found the courage to knock on the iron door. "My lord, you must come quickly."

Aramis clenched his fist and banged hard, the sound echoing in the chamber.

With Aramis' help, the butler repeated what he'd been told to say.

Oldman gave a furious growl from inside his Egyptian vault. "What in heaven's name is it, Walker?"

The servant relayed Aramis' mouthed words. "Daventry said he'll summon the magistrate. He said he'll arrest me for hindering an investigation."

They heard Oldman speaking to someone, heard banging and scraping and the crunch of metal as the lord turned the key in the lock.

Oldman peered around the jamb but could not see them hiding in the shadows. "I'm deducting a month's wages for your insolence. You're paid to turn visitors away, not disturb me when I'm studying the artefacts."

"The magistrate might force his way in."

Cursing Daventry to Hades, Lord Oldman yanked the door open and stepped into the corridor.

Christian expected to see the man in relaxed attire, maybe a banyan or even a nightshirt. He did not expect to find Lord Oldman wearing a blue silk robe and a pharaoh's ceremonial headdress.

Chapter Sixteen

Lord Oldman froze when Christian stepped out of the shadows. His arrogant mouth fell open as he stood bare-chested in a dark blue cloak, gripping a staff, the gold head styled like a hissing cobra.

Silent seconds passed before blind panic took hold and the degenerate darted towards the iron door. Panting, he fumbled with the key, desperate to secure the room—but it was too late.

A pitiful cry for help echoed from the depths of the chamber. It was faint, perhaps muffled by a gag, but a distress call nonetheless.

Christian pounced like a wolf in the darkness, knocking off the pharaoh's headdress as he grabbed the lord round the throat. With the moves of a skilled pugilist, he soon had the peer pinned to the floor.

"Get off me, you imbecile!" Lord Oldman squirmed and fought to break free but lacked Christian's brute strength. "You'll pay for this. Mark my words."

The ornate key slipped from the devil's fingers.

Isabella picked it up, hurried past them and entered the

candlelit chamber. She came to a crashing halt, finding nothing in the room but cabinets full of Egyptian artefacts.

Despite the men arguing in the corridor and Lord Oldman telling the butler he'd make sure no one in London employed him again, the sound of someone's whimpers breezed over her like whispers in the wind.

Was it a spirit from the underworld?

It certainly seemed to be coming from below ground.

Had the lord been summoning the dead?

Was the room plagued by an Egyptian curse?

"Do you hear that?" she said, sensing someone behind her.

Mr Gibbs squeezed past to examine the glass cabinets and tiled floor. He stamped on the floor with the heel of his boot. "Is anyone down there?"

The butler appeared in the doorway. "It's the f-footman. While serving dinner, he dropped a platter and ruined his lordship's best trousers." He pointed to the case containing the gold chalice. "You need to move that one to access the secret chamber."

Mr Gibbs moved the cabinet with ease to reveal a trapdoor. He raised the hatch to find a small flight of stone steps leading down into a makeshift tomb.

"His lordship keeps his treasure chests down there."

Isabella's heartbeat pounded in her throat.

Mr Gibbs did not advise against following him into the chamber. He did not assume she was plagued by the weaknesses of her sex. "It might not be pretty, miss," he said by way of a warning.

Memories flooded her mind. The punishments given to girls who misbehaved at Bramling Seminary. Hours spent in a cold, dark room until she finally agreed to a private audience with Mr Griffin.

They descended the steps.

The lit wall sconce cast a modicum of light over three large chests. A scrawny fellow was bound by the hands to a rope fed through a pulley on the ceiling.

"He doesn't hurt them, miss," the butler muttered, his shame evident. "He just shouts and curses and calls on Anubis."

"I beg to differ." She saw the abject terror in the young man's eyes. Words often hurt more than a punch until one built up an immunity. The loss of one's liberty was akin to a chokehold.

Mr Gibbs drew a blade and sawed through the rope, catching the footman by the waist as he sagged to the floor. "I took the trouble of sending word to Hart Street before we left the tavern. One of Mr Daventry's agents will be here shortly."

Punishing one's servant was not a crime. "We'll need a confession from Lord Oldman. We need him to admit he sold the artefacts knowing they were cheap imitations."

The footman made to speak, but like a baby bird, he lacked the strength to do anything other than open his mouth. When he did manage to form a word, all he said was, "Florentine."

The butler gave a resigned sigh. "They think his lordship killed Florentine. They have no proof, but she escaped wearing nothing but her nightdress and was found over a week later, floating in the Thames."

Isabella's heart skipped a beat.

A vision of the grey, lifeless woman invaded her mind.

"They?" she asked.

"James." He gestured to the poor fellow leaning on Mr Gibbs. "And Nancy, the maid."

A ripple of alarm ran over Isabella's shoulders. "Where is Nancy?" The maid had every reason to be afraid.

The butler's grave expression said he feared the poor girl was dead, too. "She was last seen this morning, scrubbing the front steps. I went to hurry her along and found nothing but the overturned bucket and brush."

Knowing Nancy had fled brought some consolation.

Yet why had she not come to Fortune's Den for help?

"What about Sarah? What happened to her?" Isabella needed all the facts before confronting Lord Oldman.

"The girl worked on a trial basis. It was Mr Myers idea. But his lordship sent her back. Complained she was cold and heartless and far too stubborn. He found it hard to find fault with her work."

"You mean he had no excuse to punish her." Isabella fought to contain her rising temper. "Where did he hire her?" She prayed there was a record of her employment, a trail leading to Sarah working in another household.

The butler shrugged.

A commotion in the basement caught Isabella's attention. By the sound of it, Christian was dragging the deranged pharaoh upstairs.

"Gather all the servants and have them pack their things," she said. "They will have new positions in better households."

Aaron Chance was in dire need of a maid or two. The man liked to keep staff to a minimum, but surely he would spare a thought for these unfortunate souls.

Noticing one chest was unlocked, she lifted the lid and peered inside. The trunk did not contain gem-encrusted pieces, not even the faint glimmer of rubies or gold. It was full of ushabti figurines. Smashing one on the floor proved all was not as it seemed.

With Mr Gibbs in tow, she joined Christian and Aramis in Lord Oldman's study. While they bound the man to the chair with his silk cloak, she explained what she had found in the chamber.

"But that's not all," she said, anger and disgust leaving a bitter taste in her mouth. "Nancy is missing. He sent Sarah back to wherever he hired her." She pointed at the bare-chested lord. "And a maid named Florentine fled this house and was recently found dead in the river."

Christian folded his arms across his broad chest and perched on the desk. He glared at the peer. "So, Florentine knew you were deceiving the collectors. You kept her in your sordid little chamber and when you released her, she ran."

Christian had missed the crucial part.

"He found her and killed her!" The desire to punish this buffoon had her blood charging through her veins. She would ensure he paid the price for all those who took advantage of the downtrodden.

Lord Oldman practically shook with outrage. "Foolish woman! Have you lost your mind!"

"Don't speak to her in that manner," Christian snapped.

As predicted, the lord spouted a list of rehearsed excuses. "I agreed to let Woodrow and Clarke along on the expedition so they could check the quality of the pieces. If you don't believe me, visit the collectors. Every piece sold is genuine."

"You have a treasure chest full of useless pottery in your basement," she countered. "Florentine died because she told the curator about your scheme. Lucky for you, the man is afraid of his own shadow, and sent her away." Not so lucky for Florentine. The curator could have saved her life had he fetched a constable.

"Snell gave me that chest. It was included with the goods given by the Vizier. I've been meaning to dispose of it but haven't had time."

Aramis stepped forward, his eyes dark and full of hatred.

"No, for recreation, you terrify the people who work for you. Perhaps you need a good dose of your own medicine. Perhaps I might resort to torture, tell all the men at the club that you pissed your trousers at the mere flash of a blade."

Christian adopted Mr Daventry's calm approach, though he was by no means less menacing. "You know we can ruin you. One word of this and the gossips will have a field day. Forget about your shady deals. The murdered woman worked here, so you'd better tell us exactly what happened before we summon the magistrate."

Lord Oldman sat in the chair like a poorly bandaged mummy. He shook his head. "Florentine was scared of the curse and refused to work without reciting the Rosary. I broke her beads, and she spent an hour crying in her room. I wasn't aware she'd left until the next day."

There was no way to prove or disprove his account.

Isabella's shoulders sagged, her spirit deflated.

"Florentine knew about the chest in the basement and must have assumed the figures sold to the museum were worthless," the lord added. "Fetch Daventry. He'll sort this damned mess out."

Aware time was precious, and that she needed more information before Mr Daventry's agents arrived, Isabella focused on the murder investigation. "Where did you hire Florentine? It wasn't through Mr Winthrop's agency."

The lord blinked and seemed surprised they were being so thorough. "I recall Quigley recommended a place to my secretary Myers. He hires all the servants. When he returns from Bristol, I'll have him visit Daventry's office."

Christian glanced at her.

They were so in tune, she could read his thoughts.

All hope of making an arrest was lost. The magistrate would not charge the lord with a crime. If anything, Captain

Snell would take the blame. Perhaps that accounted for his urgency in setting sail for Norway.

Two of Mr Daventry's agents arrived—a handsome Italian and one who looked like a dashing buccaneer. The men listened to the evidence and agreed to take the lord's statement.

"Any staff wishing to leave will be given temporary work until they find permanent positions," said the agent with long hair and a voice as smooth as honey. "I suggest you meet Daventry in Hart Street in the morning. We'll deal with matters here."

The dark-haired agent gripped Christian's shoulder. "I'd say go home and get a good night's rest but the Den must be teaming with gambling men at this hour."

Again, Christian met her gaze, the corners of his mouth curling into a heart-stopping smile. They had no plans to rest. Such was the intense nature of their relationship, they would be together in bed within the hour.

On the journey home, Christian made love to her with his compelling blue eyes while Aramis stared at the rain pelting the windowpane.

Sigmund, their burly manservant, welcomed them into the gaming hell's lavish red hall and tapped a finger to his lips. "Barker is about to lose his townhouse to Lord Patmore. You could hear a pin drop in the card room tonight."

Aramis rubbed his hands together. "Excellent. I'm just in time." He turned to Christian. "Are you ready to watch Patmore wreak vengeance on his cousin?"

"Not tonight."

Aramis understood the implicit meaning in those two simple words. He drew a deep breath, the long exhale one of resignation. "Then I'm sure you'll have no problem making your own amusement."

The men disappeared into a smoke-filled room, leaving Isabella alone with Christian. He touched her hand, entwined fingers. His breath came a little quicker as he led her slowly upstairs.

They stopped outside his bedchamber.

Nerves assailed her. What if Mrs Maloney cautioned against such sinful behaviour? After hearing the conte's vile threats, she should pack her valise and run, but she was weak against the power of Christian's magnetic charm.

Making love to him again would be a mistake.

A beautiful mistake.

An earth-shattering mistake.

One she would remember until her dying day.

"Do you not enjoy watching men gamble their lives away?" she said, afraid to mount the stairs in case Mrs Maloney put paid to their plans.

He smiled. "Gambling is like dipping a foot in quicksand. Some men sense the imminent danger. Some still profess they can swim while sinking in the mire. Denial is often more bearable than the truth."

The last comment hit a nerve.

She could not deny how she felt about this man. Once spoken, the truth was a permanent shackle. A lady couldn't run with her legs bound.

Still, she wished to convey some of what was in her heart.

She touched the diamond pin in his cravat. "Your moniker suits you. Like this precious gem, you steal my breath, Christian. I've never known a man be so hard and ruthless yet so insanely beautiful." A thousand nights with him would not sate her craving. He deserved the love of a woman who could give him everything.

He brought her fingers to his lips and brushed a kiss over her knuckles. "Aaron once said admitting you're afraid is not a weakness. I'm afraid I'm going to lose you. I'm afraid of what tomorrow will bring." He glanced at the deserted staircase. "Aramis offered you money to leave."

She swallowed. "He did."

"Will you take it?"

A knot tightened in her chest. She couldn't lie to him but she was so scared. Scared of the conte, of Mr Griffin, of trusting a man only to feel the crushing pain of disappointment.

"I can deal with the truth," he reminded her.

Something had shifted inside her. Easing his discomfort was more important than easing her own fears. Was this love? She wasn't sure, but she felt connected to him in ways she could not explain.

"I don't want to leave." She placed a gentle hand on his chest, covering his heart. "I want to stay here with you. But hardships teach us to be realistic. I'd run to the ends of the earth if it meant keeping you safe."

He captured her chin, his mouth closing over hers in a tender kiss that hurt her heart. "Don't go upstairs," he whispered. "I don't want anything to ruin our plans. Like me, Mrs Maloney is likely desperate for your company. I'll make it up to her, but I need you in my bed tonight, Isabella."

She understood.

Making love eased the restlessness. Making love made their problems seem insignificant. And the pleasure of having him one last time was far too tempting to resist.

Christian locked the door, and took a moment to breathe through the ache in his chest. Since seeing the conte, Isabella had been on edge. He was losing her. He could feel her slipping like sand through his fingers. If he didn't find a way to get rid of the bastard, he'd be left with nothing but a shattered heart and painful memories.

Love is a figment of the imagination.

It's the lies we tell ourself that hurt.

Aaron's words entered Christian's mind. The sentiment of a man who'd tolerated too much to believe in fairytales. A belief system that had helped his brother through the toughest times.

"Christian? Is something wrong?" Isabella's soothing voice caressed him. "If you've changed your mind about—"

"I've not changed my mind." He swung around. "I'll never change my mind about you." He needed to be constant enough for both of them. "Now I have you here, I'm considering chaining you to the bedpost." Yet he was the one wearing imaginary shackles, though he hoped his teasing smile settled her concerns.

Amusement danced in her eyes. "I'm sure it would be an interesting topic to discuss during dinner. As long as you don't mind eating from an upturned table."

Now was not the time to consider Aaron's black mood. Nothing would dampen his ardour. This might be the last time he'd take Isabella in his arms, and he meant to savour every second.

"Might I suggest we undress before our mouths meet?" He slipped out of his coat and draped it over the chair, gestured for her to remove her outdoor apparel. "We should be naked when our passion consumes us." Hell, his blood was already surging southward.

The minx removed her gloves, every tug of a finger

causing a powerful tug deep in his abdomen. "This room smells of you. If your bedsheets smell of you, you'll struggle to get rid of me in the morning."

He began untying the knot in his cravat. "There's something arousing about a lover's scent. Perhaps it's why your shift still hangs in my armoire."

She blinked as she shrugged out of her pelisse, her gaze darting to the wardrobe. "But you gave me back the laundered garment."

"No. I gave you one of Delphine's which looks similar." He couldn't explain it, but he'd wanted to keep something of hers. To own a small piece of the woman who drove him wild. "I'm keeping yours as payment for services rendered."

"What services might those be?"

He removed his waistcoat. "Food and lodgings." Though he was the one who owed her a debt. She'd made him see that loving someone was possible. He'd just have to pray fate granted him a boon. "And access to my extensive knowledge of Egyptian artefacts."

"You've benefited from my expertise, too." She hiked up her skirts, her hand moving to her garter. "It's only right I have something of yours."

"Leave your stockings. I wish to remove them myself." He dragged his shirt over his head and smiled upon hearing her little gasp. "Strip and I'll give you something you'll treasure forever."

Her eyes widened. "Not a child?"

He laughed. "Of course not. I'd never sire a child out of wedlock." And yet the thought of pumping his seed inside her caused a fluttering in his chest. He'd never imagined being a father. But he knew she could make impossible dreams come true.

"Life for a woman on her own is hard enough."

"If you carried my child you wouldn't be alone."

Those words hung in the air between them. Neither were quite ready to discuss what they meant. Perhaps that's why she stayed silent and focused on removing her dress.

He watched her untie the ribbons on her front-fastening stays, eager to catch sight of her full breasts and pretty pink nipples, nipples he would suck and tease into peaks.

Christian divested himself of all his clothes.

She finished undressing with the same sense of urgency.

His cock hardened in appreciation when she stood before him wearing nothing but her white stockings. "Now for the thing you'll treasure forever," he said, palming his shaft just to torment her.

Her lips parted.

He reached for his cravat and crossed the room. "This is to remind you of the man who made you come three times in one night." He placed the silk neckcloth in her hand. "And to remind you someone in the world cares about you a great deal."

Tears welled in her eyes.

She swallowed hard as she worked to keep them at bay.

"Keep the cravat in a memory box," he said, trying not to think of her sitting alone in a backstreet hovel. "Sell the diamond stickpin, so you need never go hungry again." He brushed the errant tear from her cheek and sought to lighten the mood. "And now for the gift you've been aching for all night."

When they kissed, he tasted the salt of more tears on her lips. He cradled her throat gently, knowing that no matter how deeply he drank he would not quench his thirst.

This second time felt different.

Their tongues danced together—a slow, sensual waltz, not a crazed jig. The focus was on deepening their connection, not rushing to find release. Their energy was no less compelling. The inner flame of desire burned so fiercely he might combust.

Was this silent outpouring of emotion love?

He'd felt nothing like it in his life.

But he couldn't tell her in words. Not yet. He'd not use it as a means to control her. If she wanted him, she had to make that decision on her own. Besides, the little moans escaping her throat stole his attention. The way her nipples brushed his chest had his pulse quickening.

With one hand, he cupped her buttocks, caressing the tiny dimple between her cheeks. "Tell me what you desire?" he whispered, kissing her shoulder. "Tonight, I am yours to command."

"Take me slowly," she uttered, her damp lashes fanning her cheeks. "I want to watch you when you do. I want to remember every precious second. I want to feel everything keenly."

"Then come to bed." He captured her hand, drew her to his impressive four-poster and dragged back the coverlet and sheets.

"It's rather large," she said.

"Every inch of it is yours."

"I was referring to the bed."

"So was I."

Her chuckle became a squeal as he scooped her into his arms and laid her down on the mattress. Hell, with this woman he'd act the fool if it meant stemming her tears.

"I assume you know where I might start." His gaze fell to the apex of her thighs as he imagined burying his head there and lavishing her gem. But then he had a sudden epiphany. "If it pleases you, we might do things a little differently."

Her eyes widened. "How?"

He rounded the bed and climbed in beside her. "Straddle me."

"What about my stockings?"

"Keep them on. A prim governess would never undress completely." She was by no means prudish. She was passionate and kind and the most beautiful person he'd ever known. "Although what we're about to do is most definitely wicked."

His cock wept as she climbed on top of him and gave him a perfect view of her bouncing breasts. But he'd need to temper his lust if he was to make her come three times tonight. And he was keen to prove a man could keep his word.

Isabella straddled his thighs, trying to avoid sitting on his throbbing erection. "Where do you want me?"

Everywhere, love.

He beckoned her forward. "Move higher."

"Higher?"

He smiled. "Yes, until you're straddling my face." He gripped her waist, encouraging her to scoot forward until his head was between her thighs. "Hold on to the headboard."

"But I can't see you."

"After the first few seconds, you won't care. Besides, we've the whole night at our disposal. When I enter you, you can watch me then."

As predicted the first few swipes of his tongue left her panting.

"You control the pressure, love. Take what you want."

She soon overcame any embarrassment, learning to roll her hips in time with the rapid strokes of his tongue. Her release came quickly. She shuddered against his mouth and cried his name through every ragged breath.

He didn't wait for the ripples of pleasure to subside. "Take me inside you, Isabella. Watch me when you do."

A little shaky, she moved to straddle his hips. She was so wet he buried himself deep in one slick movement.

They stilled.

Stared at each other.

Feelings he couldn't control rose to the fore, a level of arousal he'd never felt, a powerful rush of affection unlike anything he'd known.

I'm in love with you.

The words entered his head as she placed her dainty hands on his chest, her thumbs stroking his nipples. She shook the lustrous dark curls off her face, her mouth curling into a warm smile.

I'm so in love with you it hurts.

She was so damn beautiful. Like a timeless piece of art.

"Ride me, love. Every inch is yours."

She rose up on her knees as he guided her, her eyes fluttering closed as she sank slowly down, sheathing him. "Oh, Christian!"

Lord have mercy!

He watched her, drinking in the sight of her luscious breasts and dark pink nipples. She hugged his cock like she had no intention of ever leaving. Her nails dug into his chest, marking him her property.

He should lie back and enjoy the erotic play. But despite being joined in the most intimate manner, he needed to deepen their connection.

"Hold me while I move." While buried inside her, he sat up and gathered her close. "Wrap your legs around me." In this position, they could kiss and stare into each other's eyes.

The slow grinding heightened the intimacy. They kissed,

drank deeply, their bodies growing as hot as the gazes passing between them.

"You feel so good, love. Is this what you wanted?"

"Yes," she panted, wrapping her arms around him. "Though I'd take anything you had to give."

"Admit, this is better than sweet biscuits," he said, forcing his hand between them to stroke her clitoris with his thumb. "I used to watch you eating them in the garden, watch you lick the crumbs from your lips."

"I knew you were there." Her head fell back as she arched into him. "It's why I ate them outside and not in my bedchamber." A moan escaped her. "Oh, Christian. Don't stop."

He captured her nipple in his mouth, his tongue sliding over the stiff peak. In a matter of seconds, she came apart around his cock, the powerful contractions as fast as her breathless pants.

Before the pulses subsided, Christian had her on her back. He'd been holding his release at bay for the last few minutes, and he'd need to be quick if he meant to keep his promise.

He sank into her, each powerful thrust angled to give maximum stimulation. He wanted them to come together, to pour everything of himself into one last stroke. To flood her with the depth of his devotion.

Sense prevailed.

He waited for her to shudder against him for a third time before he withdrew and an explosion of sensations ripped through him. He came hard. Her name on his lips. A secret prayer echoing in his mind.

Please let her stay.

Please don't forsake me again.

Chapter Seventeen

Isabella watched Christian sleeping soundly.

Love filled her heart. Love infused every fibre of her being. But something dark lingered in the shadows. The monster that was her constant companion, in one form or another, was merely waiting for the right time to strike. Somehow, she had to find the courage to slay the demon. If she didn't, it would mean losing the man who made her soul sing.

She needed to talk to someone.

Someone who could keep a secret.

Someone who wouldn't steal her sanity with every kiss.

Quietly, she slipped into her dress and kid boots and made for the door. She stopped to glance at Christian's tight buttocks as he lay sprawled on his front in the huge bed. Her insides melted. Making love only fed her addiction.

But she needed clarity.

Being skilled at escaping in the dark, she crept from the room and mounted the stairs. She found Mrs Maloney awake in bed, reading beneath the light of a lamp.

One look at Isabella's mussed hair and the woman closed

her book and placed it on the nightstand. "I wasn't sure I'd see you tonight." She sat up and patted the bed. "I heard you were home. No doubt I should have come looking for you." She glanced at her book and chuckled to herself. "Only a fool would hire me as a chaperone."

"Mr Chance believes you're the most capable person he knows." Drawn by the woman's warm, friendly manner, Isabella crossed the room and sat on the bed.

"Aaron invited me here so he didn't have to think about you. Christian persuaded me to come because he cares."

Christian!

Her heart swelled until she could hardly breathe. She couldn't contain the words any longer. "I'm in love with him. Christian, I mean."

Mrs Maloney laughed again. "Thank heavens. Anyone who falls in love with Aaron is asking for a life of untold misery. She'd need the hide of an ox. The ability to withstand venom." She shook her head, annoyed she'd become distracted. "But Christian. That's another matter entirely."

Isabella sighed. "Loving him has made me weak." She wasn't strong enough to leave him. What if her selfishness got him killed? "I should run, board a ship for America, but the thought tears me in two."

Mrs Maloney patted Isabella's hand. "Does this have anything to do with your father and his wicked machinations?"

Secrets she had kept for years came tumbling out. By the time she'd explained about Mr Griffin and the conte, poor Mrs Maloney looked shattered. "So, you see why I cannot stay."

Silence ensued, but then Mrs Maloney said something baffling. "We took in a stray bloodhound once. Albert, we called him after he followed Christian home from a derelict house in Albert Street. When the dog ran away, Aaron said it was for the best, as it was just another mouth to feed. Christian walked day and night and refused to come home until he'd found him."

With her mind still hazy from their lovemaking, Isabella tried to find the message in Mrs Maloney's tale. "He didn't find Albert. And it was another loss he was forced to bear."

"If he thinks you love him, he'll do everything in his power to protect you. Despite every loss he's ever suffered, he would risk everything for a chance of happiness. If you truly love him, you must trust him. The man I know would never let you down."

Tears gathered behind Isabella's eyes.

"Besides," Mrs Maloney continued, noticing she was visibly upset, "despite Aaron's objections, he's given those boys everything. If Christian wants you, Aaron will make sure nothing gets in the way."

A feeling deep in her chest said Mrs Maloney was right.

If she could just find the courage to remain steadfast, happiness was within her grasp. "Thank you." Isabella gripped the woman's hand affectionately. "I'm used to mulling problems over in my mind. Your insight has been invaluable. How can I ever repay you?"

Mrs Maloney gave a mischievous chuckle and beckoned her closer. "Be a dear and fetch me a glass of Aaron's vintage port. My old legs won't make it back up these stairs."

Feeling suddenly lighter, Isabella smiled. "As long as you say nothing about me visiting Christian's room tonight." She planned to make love to him again, convince him she would fight, not leave.

"My lips are sealed. But you must confide in him, dear, not me."

Isabella took Mrs Maloney's empty glass and crept downstairs. The hall was deserted, but boisterous laughter and the hum of excited conversation echoed from the card room.

Aaron Chance kept his best port in his study, a private room overlooking Aldgate Street. The heavy curtains were open, and the black throne-like chair behind the desk gave the perfect view of The Burnished Jade.

Not wishing to remain there too long, Isabella quickly poured the port and took a sip for Dutch courage.

The sudden ringing of the overhead bell in the hall had her darting behind the curtains. The stomp of booted footsteps preceded someone opening the front door.

Don't let it be Aaron!

Sigmund spoke, his voice firm. "I'll tell you what I told you half an hour ago. This is a gentlemen's club. Women aren't welcome. Be on your way. Don't let me see you here again."

The person asked for Mr Chance, at which point Sigmund informed her all the men of that name were otherwise engaged. "Then I need to speak to Miss Lawton. It's an urgent matter that can't wait. I've important news. She's in grave danger."

"Like I said, there's no one here of that name."

The woman persisted. "Fetch her, or there'll be hell to pay."

"Move away, or I'll call the watchman." Sigmund slammed the door. He released a string of expletives as his heavy footsteps receded.

Isabella peered covertly out of the window. Unperturbed by the rain, a woman wearing a hooded cloak crossed the street before turning to stare at the gaming hell.

It was too dark outside to confirm her identity.

Thoughts of Nancy Jones entered her mind. What if the maid was forced to spend a night on the street? Perhaps she had forgotten to ask for Delphine. It wasn't an easy name to remember.

Isabella prised the study door from the jamb. Noticing the hall was empty, she hurried to open the front door. The cloaked figure stood staring at the Den, and so Isabella beckoned the woman forward.

"Hello," she called, not daring to cross the threshold. It had to be Nancy. No one else would visit a gaming hell at night. "Nancy."

She should call Sigmund, but then she would have to explain what she was doing in Aaron Chance's study. The man might think she was snooping, gathering information for her father. He'd never trust her again.

"Nancy!"

Thankfully, the woman saw her and hurried forward, dashing through puddles with nary a care. A lock of red hair slipped from under her hood.

Good heavens! It wasn't Nancy. It was Ethel Cartwright.

That's when Isabella noticed the flash of terror in the woman's eyes. Still, she was mindful to remain indoors.

Like that of a frightened doe, Ethel's gaze shifted left and right along the street. "Miss Lawton!" she cried, shaking her head.

Panic ensued, along with a feeling of immense dread.

"Sigmund!" Isabella called, the word lost against the sudden raucous in the card room. She should close the door but couldn't shut Ethel out. "Hurry!"

But two hulking men appeared in the doorway, monstrous figures blocking her view. Before she could scream, one slapped his dirty hand over her mouth and dragged her into the street while the other calmly closed the gaming hell door.

A cold chill breezed over Christian's bare buttocks and back, waking him from slumber. Too exhausted to open his eyes, he reached for the bedsheets but remembered they were bunched at the bottom of the bed, and he'd been too damned hot to care.

Isabella!

Thoughts of her entered his mind. Memories of her magnificent breasts bouncing as he gripped her hips and drove deep inside her. The look of pure satisfaction on her lips when she came apart around his cock.

Feeling the first stirrings of arousal, he opened his eyes and turned to face the only woman he'd ever wanted.

The sudden lurch of his heart forced him up onto his knees. The space beside him was empty. The deep indentation in the pillow convinced him he'd not dreamt the erotic experience.

Panic ensued.

She'd gone!

She'd gone and not told him!

No!

He fought to stem the hole opening in his chest—a cavernous hole that would consume him if he didn't gather his wits. But then he noticed her pelisse on the floor, her stays flung over the baseboard, and sighed in relief.

A woman with nothing wouldn't leave without her clothes.

He scrubbed his face with his hand.

Now he knew why his brothers kept their hearts in coffins

buried deep underground. The constant fear of loss was like a sickness one couldn't shake.

Doubtless she had gone to fetch fresh water or had crept upstairs to appease Mrs Maloney. But the din downstairs said men were still drinking and gambling and she knew not to navigate the corridors alone.

The need to ease the escalating sense of dread had him throwing on his shirt and trousers and slipping into his shoes. No matter how hard he tried to ignore the nagging voice in his mind, he knew something was amiss.

The sudden knock on his chamber door did nothing to settle his strained nerves. Three sharp raps meant it was Aaron—the deliverer of doom.

Christian's hand shook as he opened the door. It had been Aaron who visited him in the middle of the night to tell him his mother was dead. Aaron, who'd delivered the news about his father, and his missing dog.

"Is Miss Lawton with you?" Concern darkened Aaron's features, not frustration or anger. "I know she came to your room when you returned to the club."

The lump in Christian's throat prevented him from speaking. He shook his head while wrestling with his volatile emotions.

Aaron gripped his arm, firm but reassuring. "Did she tell you she planned to leave tonight? Aramis said the conte threatened to take her back to Italy. Do you know where she might have gone?"

His chest tightened. "She's gone?"

I promise you will always know what I'm thinking.
If I decide to leave, you'll be the only person I tell.

Her words rang loudly in his head.

She'd lied.

And he'd lost her.

"Christian!" Aaron swore, his temper rising. "Are you listening to me? Curse the devil! I knew this would happen if you fucked her."

The crude word hit like an uppercut to the jaw.

Christian lunged forward, grabbing his brother by the throat. "What happened in my bed wasn't fucking. I'm in love with her, you damn fool."

"No, you're not." Aaron gripped Christian's fingers, squeezing hard until he was forced to deliver a low punch or surrender. "Most people mistake lust for love. Passion is a drug more potent than opium. You'll forget about her in due course."

Though Christian wanted to rant, rage and tear the house down, he laughed. "There's no man I respect more than you. You're right about most things, but not this. You wouldn't understand. Your heart is buried beneath so much hatred you refuse to let yourself care for a woman."

Aaron firmed his jaw. "I know my limitations. Opening my heart would be like opening a blasted Pandora's box. The only thing that would come of it is untold devastation. It's the same for us all."

"No, it's not."

A discreet cough drew Christian's attention to the stairs. Aramis stood grinning at them. "If there's to be a fight, at least give me time to sell tickets. This will be the bout of the century."

Aaron raised an imperious brow. "You're supposed to be searching the rooms for Miss Lawton, not loitering and listening to our conversation."

Aramis held up his hands in mock surrender. "There's no sign of her. She's not in the house. She visited Mrs Maloney half an hour ago, and they spoke about Christian. Doubtless she had complaints about his anatomy and needed a wise woman's advice."

Half an hour ago?

Had something Mrs Maloney said made her leave?

"Miss Lawton agreed to steal a glass of your best port, Aaron, and bring it upstairs for Mrs Maloney," Aramis continued. "When the lady failed to return, Mrs Maloney believed Christian had lured her back to bed."

"Then she can't have gone far." With renewed faith, Christian grabbed his coat. "It's almost impossible to get a hackney cab at this time of night."

"Christian!" Aaron's voice held a sharp warning. "Lawton is out to kill you. You can't trawl the streets alone. And there's every chance she left of her own volition."

No! He didn't believe that.

He couldn't believe that.

"If she has left, it's because she's trying to protect Christian." Aramis sounded confident in his assertion. "I saw how she looked at him. I saw them together. Not that I'm any judge on how a woman looks when she's in love." Aramis shook his head as if ridding himself of a painful memory. "I'll go with Christian. As he said, Miss Lawton can't have gone far."

Determined to prove they couldn't trust Miss Lawton, Aaron was quick to reveal a vital clue. "Might she have arranged to meet someone? A woman came knocking, asking to speak to Miss Lawton but Sigmund turned her away."

Christian raised his hands in exasperation. "Why the hell didn't you say so before?" It could be Nancy Jones. But Isabella wasn't foolish enough to leave the house. Not after the conte's threat. Not unless she planned to leave town.

Mounting the stairs two at a time, Theo joined the fracas. "Aaron, there's someone demanding to speak to you. By all accounts, it's urgent." Judging by the tense lines on Theo's brow, it was someone unsavoury. Else why would he be so vague? "I made them wait in your study."

"You did what?" Aaron dragged his hand through his raven hair. "For the love of God. If it's Barker complaining that his cousin cheated, have Sigmund throw him out."

"It might be Nancy Jones," Christian offered.

"Who?"

"It's Miss Scrumptious," Theo declared.

Aaron seemed momentarily ruffled. "What the bloody hell does she want? If she's come to complain about the noise, send her away."

"She believes she witnessed a crime. That's all she would say on the matter. As I said, she's waiting for you in your study."

Aaron hissed a breath. "You left her in my private office?"

But Christian didn't wait for Theo's reply. Miss Scrumptious had something to confess, and it might be relevant to Isabella's sudden disappearance.

Upon inspection, the lady had most certainly left The Burnished Jade in a hurry. Her golden hair was fashioned into a braid that hung over one shoulder. The hem of her white nightdress was visible beneath her pale blue pelisse, and she wore dainty satin slippers.

"Miss Lovelace," he said, remembering not to use her moniker.

Aaron burst into the room like he might tear her head from her shoulders. Indeed, the woman straightened her spine, preparing for an attack. But Aaron took one look at her hair and faltered—albeit for a mere second.

"You'd better have a damned good reason for calling at night and in such a state of dishabille."

"A wise woman doesn't enter the devil's domain by choice," she countered. "I'm here because I happened to witness a crime on your premises, and my conscience prevents me from remaining silent."

Aaron rounded the desk. He dropped into his throne and slouched arrogantly in the seat. "Then what are you waiting for? Speak!"

Miss Lovelace folded her arms across her chest. "Not until you thank me for my trouble."

"You want my money?"

"I want your gratitude."

"You'll be waiting a lifetime," Christian said, too desperate for answers to play games. "Thank you for calling, Miss Lovelace. I pray you bring news of Miss Lawton." He breathed deeply to keep the rising panic at bay. "The lady is missing and left the house within the last half an hour. Anything you can tell us will be invaluable."

Miss Lovelace nodded profusely. "I always glance outside before going to bed. Drunken gamblers have a habit of loitering. It can be quite unsettling."

"Then what the hell are you doing living at The Burnished Jade?" Aaron's tone rang with disapproval. "And what's happened to your father? I've not seen him in over a week."

Christian shot his brother an irate glare. "Ignore him, Miss Lovelace. Tell me, what did you see in the street?"

"A red-haired lady in a hooded cloak knocked on the door, but your man turned her away. Seconds later, a woman appeared, lingering on the Den's threshold. She called out, but that's when two men slipped from the shadows. They dragged the lady outside and bundled her into a waiting carriage."

The life drained from Christian's body.

He staggered back, gripping the desk for support.

Aaron shot to his feet, his fury barely contained. "They had the gall to steal her from these premises? When was this?"

"Twenty minutes ago." There was a bite of anger in her voice when speaking to Aaron. "I would have come sooner but had to dress and wasn't sure what sort of welcome I would receive."

"Can you describe the men or vehicle?" Christian said, not that it mattered. Doubtless both were hired and untrace-able. "Can you recall anything that might help me locate her? Anything at all?"

Miss Lovelace pursed her lips. "They threw the cloaked lady into the carriage, too. One thug had long hair tied in a queue. One occupant held open the carriage door with a silver-tipped cane."

The conte!

"Did they head towards the docks?" Christian said, his pulse soaring. He would kill anyone who harmed a hair on Isabella's head. He'd follow the conte to Italian shores. He would never stop looking until he found her.

"No. I watched from the window. They were heading in the opposite direction, to Leadenhall Street." The lady touched a shaky hand to her throat. "If I'd been outside, I would have done something to stop them."

"And they'd have taken you hostage." Aaron spoke as if she were an imbecile. "These men aren't the sort of villains one reads about in stories, Miss Lovelace."

She straightened her shoulders. "I'm well aware of that, Mr Chance. Still, only a coward stands by and does nothing."

Aaron stared at her. Despite his growing hostility, he let his gaze slide down to the lady's toes. "Only a fool allows themselves to be kidnapped when they're the only witness to the crime."

"Would you care for a drink, madam?" Theo interjected, striding towards the decanters on Aaron's drinks cabinet. "A glass of port, perhaps? Something to settle your nerves?"

"No!" Aaron marched to the study door and held it open. "Miss Lovelace is keen to return to The Burnished Jade, and we have business elsewhere." Aaron turned to Aramis. "Have Sigmund empty the club. We're going out. All of us. You've ten minutes to ready yourselves for war."

The lady inhaled sharply but was not deterred. "Perhaps there's something I can do to help that poor woman. I might come with you, act as a decoy."

"Like hell you will," Aaron growled. "Go home, madam. And I'm not referring to The Burnished Jade."

The lady laughed as she made for the door. "You'll have to get used to seeing me, Mr Chance. I own the Jade and plan on starting a new venture. A club for women. A club for wall-flowers, to be precise." And then she swept from the room, leaving Aaron seething.

"The conte has a mansion house west of Tothill Fields," Christian said, ignoring Aaron's flaring nostrils and focusing on finding Isabella. "There aren't many grand houses in the area. Someone will point us in the right direction."

"We'll need pistols and concealed blades," Aramis said.

Aaron pulled himself together. "Someone send word to Daventry's office. We need the law on our side if we're to throttle Italian nobility."

Chapter Eighteen

The underground cavern was small and dim, the vaulted brick ceiling low. The place smelled of damp wood and fermented fruit. Isabella squinted in the candlelight, noting the line of empty green bottles in the corner and the array of old barrels stacked against the wall. Beyond the arched wooden doors was undoubtedly the conte's wine cellar.

The blackguard had only spoken to her once on the journey. He'd pointed a pistol at her heart while wearing an arrogant grin. "You were always destined to be mine, *cara mia.*"

The thug beside him had bound her hands and tied the blindfold so tightly he'd yanked out strands of her hair.

Ethel Cartwright had tried pleading, offering the conte every incentive to release them. From the woman's choice of words, it was evident she had been used as a pawn in the conte's wicked game.

He said no one would get hurt.

He said if I did this, I could go free.

Upon arrival at their destination, which was almost certainly the conte's mansion near Tothill Fields, it became apparent *He* was known to her.

Get them inside with the others.

You're sure no one followed you.

Her father's sinister voice had chilled Isabella's blood. She'd been shoved through cold corridors and down the stairs, tied to an iron ring in the cellar's wall. But that's not what disturbed her most.

It was the distant cries of other women.

Mournful cries, terrified cries, cries that echoed beyond the vault.

Now free of her blindfold, she faced Ethel. "Captain Snell wasn't shipping fake artefacts, was he?"

Ethel sat on the dusty stone floor, her bound hands resting in her lap. "It's best you know nothing of their plans. It's safer for you that way."

"Safer? It's too late for me. All is lost. The conte means to steal me away on his ship." Steal her away from the man she loved. From the only happiness she'd ever known.

Christian!

Was he awake and wondering where she'd gone?

Would he trust her enough to know she'd not left him?

Would he spend a lifetime feeling betrayed?

Ethel snorted. "A life of splendour awaits. It's what every woman longs for. You should accept your fate and be grateful you're still breathing."

Isabella would rather live with Christian in Mrs Maloney's tiny room than with the conte in his luxurious villa. "Yet you're in this predicament because you tried to warn me." The woman's terrified glares and hand gestures made sense now. "Tell me. How did the conte get you to do his bidding?"

"The conte? I'm not scared of that pompous fool." Ethel glanced at the wooden doors and lowered her voice. "Cross Lawton and you're signing your own death warrant."

Isabella dismissed a frisson of fear. "My father may be wicked, but I cannot believe he would kill someone."

Pity flashed in Ethel's green eyes. "No. Lawton likes them breathing, so he can keep beating them with a stick. There's worse things than death."

A sudden scream from beyond the vault sent Isabella's pulse soaring. Gruff words accompanied a woman's helpless pleas.

"Where are they taking her?"

Ethel sighed but said nothing.

Anger sparked in Isabella's chest.

"Ethel," she began sternly, though was convinced an ounce of goodness flowed in Ethel Cartwright's veins. Else she would not have warned the maids about Lord Oldman. "Within the next hour, we will be embroiled in a war. My employer, his agents, and the Chance brothers will descend on this mansion house and arrest all those above stairs." If only she could believe it, but if Isabella hoped to discover the truth, she had to convince Ethel all was not lost. "I suggest you decide whose side you're on."

The woman hung her head.

"Very well. I cannot save you."

A tense silence ensued, broken by weak pleas and the rattle of chains.

Isabella spent the next few minutes trying to piece together the facts.

Snippets of information entered her mind.

Captain Snell's mysterious shipments.

The heavy cargo.

The foreign maid working for Lord Oldman.

Sarah's pendant with the odd markings. Her pale skin and white hair. Had she come from distant shores? Had Sarah arrived on a boat from Norway?

"Whether I escape from here or not," Isabella began, "there's a warrant out for Captain Snell's arrest. We searched the warehouse and found evidence to incriminate the captain and Lord Oldman. Captain Snell smuggles women into the country and sells them."

Ethel's lips were buttoned tighter than a nun's coif.

Isabella scoured her mind. It sounded like her father was in charge here, not the conte, not Lord Oldman or Captain Snell.

And why had the ghostly woman complained about fake artefacts and not about being smuggled to England on a ship?

"My father won't risk you turning traitor," she said, trying a different approach. "At worst, I'll get to live in an Italian villa. You'll be six feet under in an unmarked grave. At best, Mr Chance will rescue me, and you will swing from the gallows." She paused so Ethel could consider the harrowing mental image. "Or I could tell Mr Chance you helped me, persuade him to give you money and passage on a steamer bound for America."

Long seconds passed.

"How do I know I can trust you?" Ethel uttered.

"Because, like you, I've spent my life longing for freedom." She'd come to learn freedom didn't mean navigating life alone. It meant finding a partner who nurtured one's soul and understood the need for independence. "I know what it's like to be at the mercy of a cruel man."

Ethel sighed. "I knew nothing about the cargo."

"You mean the women the captain smuggles?"

"Yes. I only learnt of it last year when your father began blackmailing me. Lawton said if I didn't work for him, he'd see me locked in Newgate along with Snell."

Isabella frowned, her head awhirl with confusion. "But

you took the job in the shipping office fairly recently. What possible evidence does my father have against you?"

"Snell hired me to act as his linkman. While he was at sea, I met with those who wanted to hire *The Marigold*. I took payment and managed the diary. But I swear I didn't know what was in those crates."

"But Mr Quigley is the captain's broker."

Ethel shook her head. "I'm Quigley. Few men will deal with a woman. I used to clean the stalls at a theatre in Haymarket. While there, an actress taught me how to pass myself off as a man. Though I think Oldman's secretary is suspicious."

Good heavens!

No wonder the description of Mr Quigley was so vague.

"But you told me Quigley worked at the museum."

"I had to say something to throw you off the scent."

Isabella might have scratched her head were her hands not bound. "But you've been slandering Lord Oldman when he's the captain's best client."

"That's all part of Lawton's plan. He's taken over the smuggling business. If the River Police come knocking, he plans to lay the blame at Lord Oldman's door. I'd heard the gossip about Oldman's ruthless ways and have been causing trouble for almost a year. I told his secretary where to hire the maids. Then there's proof Oldman had the smuggled women in his house."

Isabella felt her temperature rising. "So, for the past year, you've known women are being brought to England against their will?"

"Some came of their own accord, wanting work. Some are too scared to make a fuss." Ethel hung her head in shame. "Lawton would have set me up to take the fall if I'd not gone along with his plan."

"But the women will testify. The truth will prevail."

"They can't testify, miss. Most of them are shipped out of London. Some are sold at auction. Like the ones here tonight."

"Sold!" Mother Mary! Based on the nature of the crime, it would be impossible to save Ethel from the noose. Indeed, the more the woman spoke, the more Isabella felt like striking her.

But the stomp of heavy footsteps and the rattle of keys stole her attention. The door flew open with such violence the wood hit the brick wall. The beast who'd snatched her from Fortune's Den appeared.

He smiled, baring his peg-like teeth. "Stand up. It's time to make yourself pretty. Your father said you're to do as you're told, or you'll find yourself in the auction room."

Isabella obeyed. She had a better chance of escaping the house than this underground prison. "Where are you taking me?"

"To the conte's bedchamber." The thug untied her wrists with rough hands and yanked her to her feet. "You've a bath waiting, a pretty red dress and jewels. His cook has made a fancy meal. Happen you'll be treated like royalty before he has you."

"What about me?" Ethel cried.

The beast chuckled. "You'll be sold to the highest bidder like the rest, though you'll be lucky to fetch ten shillings."

Chapter Nineteen

The Conte di Barasian's grand mansion stood on the banks of the Thames to the west of Tothill Fields. Carriages lined the narrow country lane outside the high stone wall. Only a few prestigious vehicles had been granted entrance through the wrought-iron gates. Some guests had arrived by barge or wherry, the boats left moored along the elegant walkway at the bottom of the ornate gardens.

Two guards kept watch outside the gatehouse.

So what was the conte celebrating?

Christian's heart lurched. The answer did not bear contemplating. What if the conte planned to force Isabella to marry him before a room full of noble guests? What if it was too late to save her?

He stood with his brothers and Daventry's men in the wooded area opposite the conte's lavish gates. Thankfully, they'd found Daventry and his agents at the Hart Street office discussing Oldman's fate. Learning of Isabella's kidnapping, the men had joined the fray. Indeed, Daventry had assembled a small army.

"How much longer must we wait?" Christian's impatience

was like a fire raging in his blood. A fire he'd not temper until Isabella was back in his arms.

"When Gibbs returns, we'll force the buffoons to open the gate," Daventry said calmly. "Remember what I said. Once we're inside, you cannot become distracted."

Aaron placed a reassuring hand on Christian's shoulder. "We will find Miss Lawton. She will be returned to you. You have my word."

Christian looked at his brother, his desperation surely evident. "Your word means everything to me." Aaron was his hero despite the fact he was wrong occasionally. "Know I cannot lose her. Not tonight. Not ever."

"I understand."

Daventry cleared his throat. "This might be a lavish party to celebrate the conte's arrival. Yet no invitations were sent, and he has no friends in town. So one asks oneself, who are these people, and why are they here?"

Christian had spent the last half an hour piecing together the facts, trying to solve the case and find a reason for the large gathering. Something Aramis said on the journey across town made him question what Snell was hiding in the crates.

"I don't know how the conte is involved," Christian began, "but the pendant recovered from Lord Oldman's home bears an old Norse symbol. The description of the maid, Sarah, suggests she might hail from Scandinavia."

Daventry narrowed his gaze. "Snell makes frequent trips to Norway." He seemed keen to pursue this line of enquiry. "Perhaps he ships something other than spring water ice."

"It's likely. No one is allowed to inspect the crates."

"And each crate is large enough to hold three subdued women."

Aaron spoke up. "There's been a spate of disappearances from dockside taverns within the last week. The women who walk the alleyways around Shadwell Market have taken to working in pairs. Perhaps Snell ships women out of London, too."

There was no time to contemplate the matter further.

Panicked shouts rent the air.

The smell of smoke assaulted Christian's nostrils.

Black plumes billowed into the night sky.

A breathless Gibbs appeared from the darkness, brushing his hands vigorously as if proud of a job well done. "There'll be no means of escape via the river tonight."

"Did anyone see you?" Daventry asked.

"No. The watermen were drinking on the bank, and the barges were moored so closely together I only had to set one alight."

Daventry patted Gibbs on the back before addressing Christian. "Distract the guards until we're over the wall." He faced the other men. "We'll have the gate open in no time. Then we'll all enter the house together. We won't shoot unless there's no option."

Christian took a moment to step into character. He would do anything for Isabella, even if it meant acting the buffoon.

Swaggering across the road like a drunken vagrant, he approached the gate and waved his rum bottle. "You fellows fancy a swig?" While Aaron and Lucius Daventry scaled the stone wall, Christian whistled a country tune.

"Be on your way!" a guard shouted.

Christian drank from the bottle before spitting rum over the iron railings and pretending to vomit. "Tastes like horse piss. Try it yourself." He forced the stopper into the neck and hurled the bottle over the gate. It landed with a thud on a patch of grass.

The bravest guard charged forward, calling Christian

names the devil wouldn't dare repeat. "Move along before you get my boot up your arse."

Christian fumbled with the placket of his trousers. "See if my piss tastes any better."

Outraged, the guard hauled a ring of keys from his pocket and set about opening the gate. "Filthy swine! Wait until I get my hands—"

Like demons from the shadows, Aaron and Daventry struck, grabbing the men around the neck and pulling them into the bushes. Aaron could silence a man in seconds. Still, Daventry beckoned his agents forward, had them secure the guards' hands and feet with rope and lock them in the gatehouse.

They navigated the long drive to the Palladian-style mansion.

Finding Isabella was Christian's only objective, and so he suggested searching for the servants' entrance.

"We'll enter through the front door." A sinister smirk darkened Daventry's features. "Should anyone raise the alarm, we risk the conte fleeing before we can apprehend him."

With the devil's arrogance, they sauntered up the sweeping stone staircase and strode towards two liveried footmen. The servants asked to see their invitations.

"The guards at the gate took them." Daventry straightened, though the man was intimidating regardless of his height. "We'll wait here while you seek confirmation."

The servants glanced at each other, shrugged, then let them pass.

Thirty men had gathered in the extravagant supper room, eating canapés from gold platters and drinking champagne from crystal flutes. Christian recognised one or two. It soon became clear some had journeyed from as far as France and Spain to attend the conte's secret party.

Aaron handed out the champagne, and they stood with Daventry's men as if they were guests enjoying the conte's hospitality.

Daventry lowered his voice. "Sloane. Hunter. Remain in the hall. When the time comes, lock the front door. Prevent anyone from leaving. Fire warning shots if need be. Gibbs will guard the steps and be on hand to offer support."

Christian's mounting frustration urged him to say, "Can I not creep through the corridors and hunt for Isabella? I'll go alone while you deal with matters here." The more time that passed, the more he feared for her safety. What if the conte escaped and took her hostage?

Aaron gripped his shoulder. "We have the keys to the gate. No one can leave via the river. You have my word she will be in your arms within the hour. Have I ever let you down?"

Daventry was equally persuasive. "While the Home Secretary sanctioned this investigation, rescuing my agent is my main aim. To save Miss Lawton's life, we must let the conte believe she is a bargaining tool. When men panic, they silence the witnesses."

The sudden clang of a gong signalled something important.

Amid a sudden flurry of excitement, those in the supper room downed their drinks and headed towards the narrow marble corridor.

It was Daventry's turn to make promises. "Keep calm. We will prevail. I've not lost a fight yet."

They followed the crowd through the corridor and entered a mirrored ballroom lit by crystal chandeliers. Men sat in rows of padded gilt chairs before a makeshift stage. In a bid to remain as inconspicuous as possible, Aaron gestured to the seats in the back row.

The lively conversation continued.

Laughing like a drunken buffoon, Lord Hanson happened to look over his shoulder. His bushy grey brows rose in consternation as he met Christian's gaze. The lord paled as he considered Aaron, then Daventry.

Hanson stood abruptly, but then a flourish of trumpets silenced the room, and the lord was forced to regain his seat.

All eyes turned to the curtained stage.

The swathe of red velvet parted to reveal a beautiful dark-haired woman dressed in the garb of Cleopatra and locked in a gilt cage. Through terrified eyes, she scanned the crowd, rattling the bars like a crazed animal.

Christian cursed under his breath.

It took immense effort to remain seated.

The conte appeared, a popinjay dressed in blue and gold silk. He hit the gilt bars with his cane to silence the frightened girl before addressing the crowd.

"My esteemed guests." He repeated the greeting in numerous languages. "Tonight, you are invited to cast your eyes over a host of exotic beauties sourced from faraway lands." He waited for the crowd's excited applause before continuing. "Here we have our Egyptian goddess Khepri. Such striking beauty is rarely seen on England's fine shores. The Grand Vizier himself provides proof of her chastity."

The conte continued his pitch before revealing the real reason they were gathered here. This woman was to be sold at auction, and the bidding opened at a shocking twenty thousand pounds.

From all around the room, men raised their paddles.

The bids came so fast that one could barely keep track.

The conte banged the stage with his cane to signal the

winning tender—an extortionate one hundred thousand promised by an unknown Frenchman in the front row.

"I can't wait to thump the smiles off their faces," Christian muttered. "Only after I've murdered the conte, of course."

"Let me worry about vengeance," Aaron said darkly. "Miss Lawton will need you in one piece. I'll deal with the conte before I rid the world of Sir Geoffrey Lawton. I mean to ensure his daughter has no reason to run."

Christian glanced at Aaron, a rush of pride, love and respect gathering in his chest. "I'm determined to marry her if she'll accept."

Aaron averted his gaze and stared at the stage. "Good. I have other uses for your room, and your house in Ludgate Hill shouldn't be left empty."

The thought of abandoning his brothers caused Christian's heart to constrict. But he loved Isabella, and they could not make a life together while living above a gaming hell.

"You may still depend on me to work at Fortune's Den."

A faint smile touched Aaron's lips. "You're a partner in a successful business. I expect to see you each morning, promptly at ten."

Christian smiled too, but the conte carted another poor woman out for display, and anger flared anew.

Daventry insisted they sit through four more auctions while he made notes in a small black book. The Earl of Evesham's dissolute son spotted them seated at the back. He whispered to the fellow beside him, and they both shrank down in their chairs while eyeing the exit.

Impatience was like a serpent slithering in Christian's veins, but fate granted them a boon. Lawton appeared when summoned by the conte.

Christian turned to Aaron. "It seems the lord has

answered our prayers. I say we strip Lawton naked, load him into a cart and deposit him in the rookeries. We can hunt him down as one would an animal."

"Forget Lawton. He's mine."

Christian was about to protest, but chaos erupted when the conte introduced Lawton as his business partner and the father of his soon-to-be bride. While Christian sighed with relief to know Isabella was alive, a gentleman in the crowd shot to his feet and cried, "Liar! Deceiver!"

Amid the stunned silence, Lawton narrowed his gaze and peered over the sea of heads. Recognition dawned, and his temper erupted. "Sit down, Mr Griffin. Sit down, or I shall have you removed."

Griffin? What the devil was he doing at the conte's auction?

"I'll not be silenced," Griffin shouted. "You promised *me* your daughter's hand in marriage. Yet this posturing dandy claims you granted him the privilege. I paid you in good faith, yet you forced me to partake in this disgusting charade."

Mr Griffin failed to see his own hypocrisy.

The conte raised his chin and cursed in Italian. "Sir Geoffrey is powerless to act. I have a legally binding contract. Being a fair man, I shall see you reimbursed. Or you may accept another woman in return for your payment. I know a fiery red-headed creature who will serve you well. I shall have her brought up at once."

But Mr Griffin would not be deterred. "Miss Lawton accepted my suit when she was eighteen years old. Miss Blunkett from the Bramling Seminary had Sir Geoffrey sign a letter agreeing to the match."

The conte faced Lawton. "Is this true?"

Lawton shrugged. "The letter is worthless. Besides, I imagine Miss Blunkett disposed of it years ago."

"I have it!" Griffin whipped the note from his pocket and waved it vigorously. "And shall read it out before witnesses."

Christian groaned. A good barrister would have this fool dismissed from court. The conte obviously agreed and decided to vilify and humiliate the reprobate.

"You're no match for a man like me," the conte sneered. "From the poor cut of your coat, it is clear you lack refinement. Why would Miss Lawton wish to marry a mister when she can carry the title of contessa?"

Christian leant closer to Aaron. "If I'm to marry Miss Lawton, I must eliminate the competition." A less confident man might question his own worth. But he knew Isabella cared for him. It was there in every kind word, every kiss, every gentle caress.

"You're worth more than these cretins. If Miss Lawton cannot see that, she doesn't deserve you. Besides, what can Griffin do?"

Like Aaron, the conte and every other man in the room, Christian had underestimated the power of Griffin's vehemence. "You will bring Miss Lawton to me, else I shall wipe that smug grin off your face."

The conte laughed. He called for his men to intervene, the same miscreants who had aided him outside the Grapes tavern.

Much to everyone's horror, Griffin pulled a hunting knife from a satchel. Those next to him darted from the aisle, knocking over their fancy chairs. The onlookers merely gasped as Griffin threw his blade with practised expertise.

From the trajectory, Christian knew it would hit the target.

For a second or two, the conte seemed confused by the crowd's horrified cries. With an air of nonchalance, he glanced down at his expensive silk coat and noticed the knife protruding from his chest. As quick as the spread of burgundy blood, the life drained from the conte's shocked face.

He swayed, his eyes so wide the whites were visible. Then he dropped to his knees before his face hit the floor with a thud.

Only an imbecile would lock a desperate woman in a bedchamber and presume she could not escape. Only the conte would assume he could bribe a woman with a ruby necklace and a pretty red dress.

But something was amiss.

The smell of smoke and distant cries had drawn Isabella to the window. Amid the inky blackness of the Thames, the moored boats were a wild blaze of amber and gold. Men were busy filling buckets from the river to douse the flames and had been battling the fire for an hour.

Knowing the distraction would assist in her escape, Isabella listened at the bedchamber door before pulling pins from her newly styled hair and using them to trip the mechanism.

She laughed to herself.

Every miserable moment in her life had brought her to this point. Had it not been for Miss Blunkett's strict punishments, Isabella wouldn't know the first thing about picking a lock.

Armed with a wine bottle, she prised the door carefully from the jamb and peered into the dimly lit corridor. There was no one in the hallway except for the beast keeping guard at the top of the marble staircase.

She hesitated.

The servants' stairs were closest, and she'd have a better chance of escaping into the garden. Yet it would be impossible to leave via the river, and the fire would have drawn more servants outside.

And who would free the women in the cellar? By the time she sought help, they might be in carriages bound for Dover. Doubts crept into her mind. There was more chance of getting caught if she didn't run now.

She said a silent prayer, hoping the Lord would offer a solution.

The solution came sooner than expected.

The sudden boom of pistol fire and panicked cries had the guard leaving his post and racing downstairs. She waited a minute before creeping along the corridor and peering over the bannister.

Two armed men, one who looked familiar, ushered the guard and liveried servants aside, warning them to keep their hands raised.

Isabella blinked and narrowed her gaze.

Praise be! It was Mr Daventry's buccaneer agent, Mr Sloane.

A wave of emotion swept over her—relief that help was on hand and that sometime soon Christian would know she had not deserted him.

She hurried downstairs. "Mr Sloane!"

The gentleman saw her and beckoned her forward.

After a garbled attempt to explain all that had occurred, she said, "Someone needs to free the women in the cellar. Tell me Mr Daventry didn't send you here without assistance." Pulse galloping, she glanced behind her. "We must help those poor hostages before my father and the conte find us."

Mr Sloane placed a reassuring hand on her shoulder. "The

conte is dead. Killed by a gentleman here for the auction. One of the conte's men shot the assassin. We cannot enter the ballroom. Your father and his lackeys have pistols aimed at the Chance brothers."

"Christian is here?"

Mr Sloane managed a weak smile. "Yes, but they're locked in a stalemate. The Chance brothers and our colleagues have their pistols trained on your father and the men in the crowd. If one shoots, they all will."

Her heart skipped a beat.

She could not lose Christian.

Not now she had found a reason to stop running.

Not now she had found someone to love.

"I have an idea." She explained her plan to enter the ballroom. "It's lunacy, but it might give us a few precious seconds to disarm my father."

Mr Sloane conversed with his colleague.

Time was of the essence. "If I can distract my father, Mr Daventry can shoot. I'm light on my feet. Is it not better to risk one life than many?" Did the Chance brothers not deserve retribution?

A footman spoke and explained she could access the stage from the garden terrace.

"I could hide behind the curtain and strike with a viper-like snap," she said, praying she could hold her nerve.

"I'll accompany you," Mr Sloane said. "Hunter can keep watch here."

Though her heart thumped hard against her ribcage, she followed Mr Sloane into the garden. As they headed towards the paved terrace, they heard footsteps and muted cries.

Ethel Cartwright and the enslaved women burst out through the servants' door. Some were barely clothed. Some were dazed. Some were sobbing, relieved to find themselves free of their shackles.

"Ethel?" Isabella whispered, beckoning her over.

Wielding a pistol, Ethel closed the gap between them, the hostages following behind like sheep. "I planned to come looking for you, Miss Lawton, once I'd found somewhere safe to hide the girls."

Isabella introduced Mr Sloane. "There's no time to talk now." She explained her plan. "It's my only option. My father won't see me as a threat. If I strike quickly, I can catch him unawares."

Ethel wouldn't hear of it. "I'll go. You wouldn't be in this mess if I'd not hammered on the Den's door. Besides, if I can knock a burly guard out with an empty bottle, I can rid the world of the devil's spawn."

"I have a better idea. You'll assist Mr Sloane. Do everything in your power to ensure I don't die." Isabella made for the terrace doors before it was too late and someone fired the first shot.

Ethel followed, as did the foreign women who barely spoke a word of English between them. Still, they understood hand gestures and the need for silence.

They all came to a halt behind the makeshift stage.

Isabella gripped the wine bottle. She peered through a narrow gap in the curtain and assessed the scene.

"Lower your weapon, Lawton." Mr Daventry's voice echoed through the elegant ballroom. "Don't bank on me tiring. I can keep a straight aim all night."

"Take me down, and I'll take you all with me."

Mr Daventry laughed. "You'll die now or on the scaffold. Everyone here will testify against you or risk being charged with a crime. The Home Secretary is on his way. I have the place surrounded. Your men have the option to lower their weapons and save their necks."

Isabella searched the throng.

She found Christian standing firm with his pistol pointed at her father. If only Mr Daventry hadn't asked him to help at the museum. He would be at the club, out of harm's way, not embroiled in this godforsaken mess.

Please don't fire, my love!

"Don't listen to him," her father sneered. "We can save ourselves if we shoot them." He spoke to a man in the crowd. "Lord Bardsley, do you want your wife to know you came to purchase a woman for your own amusement? If we take these men out, no one need know your sordid secret."

"Does Lord Bardsley want to die?" Aaron Chance said coldly. "Does he want me to hound his son to the grave, strip him of his assets to pay for his father's mistake? You've no chance of killing us all. Surrender. It's the only option."

"Never!" her father spat.

Afraid time had run out, Isabella stepped from behind the curtain. She held the wine bottle behind her back, her hands shaking so violently she would probably miss the target.

"There's another option," she said, catching her father off guard.

"Isabella?"

"Don't shoot!" Christian cried—she would know his voice anywhere. "Don't hurt her. For God's sake, lower your weapons."

"It's too late, Father." She saw the conte's lifeless body lying facedown on the stage, a rush of relief calming her momentarily. Her gaze moved to the dead man in the aisle. A man who bore a remarkable likeness to Mr Griffin. "I shall persuade them to let you go free. I'll go with you if you leave now."

She considered her options as she edged closer.

One could not murder a man and live to tell the tale.

"As if I would trust you," her father scoffed. "You're as wicked as your mother." As expected, he aimed his pistol at her heart. "Foolish girl. What do you have behind your back, Isabella?"

"Wine, Father." With slow, measured movements she showed him the bottle, though her heartbeat thundered in her throat. "It's one of the conte's finest vintages. We can drink it together once we're away from here. If you take me as a hostage, Christian will let us leave. If you want to live, it's your only choice."

She prayed he didn't see Ethel and Mr Sloane pointing their pistols through the curtain. Prayed she wouldn't get hit by a stray shot.

Her father sneered. "Why the hell would I want to leave with you? I couldn't stand you as a girl. The woman is equally loathsome."

The cruel words failed to penetrate her armour.

Then a strange bird call echoed through the ballroom.

Mr Daventry recognised the sound immediately and waved for his men to lower their weapons. Her father's men looked at the ceiling, her cue to hurl the bottle at her father's head.

Isabella launched the bottle and threw herself onto the floor. She hit the stage with a thud, knocking the air from her lungs. It hurt to draw breath.

She didn't know if the bottle had hit her father. She didn't know who fired the two shots. But the wooden boards shook beneath her as a body hit the stage.

The smell of sulphur assaulted the air.

Then her world went black.

Chapter Twenty

Christian was running, pushing men and chairs aside to reach Isabella.

Two shots were fired. Two people hit the floor. Neither seemed to move. It happened in a split second—his hope of Isabella escaping alive instantly shattered.

"Isabella!"

Despite the chaos left in his wake, he vaulted onto the stage and dropped to his knees beside the woman he loved. He moved to touch her, but his hands shook violently, and he was too scared to check her pulse.

No! He'd sell his soul to the devil if he lost her.

Aaron was beside him, choosing to help rather than making sure Lawton was dead. "Both shots hit Lawton. I'm certain. Daventry said his man made the bird call."

He grabbed Aaron's arm and firmed his jaw. "Make this right. She's not gone. Tell me she's not gone." Tears gathered behind his eyes. His throat was so tight he could hardly breathe.

But then Isabella moaned weakly and moved her limbs.

Christian did cry then.

Relief poured from his body, soothing him like healing waters.

He dared to grip her arm and haul her onto her back.

Her eyes flickered open. "Christian!" She reached up and cupped his cheek, but her hands were so damned cold. "I feared I'd never see you again." She touched her abdomen as if something pained her.

"Are you hurt?" He could see no sign of a wound or blood. Why the hell was she wearing red? "Were you shot?"

She shook her head and heaved a breath. "The fall knocked the air from my lungs. I must have fainted." Then, as if remembering something important, she sat up. "Hurry! Help me to my feet."

Fearing she wasn't strong enough to stand, Christian scooped her into his arms. He glanced at Aaron, crouched beside Lawton's lifeless body. The look on his brother's face was unreadable. A complex fusion of sadness, relief and crippling disappointment.

"I can walk." Isabella pressed a chaste kiss to his lips. "But I need your help with something else. Will you undo the clasp on this ruby necklace?"

Amid the disorder in the ballroom and Daventry's demand that every man remain seated, Christian did as Isabella asked.

"Wait here. It's best you're not involved in my reckless decision." She turned on her heel and darted through the thick red curtain without sparing her father a fleeting glance.

Christian followed her into the garden, where she hurried to catch Ethel Cartwright and a group of foreign women.

He listened to the conversation but did not intervene.

"Take these." Isabella thrust the ruby necklace and earrings into Ethel's hand. "Hurry. Go now before the magistrate arrives. You'll hang for the part you played. I know how manipulative my father can be. I wouldn't be here if you hadn't fired the fatal shot."

Ethel looked at the priceless gems in her hand. "I can't take your jewels. You'll need them. You could go to Egypt and study those ugly figures you love."

Isabella glanced at Christian, her gaze softening. "There's nothing for me in Egypt. Take them. Go now before the authorities arrive."

Christian stepped forward. "Keep away from the main roads, Miss Cartwright. There's a pawnbroker in Compton Street, St Giles. He'll buy the jewels. Tell him I sent you. Tell him diamonds never lose their lustre."

"Go!" Isabella shooed Ethel away. "There's no time to lose."

"You can't use the front gate or the boats moored on the river," Christian said. "I'm sure I saw a door in the west wall."

Ethel nodded. She used a series of hand gestures to force the rescued women to remain in the garden. Then she took to her heels and disappeared into the verdure.

Having spent hours longing to touch Isabella, Christian cupped her elbow. "I thought I'd lost you. I've tried to remain focused these last few hours, but I've been out of my mind with worry."

She met his gaze, her watery eyes conveying the depth of her fears. "Forgive me. I shouldn't have opened the door. I kept my promise and never crossed the threshold, but the conte's men were lurking in the darkness, waiting to pounce." She came up on her toes and pressed a chaste kiss to his lips. "Once I'd given Mrs Maloney her port, I planned to return to your bed."

Christian wrapped his arms around her. He poured everything of himself into a tender kiss. Every sensual stroke of their tongues served as a reminder of what they'd almost lost.

He was in no doubt how he felt about her.

Had it not been for the group of women watching them and tittering amongst themselves, he would have confessed undying love.

"We need to deal with things here," he said before his need for her consumed him. "Then I'm taking you home, back to bed."

She ran her hand over his bicep. "We should make haste."

And yet a nagging voice in his mind said a night of unbridled passion wouldn't settle his restless spirit. While Isabella craved independence, he wanted her for his wife. His lifelong companion. But he loved her too much to take her freedom. He needed to think on the matter some more.

Aramis appeared. His dark, dominant countenance had the hostages huddling together like frightened sheep. Doubtless they believed this was hell. "Daventry has sent his agent to fetch the magistrate. He needs our help to prevent the guests leaving."

While Isabella took the women upstairs to the safety of the conte's bedchamber, Christian returned to the ballroom.

White sheets covered the dead men. Under threat of being shot for attempting to flee, the guests allowed Sloane to secure their hands with rope.

"They tried to bribe their way to freedom," Aramis said, his lips curling in contempt. "Most of these men will be set free. Only those who won the auctions will answer for their actions. The others can plead ignorance."

"Once they arrest Captain Snell, I'm sure more evidence will come to light." Christian considered Aramis' tired eyes. "I'm sorry for dragging you into this mess. When I agreed to help Daventry, I thought he'd have me scrolling through documents and cataloguing rare finds."

Aramis gave an amused snort. "I thought you knew Daventry better than that. The man enjoys watching others risk their necks in the name of justice."

"Be careful, brother. Daventry is so pleased with your efforts you might find yourself embroiled in his next case."

"Like hell. There's no way the man could tempt me to work for him. Every male agent ends up shackled with a wife." Aramis shuddered like someone had stepped on his grave. "Anyone who can persuade a Chance brother to marry is the devil incarnate."

Christian laughed, though Aramis had a point. Was Isabella so invested in the case her emotions were heightened? Had the forced proximity led to this outpouring of affection?

An idea formed in his mind. If he was wrong, he risked losing her. Still, if he was wrong, she was never his to begin with.

Two hours passed before the magistrate arrived with a dozen constables. Daventry had already sent his men to the conte's study to fetch paper and ink. Consequently, everyone presented the magistrate with written statements.

"What will happen to the ladies upstairs, my lord?" Isabella asked the Home Secretary when he arrived to oversee the proceedings.

Lord Melbourne sought to offer every reassurance. "Those who wish to return home will be allowed to do so. Those who wish to remain in England will be found respectable employment." He turned to Daventry and gave him a congratulatory slap on the back. "Well, in an effort to find a murderer, you uncovered a smuggling ring. Are we certain Lord Oldman is involved?"

"Oldman is nothing more than a naive fool with a temper," Daventry said with conviction. "Should that prove to be the case, I shall address his mistreatment of his staff."

Lord Melbourne gestured to the body being examined by the coroner. "Do you think Sir Geoffrey killed the girl because she knew about the auction?"

Isabella cleared her throat. "I beg your pardon, but I believe my father was innocent of that crime. I fear the real culprit is alive and well and has nothing to do with smuggling."

Daventry frowned. "Would you care to explain your theory?"

"Sir, if I may be excused, I should like to apprehend the villain. It shouldn't be difficult to gain a confession. Mr Chance will accompany me."

Daventry grinned. "And which Mr Chance would that be?"

"Every damn one of us," Aaron interjected. "We're not letting Miss Lawton out of our sight until the murderer is caught."

Christian glanced at his brothers gathered around in a gesture of solidarity. "Let's pray we catch the murderer within the hour." Dawn would soon be upon them. He needed to be alone with Isabella, to hold her close before he offered her an ultimatum. "We all need a stiff drink and a good night's sleep."

Daventry agreed. "I shall look forward to reading the villain's confession, though I have a strange suspicion who it might be."

By the time they reached Great Russell Street, the sun had breached the misty horizon. The journey in Aaron's carriage was a test of Christian's resolve. While his brothers looked on, he held Isabella close, kissed her brow and stroked her hair.

Aaron looked to have the weight of the world on his shoulders, but he said nothing until the carriage stopped outside the British Museum. "How do you mean to gain a confession, madam?"

Isabella smiled. "As you're all here, I thought intimidation might do the trick. It's that, or I pretend to be the dead woman risen from the grave."

Aramis tugged the cuffs of his coat. "Might I play the fallen angel here to cause mayhem? You and Christian can be the voices of reason."

Perhaps keen to forge friendships, Isabella agreed.

They made a plan before alighting.

Isabella drew Christian aside. "Aaron seems rather subdued since we left the conte's mansion. I believe he blames me for almost getting you all killed."

Christian cupped her cheek. "It's not that. He's spent years planning your father's demise. I suspect he feels robbed because he didn't deliver the fatal blow. If there's one thing my brother despises, it's the feeling of inadequacy."

"I see."

"He'll come to accept it in time."

"Surely he can put the ghosts of the past to rest now."

Christian's heart melted at her naiveté. "It would take more than Lawton's death to bring my brother the peace he deserves. I fear his troubled soul will haunt him for an eternity."

Cornelius Brown's arrival brought the conversation to an abrupt end. The man was too busy inspecting his pocket watch to notice five people loitering outside the museum. He almost jumped out of his skin when he locked eyes with Isabella.

"Mr Brown." She stepped forward. "I trust all went well in Bath. While I find Roman artefacts a little underwhelming, I'm told they fetch a handsome price."

"To find Roman ruins on English soil is reward itself." The curator observed her red silk dress and loose hair and frowned. He cast a curious eye over Christian's brothers. "I trust all is well, Miss Lawton."

"Oh yes. I came merely to tell you our splendid news regarding the Egyptian artefacts. You must forgive my odd appearance. The investigation was concluded this past hour. Might we talk inside?"

The man shifted uncomfortably. "I'm a little short of time. I'm to inspect the exhibits before we open at nine."

"Don't you want to know if the artefacts are genuine? It may surprise you to learn what we discovered in Lord Oldman's Egyptian crypt."

She pestered the man until he had no choice but to welcome them through the doors and into the elegant hall.

She persuaded him to lead them to his office. It was a vast room filled with books, marble busts and expensive walnut furniture.

"We won't keep you." Isabella gestured to the padded chair opposite the desk and sat down before the curator spoke.

Christian and his brothers remained standing.

"We have Snell in custody," Christian said, keeping his tone even. "We found a horde of fake artefacts in Lord Oldman's basement, though he assures us none were sold to clients."

Cornelius Brown paled. "You mean there might be forged pieces amongst my exhibits?"

"It's doubtful, sir." Isabella was quick to put him at ease. "You might find the truth shocking, but Captain Snell was smuggling women inside the crates. Last night, we attended an auction where these poor souls were being sold to the highest bidder."

"Good Lord!" The curator failed to meet her gaze. He stared at the papers on his desk. "How dreadful it must have been for all involved."

"Yes, you'll be sorry to hear that the ghostly figure you encountered worked as a maid for Lord Oldman. We're still gathering evidence, but believe she came to England on the promise of work, though did not expect to be employed by a tyrant. The man's cruelty knows no bounds."

The curator cupped his throat. "You think Lord Oldman killed the poor creature? She was frantic when she accosted me in the courtyard. Mumbling gibberish. Though now I think of it, she spoke with an accent."

"We're still trying to establish the facts," Christian said.

Isabella glanced at Aramis, who took it as his cue to intimidate the witness. He perched on the desk and folded his arms across his broad chest. "What exactly did the woman say to you?"

"It might help with the investigation," Isabella added.

Brown's bottom lip quivered. "I was so scared I can hardly remember. She mentioned the artefacts. Spoke of sinister goings-on—Egyptian curses and the like. Said not to trust the men who sold the treasures from Amarna."

Aramis frowned. "You're a grown man of reasonably athletic build. Do you expect me to believe you were afraid of a woman?"

The curator's cheeks burned. "It was late, and she was in a dreadful state."

"Did you not think to question why?" Aramis sounded more like an enquiry agent than Lucifer's servant. "Did you not attempt to call the watchman? Is that not what a gentleman would do?"

"There was no time. She ran before I could offer assistance."

Aramis' eyes darkened. When he spoke, his tone was as menacing as his expression. "Lying bastard. She told you Oldman was her employer, mentioned the chest of fake artefacts and told you not to trust him. Instead of helping her, you panicked."

Affronted, Brown gripped the desk and stood. "That's preposterous. I've told you everything I can remember."

Aramis jumped off the desk and Brown nearly fainted. "She was crying and threatening to tell everyone about Oldman's Egyptian chamber." Aramis held the curator in his death-like stare. "You knew it would reflect badly on the museum once others learned of Oldman's perverse antics. People would assume all your treasures were fake. Your integrity would be brought into question."

"N-no!"

Aramis grabbed the curator by his fancy cravat. "And so you silenced her. You squeezed the life from her body and threw her into the Thames." He gripped Brown by the throat. "I'll throttle you in the same manner if you don't tell me the bloody truth."

Aramis squeezed until Brown's eyes bulged.

In a feeble bid to break free, the curator thumped Aramis. His croaky words were inaudible. The second Aramis released him, he collapsed against the desk and quickly changed his story. "She attacked me. Flew at me in a violent rage. I was merely defending myself. I told her to be quiet, but she wouldn't listen. I never meant to hurt her. Just stun her into silence."

Isabella gasped.

An icy shiver ran the length of Christian's spine. Guilt assailed him. He had left Isabella alone at the museum with a man who'd already committed murder.

But how had Brown disposed of the body?

Isabella knew the answer. "On the docket from the Society of Antiquaries, it said they delivered the Egyptian artefacts in a wooden trunk. When I asked to inspect it, you said you'd returned it to Somerset House. Yet I'll warrant you used the museum's cart to ferry the trunk to the river."

Brown started squealing like a pig.

To shirk responsibility, he blamed everyone involved.

While Aramis took pleasure in restraining the villain, Aaron turned to Christian. "We should take the curator to Bow Street and give our statements. Then we should return to Fortune's Den. We need sleep if we plan to open on time tonight."

Isabella stood. The tense lines on her face spoke of secret worries. "Yes, it's been an exhausting night." The strain in her voice was unmistakable.

Christian guessed the problem. She was unsure what to do now they'd solved the case. Keen to ease her anxiety, he said, "I trust Isabella can remain at the club."

Aaron nodded, though his expression remained grim. "Only until other arrangements can be made. I'm sorry, Miss Lawton, but Fortune's Den is no place for a woman."

The two hours spent giving statements at Bow Street had left Isabella on the brink of exhaustion. Every muscle ached. The pounding in her head mirrored the wild thumping of her heart.

Once again, she found herself homeless.

This time, she'd have her wages. And the man gripping her hand as she entered his bedchamber ensured she wasn't alone.

Christian closed the door and pulled her into an embrace. He pressed his forehead to hers. "I've thought about nothing but this moment all night. I want you so badly, Isabella. It's killing me."

Frantic with need, she pushed his coat off his shoulders. "Everything aches. You're the only one who can soothe me, Christian."

Tears gathered behind her eyes.

Please don't let this end.

The case was over—but what would happen to them?

A sensible woman would keep her thoughts to herself, but she could not take another breath without letting him know how he made her feel.

"Before passion overwhelms us, let me thank you."

His sensual smile had heat pooling between her thighs. "Thank me?" He smoothed his hands over her buttocks and drew her tight against his hard body. "For what, love? For the kisses that make you mindless with need?" He claimed her mouth in a slow, hypnotic kiss that curled her toes. "For making you come hard around my cock?"

The haze of desire swept over her. She was wet, her sex already pulsing to an intoxicating rhythm. She'd be on her back in a matter of seconds, and then she might never reveal what was in her heart.

"When you're buried deep inside me, everything feels right, but that's not why I want to thank you." She swallowed past the lump in her throat. "You've been so kind to me,

Christian. You don't make me feel like a burden. No one has ever cared for me the way you do."

He tucked a lock of hair behind her ear. "I'm in love with you. Surely you know I'd die for you, Isabella."

Dare she hope it was true?

All the old doubts surfaced. "But what if you're wrong?"

"I've never known desire like this. The urge to make love is too powerful to suppress, but I'd be happy just to hold you in my arms and watch you sleep." He stroked the backs of his fingers over her jaw. "Besides, I'm not the one thinking about running away."

Her stomach twisted into knots.

How did one undo a lifetime of hurt?

How did one learn to trust?

"I love you," she whispered, the emotion behind the words clear in her trembling voice. "I love you so much I can barely breathe."

If only she could crawl into his bed and stay there forever.

His smile was short-lived. "Why do I sense your hesitance?"

"If you do, I'm at fault for giving you a reason to doubt me. Believe me when I say I'm desperately in love with you, Christian."

He tangled his hands in her hair and tilted her head. His fervent kisses left a searing trail down the column of her throat. "Never forget how I make you feel. Never doubt this is real."

Something in his tone made her look at him. What she saw in his eyes made her heart sink. "You say that as if you're the one who's leaving."

"I am."

"What?" She jerked out of his grasp.

"Let me explain before you concoct a tragic story in your

mind." He reached for his coat and slipped his hand into the pocket, retrieving two sealed notes. "I want you, in every way a man can want a woman. This letter explains it all." He moved past her to place it on the nightstand. "I could be selfish and make demands, but I love you too much not to grant you your freedom."

Her chest constricted. Fear sank its icy claws into her heart. Was this why he left her talking to Aramis while he slipped into Aaron's study?

"Christian, what are you saying?"

He placed the second note on the nightstand and closed the gap between them. He reached for her hand, linking their fingers. "You will always have my heart. I will always be yours. Let's go to bed to sleep. When you wake, you must read the notes. If you want me, I've explained where you can find me."

Confusion had her shaking her head. "No."

"I'll not force you to surrender your freedom." He kissed her forehead, then took a moment to appreciate her figure. "You look wicked in red." He removed his waistcoat. "Are you coming to bed?"

Her throat was so tight she couldn't answer. She thought of demanding to read the notes now. But she was at fault. She'd told him she planned to run. She had made it clear she sought a life elsewhere. What else was he to do but test her resolve?

"Will you make love to me?" she breathed.

"Are you not exhausted, love?"

"A little." She wanted to feel close to him and let the heat of his body warm her numb limbs. "I want you inside me, Christian."

"There's nowhere else I'd rather be."

They stripped off their clothes and climbed into bed.

He didn't find new ways to heighten their pleasure. He merely covered her body with his, his kisses as deep as his slow thrusts. He never took his eyes off her. Amid the glaze of desire, she glimpsed his pain—the fear of loss mingled with abiding love.

Chapter Twenty-One

Isabella didn't hear Christian climb out of bed. She didn't hear the trickle of water or the rustle of clothes as he washed and dressed, or the quiet click of the door closing. Yet she knew he'd left the house before she opened her eyes.

She lay still for a moment.

Was this the fork in the road Ethel mentioned, the loss she would feel keenly until the day she died? But Christian had not forsaken her. He had given her the right to forge her own destiny—a gift more precious than historical treasures or expensive gems.

Gathering her strength, she sat up and snatched the notes from the nightstand. *They smell of him*, she thought, bringing them to her nose and inhaling deeply. She didn't want the scent to fade. She didn't want to wake alone, longing to catch his aroma in the air.

With shaky fingers, she broke the seal on the letter she was meant to open first. Folded banknotes fell out. A thousand pounds in signed notes, to be precise. Christian had written a simple message inside.

If you must run, there's no need to go hungry.

A sob burst from her throat. No one had ever cared if she lived or died. But that's not what caused the tears to fall. She could imagine him writing the words, the ache of loss like a blade to his heart.

Isabella hugged the letter to her chest. "Oh, Christian."

The selfless act made her love him all the more.

She dried her eyes and opened the second seal.

If you're reading this, there's still hope.

I'm at my house in Ludgate Hill—our house in
Ludgate Hill, if you accept my proposal.
Some things you know about me.
I can fight three men with my eyes blindfolded. I'm
not as knowledgeable as you when it comes to
Egyptian treasures. I love my family and could never
forsake them. No other man will make love to you like
I do.

Now for the things you may not know.
It's all or nothing, Isabella.
I've lost too much to settle for anything less.
I cannot promise life will be perfect, but as my wife,
you will be free to pursue your deepest desires. I ask
that you do so with me.

Marriage? Christian was offering marriage?

Isabella's heart soared.

She shot out of bed but remembered she had nothing to wear but the ghastly red gown. Her only other decent dress was upstairs, though she'd not risk being waylaid by Mrs

Maloney. She could ask for Delphine's help, but the lady spent an age choosing the right apparel.

Then she saw her pelisse draped over the chair in the corner of the room and whispered a silent prayer of thanks.

Hiding the first letter and the signed notes in Christian's drawer, she tucked his proposal in her pocket and hurried downstairs. She stopped at the front door to take a breath.

Aaron Chance appeared from the depths of his study. Arms folded, he leant against the jamb. "You've not eaten."

"I've no appetite."

Was he keen to know where Christian had gone? Did he know what was written in the letters? Should she mention marriage, or would Christian want to inform his family personally?

He scanned her attire, the depth of his stare unnerving. "Gibbs is waiting outside. He'll take you wherever you want to go." He paused, the tension in the air heightening. "You and Christian work well together. You play the part of the intrepid enquiry agent remarkably well. A man might wonder what other roles you play."

Other roles?

What did he mean?

Tired of his intimidating manner, she said, "Why don't you say what's really on your mind, Mr Chance? Clearly, you have a problem you wish to discuss."

"I find women much like those little figurines you study. It's difficult to tell an original from a fake. And so I ask, what are your intentions towards my brother?"

Heavens! He sounded like the father of a famed debutante.

"I'm afraid I am not at liberty to tell you." She'd say nothing until she had spoken to Christian. "Rest assured. His happiness is my only concern."

"Indeed." Aaron pushed away from the jamb, the tense air shifting around him. "We've survived unimaginable horrors, Miss Lawton. Being part of this family means subjecting oneself to intense scrutiny. To marry a Chance brother, one must have a backbone of steel. I'm not convinced you have the mettle."

This conversation acted as a stark warning. If she wanted Christian, she had to learn to deal with his brothers. Their lives would never be their own. Aaron would always be there in the background, issuing commands.

"I have no wish to compare scars, Mr Chance. Suffice it to say, I believe we were both forged in hell's flames. Forgive me. I have pressing business elsewhere. Good day."

"Christian loves you," Aaron said as she opened the door. "He's the only one amongst us who has a chance of being happy. And so I ask one thing of you."

She inhaled deeply, though didn't look at him. "Yes?"

"If you decide to leave London, never return."

Christian had taken to pacing the length of the drawing room. The chime of the mantel clock rang like a death knell. A signal his life was doomed. That he was too wicked to deserve even a modicum of happiness.

Isabella should have woken hours ago.

The mile walk to Ludgate Hill took twenty minutes. He tried to think of all the reasons she might be late. Refused to draw the obvious conclusion. The tender way they'd made love last night had convinced him she would not run. Every fibre of his being said he could trust her.

So, where the hell was she?

The sound of the front door opening stole the breath from his lungs. Instead of the light patter of feet and a woman's curious call, he heard the thud of booted footsteps on the parquet. Three loud raps on the drawing room door confirmed it was Aaron.

Christian closed his eyes against a swell of raw emotion.

Don't come in!

Damn you! Don't come in!

Aaron failed to hear Christian's silent plea. He entered the room and scanned the empty seats, his face a mask of stone. "Am I to understand she's not here? She left Fortune's Den two hours ago."

Panic surfaced.

He forced his fears aside and sought another explanation. "What if Daventry hasn't arrested Captain Snell? The bastard might have taken her to use as leverage."

"Christian," Aaron said calmly. "Snell is in custody. Daventry sent word an hour ago. His crew made statements to save their own necks. Snell and Lawton exchanged English women for Egyptian treasures. Daventry is to lead a missing persons investigation."

All the fight left Christian's body. He flopped down onto the sofa and rested his head in his hands. The crippling sense of helplessness was worse than anything he'd ever encountered.

"I know her. Isabella wouldn't do this."

Aaron released a deep sigh. "I may not have helped matters."

Christian jumped to his feet, anger shooting through him like a lightning bolt. "What the hell did you say to her?"

Aaron's hard eyes softened. "That being part of this family meant dealing with my brash manner. That she'd need a backbone of steel. If she's gone, she's not as strong as you think."

"When will you learn to stay out of my affairs? This has nothing to do with you!"

"It has everything to do with me. The incident with Lawton and the conte proved our lives are entwined. Christian, I prayed I would arrive to find her in your arms. If something I said made her run, then I'm sorry. I never want to cause you pain, but I'm not sorry I issued the warning."

Christian dragged his hand down his face and sighed. Being part of a powerful family was a blessing and a curse. "One day, you might find yourself in love. Then you will understand how it feels to have your heart wrenched from your chest."

"I think we both know that's doubtful."

A sudden knock on the front door caught them both unawares.

Someone entered the hall. A woman and a breathless companion.

Aaron reached for the blade tucked into his boot, but Christian raised a hand to stop him. He would know that sweet sigh anywhere.

"You'll behave, or I'm taking you back," came Isabella's frustrated whisper. "For heaven's sake. Must you be so impatient? Stop it, or I shall demand a refund from Mr Warring." Then she called to him. "Christian!"

His heart almost burst from his chest.

He resisted the urge to punch the air.

"I'm in here, Isabella." He cast his brother an arrogant grin. "It seems the lady does possess a backbone of steel."

Aaron managed a smile. "I didn't doubt it."

The drawing room door burst open.

Isabella appeared, dragged into the room by a young,

droopy-eyed bloodhound. "I'm sorry I'm late. Mr Warring demanded I spend an hour with the dog before he'd agree to sell him." She gripped the lead as the eager hound pulled her around the furniture. "I'm told he's well-behaved, and this is him learning to sniff out scents. I thought we could call him Albert."

Christian swallowed deeply. He couldn't love her any more than he did in that moment. Strands of hair escaped her simple knot. There was a splatter of mud on her cheek, more covering her pelisse.

Their eyes met.

He saw his future glistening in those sultry brown pools.

"Albert?"

"Yes, though I shall make certain this one doesn't leave."

Aaron's sigh was one of relief and an unnameable emotion he rarely showed. "You know how to test a man's patience, madam."

She flashed him a brilliant smile. "Christian knew I'd come."

"I'm not referring to Christian. I thought our talk may have given you a reason to run. A better man might be plagued with guilt."

"Then one must assume your experience of strong women is limited. Might I suggest you spend more time with Miss Lovelace? Christian told me she's quite a formidable lady."

Aaron firmed his jaw. "I shall take that as my cue to leave." He stopped to stroke the hound busy sniffing his boots. "Though I loathe sounding like an overbearing parent, I suggest you both remain at Fortune's Den until you marry. For appearances' sake, Mrs Maloney will remain as chaperone."

Christian snorted. "Since when did you care about appearances?"

"Since I inherited a sister-in-law."

Aaron left them.

Christian crossed the room as soon as the front door closed. He took hold of the bloodhound's lead and brought him to heel. "I trust you'll be stricter with our children than you are with Albert."

Her hand came to rest on his chest, and he melted beneath her touch. "I believe it's important to strike a happy balance. Besides, there was no mention of children in your note, only marriage."

"I want all or nothing. Children and dogs fall into the *all* category."

"As I'm standing here, it means I'm willing to grant you anything." She came up on her toes and kissed his lips. "I understand the need to test my resolve. I love you. I mean to spend a lifetime showing you just how much."

He released the dog and took Isabella in his arms. "I love you. I'll spend forever making sure you've no reason to run." He captured her mouth, though she deepened the kiss, their tongues sliding together in a primal dance.

Lust and love made a heady combination.

Soon, they were panting as their need spiralled.

"Marry me, Isabella?" he said when she pushed him onto the sofa.

"In a heartbeat." She was gathering her skirts, waiting for him to undo the buttons on his trousers, for his erection to spring free.

"When?"

"As soon as you can procure a licence." She came to sit astride him, pushed her hands into his hair and kissed him like he was the air she needed to breathe. "In your letter, you said I'm free to pursue my deepest desires. I want you. I want you now."

He was so damn hard for her.

He pushed inside her wetness. "God, yes!"

Their groans of pleasure echoed throughout the room.

The moist sound of their joining was a potent aphrodisiac.

"Will you still want me when I'm heavy with child?" she said, sliding down onto his cock again and again. "Will you still make love to me when we're old and grey?"

Her questions proved reassuring. She spoke of raising a family, of a lifetime together. His heart rejoiced at his good fortune. "Have no fear, love. You'll be the Queen of Diamonds, and diamonds never lose their lustre."

One month later
Ludgate Hill

Daventry sat in Christian's study, grinning at Isabella like a proud parent. "It's a small token to celebrate your new position at the museum, Mrs Chance. My wife felt it was an appropriate gift. She's keen to see you rise to the position of curator."

"Thank you. It's extremely kind, but I'm quite content being Mr Purton's assistant." Dressed in a prim blue dress, Isabella sat in the chair opposite the desk and opened the velvet box. She gasped, much like she had an hour ago before their responsibilities forced them out of bed. "Christian, it's a pretty fob watch on a chain." She showed him the generous gift.

"It's beautiful." Not as beautiful as her.

They had been married for a week. A wave of emotion welled in Christian's chest whenever he pictured her reciting her vows. She had agreed to obey him, but he'd been quick to reassure her this was a partnership. A wild and passionate partnership. Indeed, he could not get enough of his wife.

Christian felt his smile broadening.

The lady wore his gift strapped to her thigh.

It was only right he examine the item before she left for work today. And he would if Daventry would drink his damn coffee and bugger off.

"My wife says a professional woman should always know the time." Daventry merely sipped his beverage. "Oh, I almost forgot. My agent found Nancy Jones working at the Nag's Head in Cheapside. By all accounts, she would rather deal with drunken louts than irate lords."

Isabella clutched her chest. "Oh, thank heavens."

"The landlady offered her food and board in exchange for extra duties. She was shocked to hear of your position at the museum and is keen to have a tour of the exhibits."

To make amends for his behaviour, Lord Oldman had taken a more progressive approach to women and had approved Isabella's appointment at the museum. She was strong enough to deal with the handful of objectors.

"You and Mrs Daventry must dine with us." Isabella slipped the watch chain over her head and examined the blue enamel case. "I should very much like to thank her myself."

"Sybil would like that. She enjoys intelligent conversation and is a keen advocate of women's rights." Daventry gripped his coffee cup like he had no intention of ever leaving. "You'd get on well."

Isabella smiled and glanced covertly at Christian.

Time was of the essence. If they were to part for the day, they needed a moment alone to indulge in passionate kisses and appease their addiction.

"Well," she said, placing the lid on the box and brushing her skirts. "I mustn't be late for work. Mr Purton is quite the hard taskmaster."

"Of course." Daventry finally took his cue to leave, but not before asking a cryptic question. "Have you heard from Aramis this morning?"

Christian glanced at the mantel clock. "At this hour, he'll be in bed. Whose bed I cannot say. Being determined not to marry, he decided to take a mistress." Aramis had spent the last month avoiding Lucius Daventry so as not to become embroiled in a case.

"Yes, I believe Lydia Fontaine invited him to join her for supper at the Belldrake Theatre last night."

"She did?" It was the first Christian had heard. Aramis was as private as Aaron. So how the hell did Daventry know? "Then I imagine he's at home. My brother despises pretentious women." And Miss Fontaine kept her admirers dangling like puppets. The actress toyed with them until the strings broke, then she cast them aside.

"Was Aramis planning a trip?"

Suspicion flared. "No, but I'm sure you're keen to prove me wrong."

Daventry smiled. "It's just he was seen in a carriage in the yard of the Copper Crown Inn near Highgate, with someone who looked remarkably like the actress. Though the rumour is Miss Fontaine has been missing for three days. In her absence, the theatre had her assistant play Hero and managed to convince the audience it was Miss Fontaine."

The Copper Crown was a thieves' den. Most men who drank there were too sotted to recall their own names.

"Perhaps Aramis was running an errand for Aaron." He might have been chasing a gambling debt. "I'll have him send word to Hart Street when I arrive at Fortune's Den." Though why Daventry should care about Aramis' illicit encounters was anyone's guess.

"I shall wait. We can journey there together," Daventry suggested.

Mother of all saints!

Christian felt his temper rising. As Daventry appreciated honesty, he considered hitting him with the truth, but it was Isabella who spoke bluntly.

"I would like to spend time alone with my husband before we leave for work," Isabella said as if she'd read Christian's mind. "I'm sure you understand."

Daventry raised his hands in mock surrender. "Of course. I shall leave you in peace. Ensure Aramis contacts me before noon. Don't disturb the butler. I shall show myself out."

Isabella waited until the front door closed before leaving her seat. "What was that all about?" She rounded the desk and dropped into Christian's lap, wrapping her arms around his neck.

"I suspect Daventry is looking to hire Aramis as an agent. Hence the need for the intriguing story." Christian laughed to himself. "Aramis isn't foolish enough to fall for Daventry's tricks."

"Unlike us," she said, running her hand through his hair. "Not that I'm complaining. I'm enjoying my wifely duties immensely."

He knew from her sultry tone what she wanted. The minx could undoubtedly feel his cock swelling beneath her buttocks. "Must you go to work today?" He stroked his hand up her stocking until he reached the thigh belt and the small sheathed dagger. "Hmm. First appearances can be deceptive. This prim dress conceals a body made for sin."

She kissed him, her tongue sweeping through his lips.

Arousal pumped through his body. He lifted her off his lap and onto the desk. "Doubtless we shall both be late for work today."

She parted her legs and hiked up her skirts, her smile turning coy. "We're hardly to blame. Wickedness is in our blood."

His gaze dipped to the dagger pressed to her soft thigh. The diamond embedded in the handle sparkled, a symbol of their eternal love. "You're definitely a little bit dangerous, my love."

Isabella slid her hand over his erection. She pulled the blade from its sheath and cut the button off his trousers. "Don't be fooled, Mr Chance. I can be downright savage."

Thank you!

I hope you enjoyed reading *A Little Bit Dangerous.*

Did Aramis meet Miss Fontaine at the Belldrake?
Why was London's most unlikely suitor spotted at a thieves'
den near Highgate?

Find out in …

Temptress in Disguise
Rogues of Fortune's Den - Book 2

More titles by Adele Clee

Gentlemen of the Order

Dauntless

Raven

Valiant

Dark Angel

Ladies of the Order

The Devereaux Affair

More than a Masquerade

Mine at Midnight

Your Scarred Heart

No Life for a Lady

Scandal Sheet Survivors

More than Tempted

Not so Wicked

Never a Duchess

No One's Bride

Rogues of Fortune's Den

A Little Bit Dangerous

Temptress in Disguise

37788386R00178